Sugar Spinelli's
Little Instruction Book

I never thought I'd see the day when Chance Cartwright let a woman summon *him* for a date. But that was before I caught a glimpse of the feisty-looking blonde—the one you just know won't take no for an answer. There were sparks aplenty flying between the two of them backstage, let me tell you. And it's been that way for a month, from what I hear. Why, that gal has chased him all the way from Texas! Calling him, sending him gifts, writing him letters, and telegrams, and faxes. She wants Chance to be in some fancy ad campaign. And when he wouldn't do what she wanted, she upped and bought him for the weekend, pretty as you please. Chance didn't look too happy about it, either!

Dear Reader,

We just knew you wouldn't want to miss the news event that has all of Wyoming abuzz! There's a herd of eligible bachelors on their way to Lightning Creek—and they're all for sale!

Cowboy, park ranger, rancher, P.I.—they all grew up at Lost Springs Ranch, and every one of these mavericks has his price, so long as the money's going to help keep Lost Springs afloat.

The auction is about to begin! Young and old, every woman in the state wants in on the action, so pony up some cash and join the fun. The man of your dreams might just be up for grabs!

Marsha Zinberg
Editorial Coordinator, HEART OF THE WEST

A BABY
BY
CHANCE
Cathy Gillen Thacker

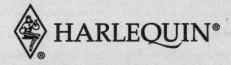

HARLEQUIN®

TORONTO • NEW YORK • LONDON
AMSTERDAM • PARIS • SYDNEY • HAMBURG
STOCKHOLM • ATHENS • TOKYO • MILAN • MADRID
PRAGUE • WARSAW • BUDAPEST • AUCKLAND

Cathy Gillen Thacker is acknowledged as the author of this work.

ISBN 0-373-82593-5

A BABY BY CHANCE

A Note from the Author

I write romances for three reasons. One, I like happy endings, and in a romance you always get a happy ending—guaranteed. Two, I think there is a special someone out there for everyone and I like to write about the search. And three, I like figuring out why people are drawn to each other and what makes their relationship work once they are together.

Of course, finding the love of your life is always a challenge, never more so than in *A Baby by Chance.* Madison Burnes is a sexy lady advertising executive in hot pursuit of the ultimate bachelor cowboy for her campaign. Madison wants what she wants—now! And she never takes no for an answer. Chance Cartwright is a successful rancher. He's got a heart as big as all Wyoming and a way with horses—not to mention women. He couldn't care less about money or fame.

Neither is looking for romance, but when they meet, the sparks are more than they can handle. Almost before they know it, they've succumbed to a passion unlike anything they've ever felt, and their lives are entangled forever. Which just goes to show, love has a way of finding us even when we're *not* looking for it.

I hope you have as much fun getting to know Madison and Chance as I did.

Happy reading!

Cathy Gillen Thacker

This book is for Julie and Eric Gerhardt, two very special people. I wish you much love and happiness in your new life together. May you always stay newlyweds at heart.

CHAPTER ONE

CHANCE CARTWRIGHT knew who it was even before he turned around. Her low, honeyed voice had haunted his dreams for weeks now. He'd gone to sleep wondering what the indefatigable Madison Burnes from Dallas, Texas, looked like. Was the ad agency exec as sexy as she sounded? As determined? As flirtatious? The answer to all of that, Chance discovered as he turned and saw her, was, "Heck, yes!"

"Hello, Chance."

That voice again. His task would have been a far sight easier if she hadn't looked like an angel, too. Chance grinned at the sexy blonde in the fire-engine red power suit, cell phone in hand. She was regarding him flirtatiously and had one hand propped on a slender hip. Her hair glinted with shimmery gold and silver highlights. It fell to her shoulders, flipped up at the ends and looked soft as spun silk, reminding him of pictures of fairy-tale princesses he'd seen in storybooks long ago. A pair of sunglasses was perched jauntily on her head. She was smiling as she looked at him—and she had a great smile. As well as soft lips, a terrific body and long, sexy legs that all but demanded a second—make that third and fourth—look as she closed the distance between them gracefully.

Chance touched the brim of his hat. "Madison Burnes, I'm guessing."

"You guessed right," she said in her soft, southern drawl.

At that moment Chance wished he were anywhere but backstage at the bachelor auction for the Lost Springs Ranch for Boys. He would've liked to spend some time with her before he delivered the bad news, but since time was short, he figured he might as well cut to the chase. What happened after that—after she knew where they stood—well, that was up to her, he figured. "The answer is no."

The angel with the delicately sculpted face edged nearer. "Now, Chance," she scolded playfully, "I haven't asked you anything yet."

Today, Chance thought. "But you're going to," he retorted, letting his glance drift over her high full breasts, slender waist and perfectly proportioned hips before returning to her pretty green eyes. He braced himself for the inevitable pitch. It wasn't long in coming.

She batted her lashes. "You know me too well, Chance Cartwright."

No, Chance thought, he didn't know her at all. But he wanted to know her. The nonstop phone calls, messages, telegrams, e-mails and gifts the last month had intrigued the heck out of him. He'd never met a woman so impervious to the word *no* in his life. But none of that changed the facts of the situation, he reminded himself. "I don't do commercials or endorsements," he told her bluntly.

Madison merely smiled and gave him a steady look. "There's a first time for everything," she said.

"There may be," Chance agreed, tipping his hat in acknowledgment as they signaled him that he was up next. "But not," he said heavily, "for this."

"REGRETS?" Lindsay Duncan teased seconds later as Chance stood amid thunderous applause.

Chance grinned at Lindsay, the current owner of the Lost Springs Ranch for Boys. She'd been having a rough go of it financially as of late. Hence the bachelor auction fundraiser and his reluctant—but heartfelt—participation. "I'm about to be sold to the highest bidder for the weekend," Chance teased his old friend as the hot Wyoming sun beat down on them and the air resounded with catcalls and whistles of distinctly feminine appreciation. "What do you think?"

Lindsay linked her arm in Chance's, and together they headed for the auction block that had been set up in the ranch's showring. The warm summer air was fragrant with the mouthwatering smells of mesquite-barbecued chicken and ribs, but any cravings in the arena were solely for the bachelors.

"Cheer up, cowboy. It's for a good cause." Lindsay smiled and patted his arm reassuringly.

How well Chance knew that. If the proceeds from this lunacy weren't going directly to the Lost Springs Ranch for Boys, he thought ruefully, he wouldn't be here. But he owed the ranch a heck of a lot. It had provided a good, loving home for him when he'd had no place to go. And now it was his turn to help provide a safe haven for other abandoned or orphaned boys who felt just as lost and alone as he had.

Lindsay winked at the audience of mostly women, and grinned as if Chance were quite a catch. "Besides, maybe someone wonderful will buy you."

Chance figured the odds of that happening were about the same as him winning the next Publisher's Clearinghouse Sweepstakes. But given all he'd been through in the past, he could survive whatever the weekend brought. He wanted the ranch to have as much money as they could raise today. Which was why he'd brought along the bouquet of red roses he clutched in his fist. Anything to get the bidding going, he thought as he looked at the risers filled with women of all ages, shapes and sizes.

"Ladies, we have here in front of us Chance Cartwright," the auctioneer said, as Chance lifted the fistful of flowers like a victor's trophy in a competition. He leaned toward the mike and said, "Hello, ladies!" His words sent paroxysms of screaming through the crowd.

Lindsay kissed him on the cheek, eliciting a wistful sigh from the audience, then stepped away from the action.

"Some of you may already know Chance," the auctioneer said as the crowd continued to scream enthusiastically, "as the premiere horse trainer in the country."

Feeling like a rock star on a concert stage and hamming it up all the more, Chance swept off his hat and began a sexy pirouette while the auctioneer ran down the rest of his accomplishments. He told the audience how Chance had started his ranch from nothing twelve years prior, and through much hard work and a commitment to excellence had risen quickly to prominence. He talked about all the celebrities who had chosen to have their horses trained by Chance, and all the Lost Springs boys Chance had helped, giving them part-time jobs as grooms and teaching them not just how to rope and ride and care for horses, but how to be men of whom the community and the ranch could be proud.

Finding the pre-bidding hype mildly embarrassing, to say the least, Chance grinned and set his hat on his head. Baffled as to what type of woman would show up at an event like this, he scanned the audience curiously, moving his gaze past a pregnant woman, another with two small children and a group of older women in jogging suits. Then there was Madison Burnes. Looking too keyed up to sit, she was positioned at the very top of the bleachers, her cell phone pressed to her ear, pacing back and forth in the small space. No doubt, Chance thought, watching her frown as she talked, she was waiting to talk to him after the auction. He just couldn't seem to convince her that he wanted no part of her fancy ad campaign.

She was smiling at him, standing in a puddle of June sunlight, one hand propped on her slender hip.

"Now, who'll bid five hun—" the auctioneer began.

Her eyes firmly on him, Madison Burnes raised her index finger, pausing in her telephone conversation just long enough to place the first bid. "Five thousand," she called out cheerfully. "Do you take American Express?"

"YOU DID IT!" Madison Burnes's colleague and best friend, Kit Connelly Smith, crowed on the other end of the phone line.

"I told you I would," Madison retorted smugly. Her high bid had cut off all others.

"And now you get to spend the entire weekend with that gorgeous man."

He was that, all right, Madison thought, letting her glance trail slowly over his broad-shouldered, six-foot-two-inch frame. In Dallas, she worked closely with incredibly handsome male models and good-looking cowboys all the time; they were a staple in the Texas-based ads she designed and created. But when it came to sex appeal, none of the men she had worked with could hold a candle to Chance Cartwright. There was just something about seeing him in person that made her quiver inside and catch her breath a little.

Why that was, exactly, she didn't know. Sure, his shoulders, abs and chest looked incredibly strong and fit beneath his starched white shirt. And there was no doubt he really filled out a pair of Levi's. Or that the short, curly dark hair peeking out from beneath the rim of his bone-colored Stetson looked touchable and soft. Or that he had the kind of very sexy, all-American good looks and appealingly masculine smile featured in every toothpaste ad ever made. It had to do with the way he moved. Confidently. With the sense of humor he had about himself and this event. Simply put, he was the perfect man for her latest ad campaign. That had to explain it, Madison told herself firmly, because she was still quivering inside, just watching him.

"Uncle Ed is going to be so pleased about this," Kit continued happily.

"He'll be even happier when I get Cartwright to say yes," Madison said determinedly. And she would, before their weekend together was finished. "Chance is headed my way." Madison's heart began to pound with anticipation. "I've got to go." She cut the connection, folded the slim cell phone in half and slid it into her bag.

"I don't know what you think you've just done." His deep blue eyes locked firmly with hers as he presented her with the bouquet of fragrant red roses. "But you haven't bought yourself anything but a date for the weekend. I am not for sale."

We'll see about that, Madison thought. "Nothing wrong with the two of us spending a little time together," she said. "Getting to know each other."

"I agree." Chance Cartwright regarded her steadily, in a way that let her know she had just grabbed a tiger by the tail. "As long as we don't talk business."

Since Madison couldn't promise him that, she flashed him her winning smile—the one she reserved for her most difficult clients—and buried her face in the sweet-smelling blossoms. Now that they were just inches apart, she could see how closely he had shaved. And that there was a faint cleft in his chin, one that gave him a dashing edge.

The rules for the weekend laid down, Chance inclined his head at the table that had been set up to handle the formality of the transactions. "There's some paperwork that needs completing before we talk specifics of our date," he told her, his mind clearly first and foremost on the charity they were supporting.

Madison bowed to his discretion. "Just show me the way," she said pleasantly, figuring the sooner they could get out of here, the better.

At the table, Madison quickly completed the necessary paperwork then handed over five thousand dollars of traveler's checks, all issued in her name as well as her company's. She had five thousand more earmarked for entertainment or wooing purposes—like first-class accommodations in whatever city Chance chose, dinners at whatever restaurants he chose and so forth. Madison could see by the prickly attitude beneath his surface civility that she was going to need every penny of it.

"Connelly and Associates, the company you work for, certainly is generous," Chance murmured.

"They're always contributing to worthy causes." Madison smiled winningly again. "I convinced them this was one of them."

Chance tilted his head as he continued to study her. "Buying you a date for the weekend?"

Warmth that had little to do with the sun shining overhead filled Madison's cheeks. "Supporting the Lost Springs Ranch for Boys," she amended dryly.

"So when do you want to do this?" Without warning, his expression became wary. Careful. As if he didn't quite trust her not to try to turn the situation to her advantage.

"How about now?" Madison asked as they walked away from the table.

She tried not to notice how easily their steps meshed as he gallantly took her elbow to usher her through the crowd gathered to watch another bachelor be auctioned off.

Chance, who'd been studying the way the light summer breeze was lifting her hair, blinked in surprise. "It's already Saturday."

Madison tucked a strand of silvery blond hair behind her ear. "Saturday through Monday is fine."

Chance frowned. It was apparent he did not like someone else calling the shots. He lifted his hat, revealing a suntanned forehead brushed with silky black curls, and resettled it on his head. "Like I said earlier, during the auction, ma'am, I've got a ranch to care for and horses to tend."

The unbending politeness of his low voice did little to mitigate his frown. "I can't just take off on a whim."

Madison was aware of that. Step One for her with every project was to do extensive research on everything and everyone likely to be involved. Step Two was to meet with the people face-to-face in a leisurely, comfortable setting. Get to know each other a little. Then, and only then, talk business.

"That's all right," Madison assured Chance pleasantly. "We can spend our date at your ranch." Not only would Chance be more at ease there, she decided firmly, it would give her an opportunity to see him in his environment and thoroughly scope out his property in a commercial sense. The director they had hired to film the commercials was going to want a full run-down from her as soon as she was back in Dallas.

Chance glanced her over from head to toe. He rolled his weight forward, so he was balanced on the balls of his feet. He seemed as puzzled by her happy-go-lucky attitude as he was disturbed by her eagerness to be alone with him. "Funny, I wouldn't have figured a city girl like you'd be at home on the range," he drawled, regarding her with unconcealed amusement.

Madison knew what he meant. And he was right. She'd never so much as set foot on a ranch prior to her entry into the business world. "No, but I'm pretty relaxed around the refrigerator," she quipped.

As Chance threw back his head and laughed gustily, Madison planted her hands on her hips and grinned. "Besides, it'll be easier on both of us, don't you think?" she continued, beseeching him cheerfully to do things her way.

"Okay." He inclined his head. "Got anything with you besides those clothes?" he asked.

Madison nodded and tried not to appear self-conscious. Which wasn't easy, given the thorough appraisal he was giving her suit and heels. "My boots and jeans are in my suitcase. I'm prepared for anything."

"*Anything?*"

"Anything you can dish out, cowboy," Madison quipped, knowing that was the understatement of the year. Shifting the flowers to her other arm, she walked over to pick up the wheeled suitcase she'd left beneath the bleachers in the small arena.

Chance took it for her and headed for the parking area. "How'd you get to Lost Springs?"

"Taxi, so we'll have to use your pickup truck." That, too, had been planned.

Chance ground to a halt. "How'd you know what I drive?" He turned to confront her. His eyes turned the deep, stormy blue of a mountain lake.

Madison shrugged. "You are a cowboy, after all." She paused. "What else do cowboys drive?"

"Depends on the cowboy, I expect." Chance studied her shrewdly even as he accepted her answer, then resumed walking and led her to a truck that had seen better days, the outside splattered with mud and grime. He opened the door and slipped her suitcase, then the flowers, behind the long bench seat.

He held out a hand to help her up. Madison tucked her palm in his larger one. Ignoring the rush of tingling warmth his touch generated, she started to step up and, to her embarrassment, immediately hit a snag. Her skirt was too short and too tight to allow her to bring her knee up as far as was required to boost herself into the cab—without revealing more than she intended to, that is.

Watching, Chance said dryly, "Need some help?" Madison noted with chagrin he didn't seem to mind how much leg she showed.

"Unless I suddenly sprout wings and fly," she said, trying her best not to look as self-conscious as she felt, "it would appear so."

Chance tipped his hat. "Toss your purse in," he ordered.

Bristling at having been ordered around, Madison obeyed.

"Okay, step in close and put your arms around my shoulders."

Trying her best to appear cool, calm and collected when she felt anything but, Madison swallowed and did as directed. The feel of her palms on his broad shoulders was electrifying, but to her mounting exasperation he did nothing to transport her into the cab of his truck. As they continued to stand there, snug as two peas in a pod, she tilted her head to his.

Chance's eyes twinkled merrily. They were at the end of the parking area, where a grassy slope angled downward toward the soccer field. In the distance was a heart-stirring view of the far-off Wind River Range. With the sun high overhead, casting a golden sheen on the broken-backed mountains, swaying grasses and sage fields beyond Lost Springs, Madison felt as if they were caught in a sensual tableau. One that was as enticing and seductive—and ultimately false—as any commercial she'd ever created. "Explain to me how exactly this is going to help?" she queried.

"It isn't. I just thought it'd be fun to see if we fit together like lock and key. Apparently—" Chance favored her with an unexpectedly wicked grin "—we do."

Shocked, Madison dropped her arms and stepped back. No man had ever had the temerity to speak to her like that, never mind with a very sexy twinkle in his eyes. She planted both hands on her hips and gave him a withering look. Had she not had a very important business deal to tend to, she would have given him his walking papers, pronto. It was clear she had a bad boy on her hands. Cheeks flaming hotly, eyes flashing, she regarded him sternly. "You're not going to be all that easy to handle, are you?"

"No, ma'am, I guess I'm not easy," he retorted, and for the barest second there seemed to be some hidden meaning in his words. "But don't you fret none, 'cause I do go down okay at night." He paused, and at her startled expression continued with comically exaggerated solemnity. "You know, out on the ranch, you go down for the night."

Oh, Madison thought with relief.

"Sort of like going down for the count in boxing." Chance paused. He removed his hat and ran his hands through the rumpled layers of his curly hair. Another beat of silence passed. He narrowed his eyes and peered down his nose at her. "What'd you think I meant?"

A fiery heat climbed into her face as Madison blushed. "That's just it. I didn't know what you meant," she mumbled. But images of ways to make love had crowded her mind at his words. And they were images of making love with him—long, slow, incredibly passionate love. She told herself sternly to get a grip. This was business. Even if Chance didn't know it yet.

Determined to get the upper hand, Madison drew a bracing breath and put her hands on his shoulders. "Let's get this show on the road, shall we?"

"You're the boss." Just that quickly, Chance slipped one arm around her back, the other beneath her knees. He swung her off her feet, cradled her possessively against his chest and lifted her into the cab. Unfortunately, in her haste to be rid of him, she sat down too quickly, and his arm and hand got caught between her thighs and the bench seat. Worse, her short skirt had hiked up almost to her panties. Mortified at the feel of his warm palm and sinewy forearm trapped beneath her panty hose and the tingles of awareness that was creating deep inside her, Madison froze.

"You're going to have to lift up if you want me to get my arm out," Chance told her. "On the other hand—" he glanced at her and grinned, obviously content with the close contact "—we could stay like this for a while." He shrugged good-humoredly. "Up to you."

Madison gripped the dash, and using it for leverage,

raised herself up. "Just get your arm out of there. Now!" she demanded, refusing to let his antics intimidate her. Nothing in her research had told her he was such a hellion. But then, she hadn't exactly talked to anyone he had dated. Just those who knew of his business reputation, which had been stellar. And of his penchant for personal privacy, which had been unremitting. Nevertheless, she knew she could handle whatever roadblocks he tossed her way. He was a fool to think she couldn't.

"Yes, ma'am." Chance slid his hand across the seat, just missing the backs of her thighs as he did so. Still grinning appreciatively at the unexpected contact, he circled the cab and slid behind the wheel while Madison tugged at her skirt, finding it wouldn't go anywhere near her knees.

"You're going to have to sit over here." Chance patted the middle of the bench seat.

Given the tomfoolery that had just occurred, she couldn't help but regard the area next to him as if it were a moat full of crocodiles. "And why, pray tell, is that?"

Chance angled a thumb in her direction. "Seat belt next to the door doesn't work. And I insist everyone who rides with me wear a seat belt. Safety, you know. So you'll have to sit here." Chance patted the place beside him again.

Madison, who was still on fire from where they had touched, swiftly decided they did not need to be sitting that close. Not now or at any other time. Doing so would take her mind off business. "I'm sure I can get it to work," she said cheerfully. She tugged at the shoulder harness. And tugged. And twisted. And tugged some more. He was right. It was stuck. So Madison did the only thing she could do under the circumstances. She scooted beside him. "Maybe I'll just sit over here."

One hand draped loosely over the wheel, Chance regarded her drolly. "Good idea," he said, and started the engine.

As she tried to get comfortable, it soon became clear

Madison had a choice. She could sit with her legs straddling the hump, which meant that her knees would be apart. Not a good idea. Or she could tuck her thighs together and keep her ankles to the right of the hump, which forced her weight, and her thighs, to brush against the side of his jeans-clad legs.

Meanwhile, she was having more trouble trying to fasten this seat belt than the other one. In her attempt, she ended up bumping arms and shoulders, hips and thighs with Chance. Perspiration beaded her lip. He looked just as tense and uncomfortable.

Finally, he said brusquely, "Why don't you let me help?" And then did. Accomplishing in two seconds what she had been trying to do for two minutes.

"Now," he turned to her and asked, "all set?"

As well as out of breath. Madison wasn't used to feeling so darn aware of a man she would be working with.

His heated glance slowly scanned her face. "You okay?"

"Yes." *I just don't like the fact that you got the upper hand between us without even half trying.* Madison forced a smile and struggled unsuccessfully against a blush. "Why?"

He paid no attention to the running motor or the cool air coming out of the dash air conditioner. "You're breathing kind of hard."

More heat flooded Madison's cheeks. Sitting this close to him had caused a greater reaction than she'd bargained for. There was a tingling in her stomach. Her thighs were fluid, her knees suspiciously wobbly. Higher still, a buttery warmth spread across her chest, culminating in her breasts. "It's the heat," Madison said flatly. It had to be. She did not get this turned on just sitting next to a man, no matter how ruggedly handsome he happened to be.

Chance sent her a sideways glance as he backed his truck out of the parking space and thrust it into gear. He drove carefully between the rows of vehicles, past the news vans that had been set up to cover the event, then onto the narrow lane that connected the ranch with the highway. A split rail fence lined one side of the road. In the distance, a herd of horses grazed in a sun-splashed pasture.

"Doesn't feel that hot to me," Chance observed.

Oh, yeah? Madison thought. Then why had a bead of perspiration broken out on his temple? And why did he suddenly appear every bit as physically aware of her as she was of him, she wondered, catching a whiff of his deliciously sexy leather and spice cologne.

Chance stopped to make sure the road was clear. He looked both ways, then turned his truck onto the main highway. He continued to study her off and on as they headed in the general direction of the Wind River Range. "So, do you date a lot of cowboys or am I your first?" he prodded.

Aware he had completely misinterpreted the reason for her interest in him, Madison studied the occasional stands of aspen and pine. "You're my first."

"How come?"

Madison shrugged. "I don't meet any. I work in the city, remember?"

He fidgeted in his seat, his hard-muscled thigh nudging her much softer one in the process. "Then who do you date?" he persisted.

His questions were awfully personal. But maybe that was good, Madison thought. She needed them to get to know each other if she was going to persuade him to do what she wanted.

"To be perfectly honest, I don't normally date a lot."

Chance lifted a brow. "That a fact?" he asked, clearly disbelieving.

Madison sighed, not sure how they'd gotten on this topic. Her personal life had been disappointing as far back as she could remember in just about every way. "Afraid so," she said lightly.

"Why not?"

"No time."

He raised a brow.

"I work in advertising," Madison explained. "For one of the most demanding and high-paying firms around."

"I know that. Still, you must get plenty of offers." Chance persisted, clearly more interested in her social life than her career.

Madison watched Chance bypass the road to Lightning Creek, the closest town, and turn the truck onto the bridge that crossed Sand Creek. "I guess."

"And yet you turn them all down."

"Most of the time, yes." Without so much as a regret. She didn't believe in wasting time, hers or anyone else's.

He smiled. "So why—if you're so particular about who you go out with—did you want to date me?" Chance asked lightly as they rounded a bend in the road. The sexy promise in his voice sent shivers of awareness racing across her skin.

"You know why?" Madison spoke flirtatiously, ready to do whatever she needed to build his ego to the point where he'd agree to be spokesperson for the Ranchero campaign.

Chance abruptly steered the pickup to the side of the road. He stopped so suddenly she lurched against him. The way he considered her, she knew she was going to have to come up with something convincing if she ever hoped to win his respect. "I liked your…smile." *And the way you fit into a pair of jeans,* Madison added silently. "And…the way you pirouetted around on stage to make all the women laugh. And the roses. I liked the fact you thought to bring roses today." She finished with a burst of inspiration.

"It seemed the least I could do for anyone who helped the ranch out with a contribution. Still—" Chance paused dramatically as he gave her another supercharged look "—five thousand is a lot to pay for a date."

Madison drew a deep breath and steeled herself with resolve. "Like I said," she retorted determinedly, "the money wasn't really mine, and it's going for a good cause—the boys' ranch. I'm just here on behalf of my company."

"To grease the wheels...smooth the way to my cooperating with Connelly and Associates?"

Madison was glad he was being so grown-up about this. "You've got my number, cowboy."

Without warning, he thrust the truck into gear and guided it onto the road so swiftly she lurched against him once again. "So what do you want to see first?" Chance asked long minutes later as he turned the pickup into a lane and drove beneath the wrought-iron archway of his Double Diamond Ranch.

Madison studied the acres of velvety green pasture interspersed with wildflower-strewn meadows, rocky outcroppings and thick stands of cottonwood and blue spruce. A picturesque creek wound like a ribbon through the property. In the distance, the jagged peaks of the Wind River Range seemed closer. In between, the foothills were rimmed with juniper and sage. It was wild and civilized, beautiful and rugged all at once. Nearly two hours from town, awesomely untouched, with a dozen beautiful horses grazing here and there—the perfect place for an ad to be filmed. The perfect place for American Motor Vehicles' latest product to be launched.

Madison turned to Chance as they approached a small, two-story log-cabin-style ranch house and several barns. All were as immaculately maintained as the rest of the ranch. "First, I'd like to change." She felt the pitch would go better if they were both wearing jeans, not just Chance.

Something flickered in Chance's eyes as he parked in front of the house, but was gone almost as quickly as it appeared. "Why change when you're perfect just as you are?" he retorted glibly, cutting the engine.

Madison told herself it wasn't distrust she had seen.

"Into jeans," she explained, releasing the seat belt. She had to get him to stop looking at her legs or he'd never be able to concentrate on business. She'd counted at least ten surreptitious glances while he was driving.

Unfortunately, Madison had the same problem getting out of the truck as she had getting in. It wasn't possible to do it alone, at least not gracefully. She scooted to the edge of the seat. He was right there to open her door, a grin of sheer male anticipation on his face. "Put your hands on my shoulders," he directed.

And see if we fit like a lock and key again? "Very funny," Madison said.

Chance tilted the brim of his hat. "I'm serious."

"So am I," Madison returned matter-of-factly. "I'm not falling for that again." If they were going to talk business soon, she had to get things on a serious footing, pronto. "Just put your hands on my waist and lift me down, Chance. Now."

Chance shook his head in a way that let her know he thought she was foolish beyond words, then did as ordered, his hold on her firm, his action purposeful.

Unfortunately, her plan to hold herself as physically aloof as possible during the transfer from truck to ground did not work. With nothing to hold on to, her arms flapped like a chicken. Thrown totally off balance, she crashed into him.

"Whaddya know, you can fly," he quipped upon contact as she slid down him, thigh to thigh, the full body contact even more disturbing than before. Sparks flew between them, visibly arousing both of them.

Heart pounding, she pushed away from the hardness at the front of his jeans. Leave it to her to make a fool out of herself. Leave it to him to assist her in doing so. "Like I said," she murmured tightly, "before we continue with this *date* of ours, I have got to get out of these clothes." *Especially this skirt!*

"Works for me," Chance drawled, letting go of her with visible reluctance. He reached behind the bench seat to pull out her suitcase, flowers and purse. "Since I don't have a guest house you'll have to bunk with me." He shot her a look over his shoulder. "That okay?"

Madison tried not to notice how delicious he smelled, how very clean and male. "Perfect."

They fell into step and headed for the covered front porch with the chain-held swing. "You sleep on the left or the right?" he teased.

Madison's spine stiffened. "I sleep alone." Account or no, that was one thing they needed to get perfectly clear from the get-go.

Chance quirked a brow and made no effort to mask his disappointment.

"So if that means the sofa..." Madison continued, telling herself he was the only one disappointed. She didn't mind the fact he was off-limits to her romantically at all. Men who constantly had to get the upper hand were not her type.

Chance grinned as if he'd read her mind. "Not to worry. I've got a bed and a room just for you," he drawled as he pushed open the door and ushered her in. "We'll have to share the bathroom, but I reckon we can take turns. Unless you're in a big hurry. Then I guess we could shower at the same time."

Madison rolled her eyes at the sexy promise in his low voice. "I'm not ever in that much of a hurry, cowboy," she drawled, mocking his glib, teasing tone to a T. "I reckon we can take turns, too."

Chance grinned, then strode through the sunlit living room, Madison on his heels. It was clearly a man's abode. And the woman in Madison couldn't help but love every inch of it. A dark brown leather sofa and two armchairs formed a conversation area in front of the stone fireplace. Navajo rugs provided splashes of color on gleaming wood floors. A rolltop desk was covered with stacks of paper, a laptop computer and phone. Next to it stood a rough-hewn table with a fax and printer. There were shelves of books—most appeared to be on horses or ranching—and there were several large wooden file cabinets. At the other end of the living room was a dining area with a large oak table, and a kitchen that was at once compact and well-equipped.

"Bedrooms are upstairs," Chance announced brusquely. "I'll show you the guest room."

Madison followed Chance up the stairs, past a master bedroom dominated by a king-size bed covered with patch-work quilts. An old-fashioned cedar chest sat at the foot of the bed. The guest room sported a mirrored bureau and a double bed with a plain white cotton spread. Both rooms had spectacular views of the ranch and the mountains in the distance. As she looked at the view, Madison couldn't help thinking about the commercial. "This is just wonder-ful," she murmured. Sort of a rugged, everyman's dream domain. Properly lit, it would be the perfect backdrop for the Ranchero commercial.

Chance set her suitcase on the floor, then straightened unhurriedly. "Thinking about moving in?" he drawled, his blue eyes assessing hers as if he could suddenly read her mind again and disapproved thoroughly.

She brushed off his remark cheerfully. "Just appreciating what you have here." More determined than ever to win Chance Cartwright over to her way of thinking, Madison opened her suitcase and brought out a pair of jeans. "Where shall I meet you? Inside or out?"

"I'll be downstairs, checking my messages," Chance said.

Madison nodded. The sooner she made her pitch, the better. "I'll be down shortly."

CHANCE WAS nearly to the phone when it began to ring. He expected a client. It was Russ Hall, another Lost Springs

alum and auctionee. He and Chance, both avid supporters
of the ranch, had been friends for years. "Where are you?"
Chance asked.

"Backstage waiting my turn on the auction block."

Chance sympathized immediately. "Dreading it?"

"What do you think?" Not waiting for a reply, Russ
chuckled and asked, "How's your date going? The two of
you hitting it off?"

Almost too well, Chance thought, given the fact that he
had known the minute she bought him for the weekend that
Madison Burnes was not the woman for him. Sure, she was
sexy as hell. He admired her drive and determination and
the way she wasn't afraid to go after what she wanted, no
holds barred. But when it came to being her quarry, in a
business sense, he drew the line. Which was why he'd been
working so hard to scare her off. He wanted her to think
he was too hot to handle. He wanted her to decide on her
own to cut short their "date" and go home.

"She likes you?" Russ persisted.

Chance grimaced. "Oh, yeah." Too much, considering
what she had in mind for him. She reminded him of the
social worker who had sent him to the Lost Springs ranch.
Everyone had told him he'd love it there, and they had been
right. He *had* loved it in the end. But that didn't mean he
wanted to be told what to think or how to feel. And Madison Burnes, he was willing to bet, was determined to do
both.

On the other hand, he'd made a commitment when he
signed up for the auction. A five-thousand-dollar donation
for the ranch was riding on this. He'd do his best to be
hospitable and hope in the meantime she would reconsider
and not make her business pitch.

Russ paused as the public address system rumbled in the
background, then thunderous applause. "Think you might
get lucky?" he asked.

The last thing Chance needed was to bed down with

someone who only had plans to use him in an ad campaign. On the other hand, should her interest in him become personal instead...

Chance cast a look over his shoulder, all too aware how sound carried in his tiny ranch house. "It's too soon to tell," he murmured. He had felt Madison's trembling when he had lifted her in and out of his truck. Breathed in the lily of the valley scent of her. If she'd been anyone else, been from anywhere else except that annoyingly persistent advertising agency, he would have already tested the chemistry between them with a long, heart-stopping kiss.

"Whoops," Russ said on the other end. "I'm up next. Gotta go."

"Good luck," Chance said absently.

"Same to you, buddy," Russ returned. Their connection ended with a click.

Madison came down the stairs. She was wearing a vivid blue camp shirt, stonewashed jeans and boots, and had a thirty-five millimeter camera slung around her neck. She looked even more beautiful than she had in the sexy red business suit. "Okay, cowboy, I'm ready. Show me everything there is to see."

Curious as to how long it was going to take her to work up to her sales pitch, Chance walked her through the stables and around the grounds close to the house. He showed her the corral where he trained horses that were new to the ranch.

"It's beautiful, Chance, absolutely beautiful." Madison looked enthralled. She turned to him, pink color highlighting her cheeks. "Mind if I snap a few photos?"

Chance shrugged. "Suit yourself."

"Ready to show me those horses of yours?" Madison asked when she'd finished.

"I don't own most of them." Chance took her elbow and ushered her to a pasture. "I just stable, train and care for them. Most are owned by wealthy businessmen, movie stars and the like.''

Madison studied the two dozen horses in the south pastures. Ranging in color from light gray to dark brown, all were sleek and beautiful. But it was the big black stallion, pastured alone, that really caught her eye. Chance wasn't surprised. Shiloh was one of the most magnificent animals he had ever seen, too. ''What about that one?'' Madison said.

Chance watched Shiloh graze contentedly. He looked docile as a lamb, but appearances, as Chance well knew, could be deceptive. ''That's Shiloh. He's one of mine now.''

''Why isn't he pastured with the other horses?'' Madison took several pictures of Shiloh, all from different angles.

Chance got angry just thinking about what had happened to Shiloh. ''His original owner tried to train him with cruelty instead of love and patience. Not surprisingly, that method didn't work. Now he's dangerously unpredictable and afraid of people, too. The owner thought the fault was with Shiloh and wanted him put down.'' Chance shook his head in disgust. It would have been criminal to have such a beautiful, spirited animal destroyed because of maltreatment. ''The local vets resisted and offered to find Shiloh a home instead. I heard about it via the grapevine, intervened and brought him here.''

Madison regarded Shiloh with compassion, as if her heart went out to him, too. She took a few more pictures then turned to Chance. ''Does he trust you?''

''Not yet,'' Chance told Madison ruefully. Then he went on to promise confidently, ''But with time and patience, he will. In the meantime—'' his voice dropped a protective notch ''—you should stay away from him.''

Madison sighed, her disappointment clearly evident. She obviously would have liked a closer look. And perhaps a few more pictures, as well. "I suppose that applies to the Lost Springs boys who have part-time jobs here, too."

Chance nodded. "They're under the same restriction." He turned to Madison. "Do you ride?"

Madison's lips curved up wryly. "Not unless you count riding the pony around the ring at someone's birthday party," she admitted with regret.

Now, this was something he could see them spending the weekend doing. "Want to learn?" Chance asked on impulse.

"Maybe someday." Madison smiled and took a deep breath. "But first, now that I've seen what I needed to, let's talk business."

CHAPTER TWO

MADISON PLASTERED a too-bright smile on her face and plunged on recklessly. "You already know there's a sexy new pickup truck—the Ranchero—that's being introduced at the end of the year by AMV—that's American—"

"Motor Vehicles Corporation, I know," Chance interrupted impatiently. Clearly, he was anxious for her to get to the point.

"Yes, well..." Madison drew another bolstering breath. "I've proposed they use a real rancher, someone who works with horses, someone with charisma—like you—as a spokesperson." Although Chance was giving her no encouragement whatsoever, Madison pushed on enthusiastically. "AMV agrees you're perfect for the job. All we have to do is work out the details."

Chance glared at her for a long moment then swung away from the pasture and headed toward the ranch house at a staggering clip. "There's nothing to work out," he growled without so much as a backward glance at her. His broad shoulders were rigid with tension. "I'm not going to advertise any product."

Madison raced to catch up and jumped in front of him. To her dismay, he didn't slow down in the least or try to move around her. Which left her with only two choices. Get out of his way or jog backward and keep talking. She chose the latter. "It's not just a product, Chance." Madison stumbled slightly on the uneven terrain as she struggled to keep up. Determined to persuade him no matter what it took, she kept her chin up, her eyes locked firmly on his. "The Ranchero is the most rugged pickup to come out of Detroit in years. If you don't believe me, well, look behind the barn."

That stopped him cold. It wasn't a pleasant experience.

The scowl lines on either side of his face deepened. Chance strode around the barn to the small parking area in the rear, the one his part-time help used. Parked there was a brand-new forest green Ranchero that put his battered pickup to shame. The agency had had it delivered while he was at the auction. Madison opened the door, revealing a plush leather interior with climate control and state-of-the-art stereo system. "It's a great truck, Chance. Competitively priced so most ranchers and families can afford it, luxuriously equipped, built for extremely rugged terrain and all kinds of weather, environmentally friendly and, best of all, AMV is going to make a five-hundred-dollar donation to American parks and wildlife for every model sold."

A muscle worked convulsively in his jaw. He charged forward and slammed the door. "You've got the wrong guy."

"I know you're not a professional model—"

He whirled on her. "I train horses, Madison."

"And I know you've turned down other offers," she continued hastily.

"So what else do you need to know?" Chance stormed. He strode closer, every inch of him primed and ready to do battle.

Madison paused, her heart pounding in her chest. She was unsure just how hard to push, yet also knew this might be her only opportunity to convince him. She could not let it go without giving it her all. "So why did you turn down the saddle maker, the creosote fence ads, the horse grooming aids and the electrically heated barn commercials?" she asked curiously, determined not to make the same mistake her predecessors had, whatever it was. "Did you just not believe in the products?'' Tilting her head in a beseeching manner, she stepped closer. ''Or was it something else, like the terms of the endorsement contract, that turned you off?''

''This is beginning to sound like a business meeting,'' Chance warned gruffly. And he obviously wasn't happy about that.

''That's because it is one,'' Madison countered flatly, dropping all pretense that it had ever been anything else. ''But don't worry. You don't have to tell me,'' she soothed pleasantly. ''I'm just curious, since there was so much money involved on those other projects.''

Chance's gaze narrowed. ''How'd you know that?''

''Because people talk.''

Chance whipped off his Stetson and shoved a hand through his hair. ''I didn't tell anyone.''

''Word still gets around.'' Madison smiled at Chance winningly and returned to the Ranchero. She let down the tailgate and hopped on it, letting her legs swing off the side. ''And it's not hard to understand why. You've got a national reputation for training pleasure horses. You're the one all the rich and famous are coming to now. It only follows that requests for endorsement of ranch or horse-related products would follow.''

Chance wasn't about to debate Madison over that. He had worked hard for every iota of his success. And along with it, he had also regained the privacy—and freedom—he had yearned for since he'd been sent to the Lost Springs Ranch for Boys years ago.

Chance regarded Madison stonily. ''What do you get out of this?'' he demanded. Odds were, a lot, if she was willing to go to all this trouble.

''A vice presidency, a big jump in salary and a big corner office.''

Chance sighed. Leave it to him to get stuck with someone who had a cash register in the place where her heart should have been. His dad had tried to buy him off, too, whenever he had been in the wrong. It hadn't worked then. It wouldn't work now. "You'll have to earn it some other way."

"Not even if you donated all your earnings to the Lost Spring Ranch for Boys?"

Chance propped one foot on the truck bumper. One forearm resting on his upraised thigh, he leaned toward her, not stopping until they were face-to-face. Then he said ever so softly and disparagingly, "You don't get it, do you?"

His lazy drawl held an edge of menace, and her stomach twisted. "Get what?" she asked, as innocently as possible.

His gaze slid over her, lingering on the open V of her vivid blue cotton camp shirt before sliding down over her breasts, abdomen, thighs, and up to her face again with disconcerting ease. "I can't be bought."

He was talking nonsense. Madison planted her hands on the warm metal edge of the truck bed and crossed her blue-jeans-clad legs indolently at the knee. "Everyone has a price, Chance." Even if the price was not for yourself but for charity, as the bachelor auction had been. Even though her mother had been devastated by her father's constant betrayals, she had been bought off with diamonds and furs and expensive trips to exclusive spas. The lavish gifts hadn't solved the problems in their marriage, of course, but the luxury had certainly eased her mother's pain to the point that she was able to continue with the marriage. Just as Madison's generous salary and the luxuries it had bought her had eased the pain of her loveless life. She didn't see why a lot of extra money couldn't make his life easier, too.

Chance planted a hand on the truck bed next to her and leaned in close. "Everyone has a limit," he decreed, his tone brooking no disagreement. "And I've just reached mine." He straightened abruptly, planting both feet on the ground. "You want to stay?" He reached over, took her hand and tugged her off the bed of the truck so she was standing in front of him. "You want to follow through on the date you bought? You won't bring the subject up again."

He was being so closed-minded and mulish, it was all Madison could do not to stomp her foot. And she was not the type of woman who ever stomped her foot! She gritted her teeth instead. "Just tell me what it will take to get you to say yes!"

"Well, let's see. I'm already famous—in horse circles." Taking her wrist, Chance pulled her away from the truck, slammed the tailgate shut and ushered her willy-nilly toward the ranch house. "And I didn't have to do anything I didn't want to do to get there. As for money," he said, forcing her to practically run to keep up with him, "I've already got more than I'll ever need."

Madison knew that, damn it. She used her free hand to grab his arm, simultaneously digging in her heels. The dual effort worked to at least slow them down. "You could be named the sexiest man alive by the time we've finished launching the truck."

"And lose my privacy?" Chance skidded to a halt. Bristling with outrage, he shook his head. "Forget it."

So maybe privacy was important to him. Madison guessed that in his years as an orphan, he probably hadn't had enough of it. Not nearly. But times were different now. He had choices that he hadn't had then. She had to make him see that.

"Look, I'm sorry if I appear to be pushing you into this," she said hurriedly, cringing at the desperate sound of her voice. She drew a bracing breath and lowered her voice to a persuasive murmur. "I wouldn't do it if I didn't think it would be a winning proposition for all of us. You, me, the truck manufacturer, the ad agency I work for, the Lost Springs Ranch for Boys."

"Okay. That's it." Chance looked at the blue sky and fluffy white clouds overhead. "Heaven knows I tried." He turned to Madison, stepped in closer and looked at her. "Forget the weekend, and the five thousand dollars you paid. You—" he pressed his index finger to her chest "—are getting your money back."

Madison's jaw dropped. Knowing from her research what a truly generous man he was, she hadn't figured this would happen. "You'd really deprive the ranch of five thousand dollars?" she asked incredulously.

Chance's lips tightened into a thin white line. "No, of course not," he growled bad-temperedly. "I'll make it up to the Lost Springs coffers myself."

Stung, Madison could only gape at him. "You can't cancel our date!" She would never live it down if he did. Her career at Connelly and Associates would be ruined!

Chance moved past her, making sure he knocked into her shoulder as he did. "Watch me," he said.

With Madison hard on his heels, he stormed into the house. She followed him in and up the stairs. He charged into her room, stopping dead when he saw the clothes she had already laid out for the celebration she had planned for the two of them that evening. He looked askance at the short, sexy evening dress hanging on the back of the closet door. "You planned to wear that on a ranch?"

"Don't be silly. I had plans to charter a plane and fly us both to Denver this evening for a congratulatory meal."

Chance grabbed the lingerie she'd left on the bed and tossed it and her evening dress into her open suitcase.

Madison lounged in the doorway, folding her arms. If he thought she was going to give up this easily, he had another think coming! She had nothing—no family, no children, no life outside the office—beckoning her elsewhere. Her job was her entire world. Signing Chance was the key to her advancement. She wasn't letting him—or the promotion she had hanging in the balance—go without one hell of a fight. Because that vice presidency was the key to her happiness. That vice presidency would give her security like no man ever could.

"If you will just calm down, I know we can make a deal." Madison fixed Chance with a matter-of-fact look. "Just tell me what you want. I'll see you get it, I promise."

"I'll just bet you would," Chance drawled, wishing she didn't look so damn pretty standing there in jeans and a shirt, the blush of sun on her upturned face, the fire of her considerable ambition in her eyes.

Madison shrugged, unable to see the problem. "Then..."

Chance took a deep breath, summoning the very last ounce of his patience, then spoke in labored tones she couldn't possibly fail to understand. "I don't want to make a deal with you."

Once again, to Chance's frustration, Madison refused to back down. "Why decide now?" she asked pleasantly, pushing all the harder for what she wanted. "You can take the whole weekend to make up your mind, Chance."

"I don't need the whole weekend to make up my mind. I'm not doing it. Not now. Not ever," he stated flatly. He wasn't climbing into bed with her or the people she represented—even if he couldn't seem to stop imagining how she'd feel beneath him or wondering if she'd kiss with as much gusto and aggression as she lived. As much as he hated to admit it, he was turned on by her confidence and drive, her take-no-prisoners personality. More damning yet, he wanted to see some of that fire turned on him behind closed doors.

Madison stared at him, incensed. "That's a lousy attitude to have. Particularly when you haven't even bothered to hear me—or my agency, or the people from the AMV Corporation—out."

Maybe it was. Maybe it wasn't, Chance thought, but that's how it was going to be, and it was high time Madison realized it. He didn't have to be fair. He didn't owe her anything.

Figuring this was one city girl who had been designing events to suit herself long enough, he took her by the arms and backed her up. Ignoring her soft gasp of dismay, he closed the distance between them, aligning his body against hers, trapping her against the wall. "Just how far would you go to close this deal, Madison?" Chance taunted softly, watching her chin jut forward and her eyes turn a hot, fiery green.

She tried to shove him away.

Determined to ruffle her all-business facade, he caught her hands and held them on either side of her. "Would you go this far?" He ducked his head and touched his lips to hers, softly, evocatively.

He expected her to cry uncle immediately, of course. Realize she'd gone too far in her pursuit of him, promise to leave immediately and never darken his doorway or intrude upon the life he'd made for himself again. Instead, she kissed him.

Chance had known this woman had the potential to be trouble with a capital T the moment she had contacted him about being the Ranchero spokesperson. And that feeling had only intensified when she'd bought him for the weekend. Something about the way she had looked at him. As if he had the power to make her professional dreams come true. And that look had set forth an answering fantasy deep inside him. Only his fantasy had been about this, Chance thought, continuing to kiss her deeply and without restraint. The truth was, he'd been wondering if she would stay even after he turned her down yet again—wondering if they would ultimately act on the potent sexual attraction between them and make love before going their separate ways. Yet he also knew full well Madison Burnes was exactly the kind of career-driven city girl he had always shied away from. And for good reason. Impatient, demanding, far too stubborn and single-minded for her own good, she was the kind of headstrong woman who wanted what she wanted—now! And, as her kisses were fast proving, she would do anything to get it.

If he were smart, he'd stop kissing her this instant, Chance scolded himself sternly.

Then again…

How long, he wondered, as he tangled his hands in the softness of her white-blond hair, since he'd been presented with such a challenge or been near a woman he wanted even half as much? How long, he wondered, as her fingers dug into his shoulders and she kissed and tormented him beyond his wildest dreams, since he'd ached with pleasure, just said to hell with it and thrown caution to the wind?

Her lips were soft and warm and infinitely sweet, and she kissed him fiercely, with absolutely nothing held in check. She wasn't the kind of woman who'd give up or give in easily. Chance knew that. Yet she'd allowed him, however briefly, to overpower her and impose his desire on her. Her surrender excited him. The familiar surge of need, so long forgotten, so long ignored, came crashing back. Her lips parted, inviting him in, and her tongue sought his. No shy maiden, she gave an intense physicality to their embrace. And once he'd felt her quick response, felt her rising up to meet him, there was no stopping with just one kiss. No pretending something extraordinary wasn't happening between them.

With her persistent phone calls, letters and gifts, her hell-for-leather pursuit of him, Madison had gotten under his skin the way no woman ever had, and with her blazing like a bonfire in his arms, he knew there was only one way to extinguish the flame. With every brush of her lips against his, every soft stroke of her tongue, every searching caress of her hands, she was compelling him to make love to her the way she deserved to be made love to, and he was damned if he could say no.

It didn't matter that they were as different as night and day and would probably regret this the second it was over,

Chance thought as he sifted his hands through the ribbon softness of her hair. Nor did he care she was probably using this as a means to an end. He wanted her with all his heart and soul. And since he had never in his entire life done anything halfway, he gave it his all.

Madison had never felt such overpowering need, such urgency. Her meticulous research had told her that Chance Cartwright, bachelor cowboy extraordinaire, was sexy and drop-dead handsome and loaded with charisma. What she hadn't expected was that he would make her—the reputed ice queen of all time—tingle all over and feel soft and sexy and weak in the knees. She was not the kind of woman who could be swept off her feet, damn it! She was not the kind of woman who let passion rather than common sense rule her thoughts and actions. And yet, as Chance backed her up to the wall and spread his legs on either side of her, pressing his lower half ever so sensually to hers, all she could think about was what it would feel like to be held in his arms with nothing at all between them except their hot, silky skin. What it would be like to have Chance Cartwright know her as no man ever had, totally and completely. What it would be like to be possessed by him, protected, taken by him heart and soul.

His eyes locked with hers. His breathing was every bit as ragged and out of control as hers. "I want you," he whispered huskily.

And I want you. Madison didn't want to think about his desire for her or hers for him. Didn't want to remember how many nights, after getting off the phone with him, she had secretly fantasized what it would be like to be the woman—the only woman—in this cowboy's life. She'd come to see him to get her promotion, but had ended up getting so much more than she'd bargained for. Passion. Pleasure. A break from everything that was dull and predictable in her life. Like it or not, Madison thought, feeling him grow even hotter, harder, he made her want as fiercely

as he did. He made her react with everything that was feisty
and feminine within her. And they were only just getting
started, she knew. Worse, he was the first man—the only
man—who had ever really captivated her. But none of that
altered what had brought her here and kept her here still.
Undaunted, she told him breathlessly, "I want a promotion."

Chance's deep blue eyes narrowed. His low voice burned
with quiet urgency that had nothing to do with ego and
everything to do with desire and a willingness to please.
"Yeah, but what do you *need,* Madison?" His mouth
moved on hers effortlessly, taking complete control of the
kiss. "What do you need?"

A riptide of heat flooded through Madison, pooling between her thighs.

Chance pressed even closer, so she could feel the po-
tency of his arousal and the heat and strength emanating
from his tall, sinewy frame. "Could it be me? Could I be
the man you've been waiting for all your life?" he teased,
looking more than willing to volunteer for the job if that
was indeed the case. "Is that why you're trembling?"

Madison shot him a quelling look, stubbornly refusing
to pull away. How dare he imply that he could in any way
be the man for her. Never mind erase the uncertainty and
anxiety she always felt when it came to even the idea of
beginning an intimate relationship.

She wanted this to be business and nothing more, damn
it. Anything else got in the way! She glared at him. "You
want to make love?" she snapped. Ignoring the ribbons of
need unfurling throughout her body, weakening her knees,
making her feel all fluid-limbed, she went on tersely, "Because if that's what it will take to clear the air and get rid
of this *newfound tension* between us, I'm all for it. So long
as I get what I came here for, too, of course."

Chance looked Madison over from head to toe and gave
her an infuriating grin. "I should've known you'd frame it

like that," he drawled, all too aware that the fury in her eyes might have discouraged most men. But not him.

"It's the truth." Her whole body thrumming with pent-up need, Madison shoved away from the wall, tried to step past him, to take charge of the business between them once again.

"Is it?" Chance countered, using his body to block her way, forcing her back to remain against the wall.

Even as she denied it, she knew he could see the vulnerability in her eyes. He stepped closer and took her in his arms again. His lips moved over hers, and though Madison's mind was still fighting him, her body had long ago turned traitor on her.

"I could have sworn it was something much more basic and inevitable," Chance whispered, his hand ghosting over her ribs and moving ever upward toward her breasts.

"Like what?" Madison demanded, irritated by the increasing breathlessness in her low voice. She had never in her life experienced such tender, invigorating kisses, and she feared she never would again. That alone was enough to make her want to continue, to see where this would lead. And if this was what it would take to finally be able to cement the deal with him, well, that wasn't such a bad thing, was it?

Chance inclined his head. He rubbed his thumbs across her lips, erasing the dewy residue of their previous kisses. "Like maybe the two of us were meant to be together like this."

"You can't believe that," Madison scolded, letting him know with a glance she was no naive simpleton. It had to be some sort of cowboy pickup line he was using on her. But she saw, looking into his eyes, that he believed it.

"All I know for sure is I want you." Chance slipped his hands beneath her shirt to caress her breasts. "And...you can deny it all you want, excuse it all you want...but you want me."

That was because she had never felt passion like this, Madison thought as her nipples beaded against his tenderly caressing palms. She had never been wanted like this, so completely, so inexorably, so quickly. The past few years there had been so little excitement in her life, so little possibility of bliss on any level. To feel it now, at just a kiss or two or three, was overwhelming. And yet there was no denying it. When Chance's lips had touched hers, he'd made her feel alive, made her feel wanted. And for the moment, anyway, he made her feel cherished. Appreciated. In a very womanly, very exciting way. As foolish and reckless as that might be, Madison realized abruptly, there was a part of her that was ready and willing to explore all that— for the sake of the deal, of course, she reassured herself firmly.

"You're right," Madison murmured. Why should hard-loving cowboys be the only ones who could compartmentalize their lives, worry about business one moment, pleasure the next? Why should cowboys have all the fun? "Maybe—just maybe—this is exactly what we both need here."

There was nothing tentative or questioning about what they brought each other then. She wanted control. He understood she needed it, and he gave it to her. Then it was all raw primitive passion. Throaty moans. Her hands more bold than his.

Her lips were hot and soft, her kiss wild and sensual. Groaning, Chance deepened the kiss, meeting her tongue, stroke for enticing stroke. He swept her mouth rapaciously, leaving not a millimeter unexplored. She kissed him as if she couldn't get enough of him. Then opened his shirt, his jeans, slipped her hands inside his briefs. Her hands were everywhere, cupping him warmly, gently exploring and caressing, touching, teasing, tormenting, until goose bumps rose on his flesh and the blood rushed through his veins.

Madison deepened their kiss even more, her tongue parrying evocatively with his. Chance groaned, the sound one of deep male satisfaction, then swept her into his arms and carried her down the hall to his bedroom. His heart pounding, he lowered her to his bed. Her eyes darkened impatiently, and she watched as he hurriedly stripped off his clothes and dropped down beside her.

"Finally," Madison murmured.

Chance's soft laughter mingled with hers, the intimate sound echoing through his empty house. Still smiling, her mouth swollen from their kisses, she put her hand to the side of his face and eagerly brought his lips to hers. They kissed again as he stretched out beside her, deep, hungry kisses that had no beginning and no end. And then it was his turn to unbutton her shirt, her jeans, push aside her bra and bikini panties, not stopping until she was as gloriously naked as he. His glance trailed hungrily over the soft, rounded globes of her breasts, the graceful indentation of her waist, the silken flare of her hips, moving lower still to the triangle of golden curls, long, slender thighs, sexy calves and dainty feet. She was perfect, every breathtaking inch of her.

"You're beautiful," he said, pausing to kiss the perfect crests.

Looking more vulnerable than he ever could have imagined her being, Madison drew in a trembling breath. "You make me feel that way," she said, her eyes filled with an emotion he couldn't quite read and a yearning he could. And then there was no middle ground. Everywhere he looked, he touched. Every place he touched, he kissed. Caressed. Loved. Until she was hot and wet and open to accept him, arching off the bed, crying out her need.

The mattress gave beneath them as he stretched over her, the warmth of his body draping hers. Remembering the need to protect her, he reached into the bedside table. The time it took him to roll onto his back and rip open a packet was all she needed to get her mind on her first and foremost priority.

"Tell me you'll be the spokesperson," Madison demanded breathlessly.

Chance finished sheathing himself and tossed the empty packet aside. He caught the look on her face and knew her maneuver for what it was, an attempt to cover her vulnerability and need. But it was too late for that, much too late. He saw the fragility in her eyes, he'd seen the way she opened herself up to him, he'd felt the way she had kissed and clung to him, and he knew how much she wanted and needed him, even if she wouldn't yet admit it to herself.

He caught her chin in one hand and turned her face to his. "I'm yours," he said.

And then in one long, slow stroke, he entered her, possessing her to the fullest. When she would have hurried the pace, he held back, making her understand what it was to feel such intense, burning need. And then there was no more holding back. They clung together, savoring the hot rise of passion, the culmination of need and the wonder of finding each other at all. And then they were soaring through space, stepping away from the loneliness of the past and into the excitement of the present.

"NOW THAT'S SETTLED, where do I sign?" Chance asked.

"One thing at a time, Chance," Madison demurred, having barely caught her breath before the regrets started settling in. Very much aware of his reluctance to let her go, she extricated her trembling body from his. "Just let me get dressed." She sent him a careless smile meant to disguise all the turmoil she was feeling inside. And of that there was plenty!

Chance Cartwright might not know it, but Madison had never made love with anyone she had to work with, and she'd never lost sight of a business goal in her life. Because business—and the sheer predictability of it—was just an extension of the success-oriented goals that had sustained her throughout her turbulent childhood, through her teens and into her twenties. And now, at age thirty, to find herself on the verge of achieving the biggest plum of all—the vice presidency at Connelly and Associates—only to get off the track by becoming hormonal over a sexy rancher. Good grief, she couldn't believe she'd just made love with Chance Cartwright, even if it had been the only way to get his attention long enough to close the deal.

Well, there was one way to show him this was a hopelessly sexy interlude that would never happen again. They were business associates and nothing more. This part of their relationship was over. Finished. Their curiosity about what it would be like to make love to each other had been completely and utterly satisfied. They would close this particular chapter before they got entangled any further. Before either of them could be hurt.

Feeling her cheeks pinkening self-consciously, Madison rose with as much dignity as she could muster. Her motions as smooth and elegant as she could make them, she began putting on her clothes once again. It had been a mistake to let down her guard. But there was no changing what had just happened. All she could do was move on.

Chance lounged against the headboard, naked beneath the sheets, watching. The somber descent of his brow couldn't begin to disguise the pleasure he'd felt at having her in his bed. He nodded at her clothes. ''A little late for that, don't you think?''

Madison flashed him a tight, officious smile and tried to ignore the fact he'd made her want him in a way she had never wanted any man. With effort, she met his mesmerizing blue eyes, cleared her throat and managed a patently false chuckle. ''Now, Chance, it's never too late to get dressed.'' *Might I suggest you take the cue and do the same?*

But to her frustration—she was sure he knew exactly

what she wanted him to do—he remained right where he was, naked and in bed. Lazily propping his forearm on his upraised knee, he studied her with a mixture of tenderness and curiosity. "Let me guess what burr's gotten under your saddle. You're upset because we made love even though we're now going to have to work together."

Which was something he was clearly looking forward to doing, Madison thought. Probably in just as intimate a fashion!

She was upset because he'd made her feel vulnerable. She bristled as she tugged on her clothes. "Come on, Chance." She slid her feet into her shoes. "We're both adults here."

He lifted a brow. "That's what I thought."

It didn't matter what had happened today, Madison told herself. She could get past it the same way she had gotten past any other problem in her life. She regarded him levelly. "We are going to put this behind us, Chance. Forget it ever happened."

Madison expected Chance to jump at the graceful out she was giving him, to bring this reckless, passionate incident to a close and be very happy they would never have to think about such an embarrassing episode again. But he didn't.

To her dismay, he lounged even more comfortably on the bed. "Now, why on this green earth would we want to do that?"

"Because I am not in the market for anything more," Madison explained impatiently. And there was good reason for that. From what she'd seen, getting involved in passionate love affairs seemed to turn people's lives upside down. Whereas she liked her life just fine the way it was. All work and very little play. Her work had never let her down in any way. Her work was a great lover to have and—unlike play—provided great benefits.

"You know what I think?" Chance retorted, still studying her.

"No, but I'm sure you're going to tell me," Madison said, catching sight of her disheveled hair and kiss-swollen lips in the bureau mirror. Embarrassed by how thoroughly loved she looked, she picked up a brush and began running it through the tousled layers of her hair.

"I think you're afraid we might have found something special here—"

Madison shot him a look over her shoulder and rolled her eyes. "Chance, please!"

"—and you don't know what to do with that."

Madison dropped the brush with a thunk. She whirled to face him. No sexy cowboy, no matter how intuitive, was going to analyze her. "Oh, I don't, do I?" Madison asked.

Chance nodded. "And you know why? Because it upsets all the tidy little plans you've already made."

"You're right," Madison agreed calmly, refusing to admit to herself how sexy he still looked, lounging around that way, or how much she wanted to forget all this and climb right back into bed with him. "I don't like distractions. They disrupt my ability to do business. Fortunately, I managed to do what I was sent here to do—snag you as spokesperson for the Ranchero account." Furthermore, Madison reminded herself sternly, she wasn't the first woman he'd made love to here. The box of condoms he'd had at the ready told her that. And she probably wouldn't be the last, either. Only a fool would make their lovemaking out to be more than a casual roll in the hay for him, and she was no fool.

Chance regarded her disparagingly. Obviously that was not what he had expected or wanted to hear from her so soon after they'd made love, even if it was the truth. "I should have known that was all you wanted," he muttered beneath his breath.

What she wanted, Madison thought as she went into her

room and returned with the contracts she'd stuck in her suitcase, was to get rid of this warm and fuzzy feeling he'd given her. What she wanted was to stop glowing all over.

It was time to get back to something she could control.

She walked into the bedroom and handed Chance the contracts. "Everything is spelled out pretty plainly," she said.

Chance grimaced as he flipped through them. "So I see."

Madison perched on the far end of the bed. "The AMV executives are going to want to meet with you in Dallas as soon as possible. You'll get your signing bonus then. In the meantime, since you've already agreed to do this," Madison reminded him nicely when it seemed, for one heart-stoppingly tense moment, that he might be going to renege on his promise to her, "I'd like you to sign on the dotted line now."

She handed Chance a pen.

He made a few changes in the margins, then scrawled his signature on the bottom.

"You won't regret this," Madison told him enthusiastically.

He looked at her as if he already did.

Wordlessly, Chance flung the sheet away from him. Gloriously naked, gloriously handsome, he rose. "You better leave."

He tugged his jeans over his hips, then zipped them swiftly.

Madison sighed and tore her eyes from his ruggedly imposing form. Damn it. He was back to being the impossible cowpoke again. "We have to go over all this," she told him. "We need to set a date for the meeting. Arrange for your travel—"

"Not now, Madison," Chance said gruffly.

Madison was not about to be put off, not after all the hard work she'd done and the month she'd spent chasing him. "Give me a break here, Chance." Once again, she pulled out the smile she reserved for her most difficult clients. "I know this is a bit awkward." She was struggling with the fact they'd just made love. "But you should at least give me an opportunity to—"

"Oh, I gave you an opportunity, all right." Chance spun around. He glared at her as he shoved his arms through his shirt and buckled his belt. "I gave you plenty of opportunity. And, lady, you blew it."

CHAPTER THREE

URSULA RODRIGUEZ, the marketing director in charge of the AMV corporation's new Ranchero pickup truck, studied the photos Madison put in front of her with a critical eye. "I thought Chance Cartwright was supposed to be at this meeting today," Ursula said with a frown. As always, her jet black hair was pulled into a sleek chignon, her makeup flawless, her jewelry stylish but understated. She wore a sleek black Armani pantsuit that complimented her thin, statuesque form.

"He was," Madison said.

Ursula's dark eyes flashed in disapproval. "So where is he?"

I don't have a clue, Madison thought unhappily. Chance had been ducking her phone calls and ignoring her messages since she'd left Wyoming several weeks ago, signed contract in hand. "He called and left a message on my voice mail late last night…something about a problem with a horse he was training. He said he was not going to be here today." And that was all he'd said.

Ed Connelly—the president and founding partner of Connelly and Associates—sent Madison a narrow glance that spoke volumes about his displeasure with her. "Cartwright understood how important it is for him to make himself accessible to us?" Ed barked.

Madison nodded. "I've explained it to him, yes." Countless times. In person, on his answering machine, via letter, fax, telegram and express mail. Madison knew Chance was a decent guy. Her research had told her that. He honored his business commitments.

And this was business.

"And..." Ursula tapped her pen against the table.

"And he's not an easy man to handle," Madison explained.

"You managed to get him to sign on the dotted line," Ed said.

Yes, but that was all she'd managed to make him do thus far, Madison thought. "I'll see it doesn't happen again," she promised. If she had to go to Wyoming and haul Chance back with her in person.

Ursula stood and closed her Filofax with a decisive snap. "You've got until the end of the week to get Cartwright to Dallas. Then we go with another firm. One that doesn't promise what they can't deliver." She spun around on her heel and exited the office in a cloud of Shalimar perfume.

As she watched her boss shut the door to the conference room, Madison felt ill. Ed Connelly turned to Madison, who had remained standing. "Who else have you got lined up to back up Cartwright?" he demanded brusquely.

No one, Madison thought in mounting frustration. Nor did she want anyone else for the commercial. She wet her lips, aware the stress of the meeting had left her feeling just the tiniest bit nauseated. "Men of Chance Cartwright's caliber aren't easy to find." Boy, was that an understatement, she thought, recalling how exquisitely Chance had made love to her. She hadn't known lovemaking could be like that, so potent and all-encompassing. Aware she was digressing yet again—a common occurrence when it came to Chance, the kind of sexy cowboy who inspired daydreams—Madison forced her thoughts to the task at hand. Surreptitiously blotting her damp hairline with her fingertips, she said, "As you just saw, Ursula wants the real thing, not some drugstore cowboy who doesn't know the back end of a horse from the front."

Ed ran a hand over his balding head. "Of course she does," he exploded, exasperated. "You sold her on the idea of using a sexy, well-known rancher to sell the Ranchero. And it was a damn good idea, too. Who better to promote the fact it's American made and environmentally friendly? But if this cowboy proves unreliable, we've got to replace him."

Madison had an idea that was exactly what Chance Cartwright was counting on. Unfortunately, it wasn't that simple.

Feeling a little dizzy, she curved her hand over the back of the chair to steady herself. She took a deep, bolstering breath, willing her nausea away as she met Ed's distressed gaze. She could get through the rest of this meeting; it was silly to think she couldn't. "I can find real ranchers in abundance, Ed. No problem. Sexy, handsome men who would look good in a pickup. Also no problem. We just looked at the portfolios of darn near thirty of them. But to find a sexy, single, talented man who really makes his living that way, who has the respect of everyone in the ranching and horse training community, who also just happens to rub elbows with the rich and famous and owns his own ranch on some of the most beautiful land in all Wyoming— to find someone who's a ladies' man and a man's man all rolled into one—well, that's something else indeed."

"Then you better find a way to get Cartwright in line," Ed ordered flatly.

Her knees had turned to jelly. Like it or not, Madison had to sit down before she fell down. Doing her best to look calm and in control, she eased into her chair, dropping her notepad on her lap. "I'll book a flight to Wyoming immediately." Despite the fact she was sitting down, the rubbery feeling in Madison's knees intensified and her stomach began to take on an increasingly queasy feeling.

Ed jerked loose the knot of his tie and gulped coffee like

it was going out of style. " I don't have to tell you how much money is at stake here."

Just thinking about the potential loss of revenue for the agency made Madison grimace.

Ed, who was nothing if not a straight shooter, folded his hands in front of him and told her bluntly, "Land the account for us, Madison, and the VP slot opening up in September is yours—no question. Lose it and…" Ed let his voice trail off.

The sick feeling inside Madison moved up to her throat. There was no helping it; she was going to have to cut this meeting short. "Excuse me—" Leaping from her chair, her hand over her mouth, Madison dashed from Ed's office.

"I'VE HEARD of the pressure to succeed around here making people sick," Kit Smith remarked, "but this is ridiculous."

Madison looked up from the rim of the commode in the executive washroom. Her copper-haired colleague with the maternal air wet a paper towel and hunkered beside Madison on the gleaming marble floor. Wordlessly, Kit helped Madison—who was perspiring profusely—take her suit jacket off. She hung it over the back of the door and returned with a paper cup of cold water that she pressed into Madison's hands. "Uncle Ed said you ran out of his office, your hand over your mouth."

"It had nothing to do with what we were discussing." Ignoring the tears seeping from the corners of her eyes, Madison pressed a cold, damp paper towel to the back of her neck.

"Good. Because I wouldn't want you to worry about me usurping the VP slot. I want one, too, now that the twins are about to enter college. Make no mistake about that. But not in your place."

Kit knelt beside Madison. "Think it was something you had for lunch?" she asked gently.

"Maybe." Madison took a small sip of water, rested her forehead on her upraised hand. She sighed. This wasn't the first time she'd battled nausea recently. "Then again, maybe it's just stress. I've been feeling strange for weeks now." Deciding she felt better, Madison struggled to her feet with Kit's help.

Kit helped Madison, who was now shivering slightly, put her jacket on. "Ill how?"

Madison shrugged and walked, albeit a little unsteadily, to the sink. "Woozy, dizzy, tired." She bent and rinsed her mouth, then rummaged around for the travel-size toothbrush and toothpaste she carried in her purse. "All I want to do is sleep."

Kit shook her head. "If I didn't know better, kiddo, I'd think you were pregnant, but you'd need a man in your life for that. Unless—" Kit paused. "You didn't go the artificial insemination route, did you?"

No. But she had recklessly made love with Chance at what would have been her most fertile time of month, Madison realized uncomfortably. They'd used a condom, of course. But…was it possible? Pushing the unsettling thought away, Madison threw the paper towel in the trash, put her toothbrush and toothpaste back in her purse.

"Maybe you should see your doctor before you head back to Wyoming," Kit suggested.

"Good idea," Madison said. One way or another, she had to know.

THE SUN was shining brightly as Madison drove through the gates of Chance Cartwright's Double Diamond Ranch shortly after noon the next day. The meadows in the distance were alive with tall yellow grass and multicolored wildflowers, and the tops of the granite mountains were white against the bold blue of the summer sky. Late July, it was hotter than it had been when she had been there before, the temperature inching into the eighties. As Madison neared the house, she saw a van from the Lost Springs Ranch and a group of teenage boys in T-shirts, boots, jeans and hats mucking out stalls and grooming the horses with long, patient strokes. Chance was standing in the pasture closest to the house, instructing two of his part-time workers as they exercised his horses. They looked as if they were having the time of their lives. Chance looked equally happy. Until he saw her, that was.

He said something to the boys, then turned and strode toward her as two blue jays swooped down on them from overhead and disappeared in the cottonwood trees by the ranch house.

Her heart racing, a million butterflies jumping around inside her stomach, Madison emerged from the car, deliberately keeping her sunglasses on. Wanting to immediately telegraph the fact she'd come to make peace with him, she'd taken care to dress in jeans, boots and cotton shirt. Still, her hands were sweaty as his long legs ate up the ground between them.

Sweat dripped down his face, and the fabric of his blue chambray shirt was damp in patches. He was more deeply suntanned than he had been the last time she had seen him. And there was a wariness in his eyes when he looked at her that was new, too.

He tipped his hat in cursory politeness as he neared her. "Miss Burnes."

Madison nodded, dismayed to realize he wasn't nearly as happy to see her again as she was to see him. Because despite everything, she still desired him. "Mr. Cartwright." Her tone was the low, exceedingly pleasant one she reserved for her most difficult clients.

He regarded her grimly. "I wasn't expecting you."

Madison gave him a parody of a smile as she whipped off her sunglasses so he could see her eyes. "I figured if you'd known I was coming, you would have been sure to duck out."

Chance rubbed his jaw and tried not to grin at her cheeky attitude. "Missed a few of your phone calls, have I?" he taunted.

"As well as a command appearance in Dallas." *Which you very well know.* He let his gaze rove insolently over her from head to toe, and Madison drew a long breath. She figured she might as well be blunt. It didn't matter if this was awkward. Or something she'd rather not do. She wasn't going to be like her father. She wasn't going to lie just to make things easier and less complicated for herself. Because dishonesty never worked. "You know you could be fired as the Ranchero spokesperson for behaving this way."

"Is that a fact?" Chance drawled, not the least bit upset by her warning.

Temper simmering, Madison stepped closer until they stood toe to toe. Was this what it was going to be like— Chance passively resisting her at every turn? "We had a deal, Chance," she reminded him bluntly.

As Chance looked at her, Madison had the sharp suspicion he wanted to haul her against him until they were situated like lock and key. "I agreed to sign your papers so we'd have more time to spend together."

"In bed," Madison guessed grimly, sure she knew where all this was leading.

"And out of bed," Chance said, looking very much as if he wanted to make long, slow, passionate love to her again. "When you made it clear that wasn't going to happen—" he shrugged his broad shoulders restlessly "—you might say I lost interest." The corners of his mouth tilted up. "I'm never a very good worker when I lose interest."

"So find a way to get interested," Madison advised curtly, infuriated to find he was not going to keep his promise to her. She'd thought—erroneously, it appeared—that Chance was different from most men in that respect.

Chance looked at her from beneath the brim of his hat.

"Now, Miss Burnes," he scolded facetiously. "Are you propositioning me?"

"No!" Madison retorted, apparently too quickly and vehemently to be believed.

His sexy smile widened at the growing heat in her upturned face. A challenging gleam appeared in his blue eyes. "Then why are you here?"

Madison blew out a thoroughly exasperated breath. "Because I'm trying to save my career."

The mirth faded from his eyes as swiftly as it had appeared. "Knowing you," he said disparagingly, "I'm sure you'll find a way."

He took her by the arm and started to lead her to her car. Aware he was about to suggest she leave, Madison dug in her heels. She didn't want to tell him this now. She knew he'd perceive it in the worst possible way. But she'd come all this distance and she had no choice. If there was even a slim chance the news would make him the least bit cooperative, for all their sakes, she had to use it. "I'm pregnant."

For a moment, Chance was utterly still. His grip on her arm tightened, his fingers strong and firm. "You trying to tell me it's mine?" Disbelief edged his ruggedly handsome features.

"You trying to tell me it's not?" Madison retorted.

Chance blinked. "We were only together once."

As if she needed reminding of that! Not a night went by that she didn't dream about what it had been like to lie in his arms and make wild passionate love with him, or wake up yearning to do it all again. And again.

"And we used protection!" Chance objected.

"Tell me about it!" Madison muttered. She'd been as stunned as he was by the test results.

"Then how—" Chance demanded roughly.

Madison shrugged and threw up her hands. She'd had a little more time to think about what was happening, come to terms with the situation. It did seem as though the fates were conspiring against them by continuing to pair the two of them together, despite the fact they were anything but a match made in heaven. "Your guess is as good as mine. Although," she mumbled, beginning to get embarrassed at the frank talk, "my doctor said no method of birth control is one hundred percent foolproof. Sometimes these things just happen, he said. And this just…happened, Chance."

Chance was silent. He continued to study her, looking every bit as stunned as she'd felt upon receiving the news. Finally, he said, somewhat indifferently, "Given the circumstances…" He paused, cleared his throat. "You sure it's mine?"

Deciding *that* was uncalled for, Madison slapped him across the face.

Chance stepped back, looking as shocked as she was by what she'd done. He rubbed his face. "Guess so," he conceded.

Abruptly aware they had an audience of young workers, Chance frowned. "We can't talk here. Not without being interrupted, anyway. Let's go down to the south pasture. I need to check on Shiloh. Go get in my pickup truck."

"Chance—"

"Just do it, Madison. Now." He stalked off toward the gaggle of Lost Springs boys in his employ.

Fuming at the imperiousness of his order, Madison stormed to his battered pickup and climbed inside. She watched as he said something to the boys—something that apparently explained why he was going off with her—then grabbed a halter that had been looped over the corral fence and headed toward her. By the time he had tossed the halter in the back of the truck and climbed behind the wheel, the boys were already back at work.

Wordlessly, Chance drove the quarter mile to the pasture where Shiloh was grazing alone, well away from the other horses. "Okay." He cut the motor and jumped out of the truck. After grabbing the halter, he circled around to help Madison out of the truck. Together, they headed for the pasture gate. "I'm listening."

"There's nothing else to say," Madison stated, a lot more calmly than she felt. Emotion rippled through her, tightening her insides. "I just thought you should know you—and I—are having a baby and that baby will be born nine months to the day—most likely, anyway—from the time we were together."

Chance frowned. "I don't want kids, Madison. I never have."

Madison paused, aware her heartbeat had sped to triple time. Struggling to maintain her equilibrium, she slid her hands in the back pockets of her jeans and forced herself to look at him. "I'm not asking you for anything."

"Not even child support?"

Madison shook her head. "I don't need it. But at some point when he or she is much older, our child may want to meet you at least once. I thought you should be prepared for that."

The self-assured speech she had practiced over and over in her head on the way there fell flat. Chance's lips tightened. "What happens if I decide I want to be involved in this?" he asked mildly, studying her closely.

Panic flared in Madison's chest. The two of them couldn't get along for two seconds. The only time they had gotten along was when they were in bed. Madison stepped away from him. "Be realistic, Chance," she counseled softly. "We live in two different states, hundreds of miles apart."

Chance leaned against the pasture fence. Lazily, he hooked his heel on the bottom rung. "There are planes, trains and automobiles. Not to mention buses and horses and—"

"Fine, then." Madison cut off his recitation and put her sunglasses on, less to shield herself from the hot afternoon sun than to veil the emotion in her eyes from his coolly assessing gaze. "You can come and see your child whenever you want," she announced in the interest of fairness. "I won't stop you." Although she couldn't imagine it happening very often at her behest. Every time they saw each other, she'd remember how glorious their passion had been and be tempted to get into bed with him again.

Behind Chance, Shiloh began to approach slowly, a step or two at a time, occasionally nickering soft and low and bobbing his head.

Chance motioned to the magnificent black stallion, calling him over, then smiled tightly at Madison. "How generous of you."

Madison stiffened. Why was he making this so difficult? "I thought so," she told him coolly.

Chance continued to study her closely. "I guess this means you're planning to keep the baby and bring it up yourself?" he said, in a low, inscrutable tone.

"Of course." Once Madison had gotten over the shock—and because she was such a practical person, that hadn't taken long—she'd been deliriously happy about the baby she was expecting. Having Chance involved, of course, complicated matters immensely. But she was sure she could handle the situation as long as she approached it like any other business problem, coolly and with determination and a commitment to do whatever was necessary to make things work out.

"Are you and the baby planning to show up here a lot on a whim?"

This was trickier territory. Madison wasn't sure what answer Chance wanted her to give. Not that it mattered. These were her decisions to make. "No," Madison said with forced graciousness. "In fact, given the way things stand between us right now, well…I just can't see myself coming back here once the Ranchero account is wrapped up." Not even if they were invited. It would be too painful. She'd thought Chance, unlike her cheating, deceiving father, was a man of his word. To have him state, ''I'm yours,'' and then renege, to find out his promises to her were meaningless, too—well, to say it was a major disappointment was an understatement in the extreme.

At the mention of the contract he'd signed, Chance scowled at her and pulled the brim of his hat over his eyes. ''I suppose your attitude would change completely if I were to become a crackerjack spokesperson for the Ranchero pickup truck,'' he told her sarcastically.

Madison moved her shoulders in an elegant shrug. Although she sensed it would buy her some points with Chance, she refused to pretend otherwise about something as important as this. Aware her heart was pounding in her chest, she regarded him steadily. ''I don't deny my opinion of you would definitely become more positive again,'' she told him coldly.

Chance draped the leather lead over the fence. He turned to her, blue eyes grim, and regarded her with increasing cynicism. ''Don't pull any punches, do you, Madison?''

Madison struggled to remain calm as her emotions soared and crashed and then soared all over again. ''I call it like I see it. Always have. Always will. And right now, Chance—'' ever the businesswoman, Madison took the opportunity to drive home her point ''—you're letting down an awful lot of people with your behavior.''

Chance smirked and rubbed his clean-shaven jaw. ''Back to business as usual, right, Madison?''

Aware he was getting under her skin again without even half trying, Madison stiffened. Willing the warmth in her cheeks to go away, she stepped back a pace and clamped her folded arms closer to her midriff. ''At least I do the job I was hired to do,'' she told him archly. She gave her words a moment to sink in, waiting for them to have their desired effect, before she pushed on professionally once again. ''So when can we expect to see you in Dallas?''

Chance's eyes darkened as Shiloh finally came up behind him, stretched his nose over the fence, touching it to Chance's shoulder, demanding attention. "You can't," Chance said grimly.

Infuriated, Madison glared at Chance even as she marveled at the trust Shiloh exhibited toward humans. Six weeks ago the magnificent stallion had been completely unapproachable. Now Shiloh stood quietly while Chance scratched him under the chin and down the throat. "You really want to be fired by AMV?" Madison asked incredulously. She'd thought he cared more about the boys' ranch than that.

"Frankly, Madison, I don't give a damn what AMV does or doesn't do in regard to me." Chance gave Shiloh a final pat, straightened and pushed away from the fence. "You and the baby, on the other hand, are another matter," he warned her heavily.

This was the Chance who had the potential to rock her to her soul, Madison thought.

He grimaced and let out a deep breath. "I know you're not looking for a marriage proposal."

Nor was he about to give her one. "You're right about that," Madison told him in a matter-of-fact tone. She reached across the fence and took a turn petting Shiloh. "We barely know each other."

Worse, Chance thought unhappily as he watched Madison stroke a delicate-looking hand down Shiloh's throat, he and Madison apparently had very little in common besides breathtaking passion and the baby on the way. It sure wasn't much to build on, he thought ruefully, remembering without wanting to how soft and giving and totally without inhibitions Madison had been in bed. If only she could be that way out of bed, too...

Madison turned to Chance and continued with a pragmatism that cut him to the quick. "So maybe we should just consider that both of our obligations have now been met.'' She folded her arms beneath her breasts and assumed a militant stance. ''You know about the baby, and you know I'll take care of it.''

How Madison, Chance thought. How very Madison.

She was perfectly willing to step forward and do the decent thing by telling him about his paternity so she could then go off with *their* baby and live *her* life as if he had no real part in it, at least not day to day. She wanted a clear conscience, the freedom to do as she pleased, to take care of her needs and desires and those of their child, leaving nothing at all for him. ''I'm willing to do my share, Madison,'' Chance told her curtly. Whether she had meant to or not, she had really hit a nerve.

Studying his face, Madison paled. ''I'm not asking for that much involvement, Chance.'' Not anything like it!

Well, too damn bad, lady, because this is my kid, too, we're talking about.

Chance didn't know what kind of daddy he'd make. The thought of diapers and so on, not to mention trying to parent and love a child long distance, terrified him. ''But whatever happens, I promise I'll do the right thing for the baby,'' he told her steadily, looking deep into her green eyes, knowing the repercussions of any further mistakes between them would be severe indeed, because they would end up affecting the baby. ''That's all either of us can do,'' he said wearily.

Madison regarded him critically. ''It sounds like you're making excuses already,'' she told him haughtily.

And maybe he was, Chance thought, but only because he wanted her to understand what they were getting themselves into here. ''My own dad wasn't exactly a warm and fuzzy guy,'' Chance told her gruffly.

''So what does that have to do with us?'' Madison asked irritably.

Behind them, Shiloh—upset by their rising voices and increasingly tense posture—snorted and pawed the ground, then wheeled away and raced for the other end of the pasture, halter still on. Chance swore softly. Had he known how heated their discussion was likely to get, he wouldn't have brought her here to see the skittish horse. Figuring he'd tend to his horse later, he turned to Madison and forced himself to do what the ranch staff at Lost Springs had taught him—admit his own culpability in an unhappy past and then move on.

"I'm saying what happened between me and my dad was a two-way street," Chance told Madison impatiently. "My dad loved me and *he* didn't know how to show it. I loved him and *I* didn't know how to show it. Things that should have brought us closer together always ended up driving us further apart."

"Are you telling me you don't know how to love?"

Chance shrugged and pushed away the pain he always felt when he thought about his dad and what should have been. "I can train horses. I can be a friend, a good one. Beyond that…" He let his voice trail off. When it came to normal family relationships, trying to be a father without being a husband, trying to forge a normal family life without being married or even living in the same state…well, they'd be making it up as they went along. He felt Madison should know that, be prepared for it.

For a moment, Madison looked as if she had the same fears. Not about him this time, but about herself. And Chance's heart went out to her. He and Madison were both sure of themselves when it came to their work. They were both damn good at what they did. It was their relationship with each other—flirtatious and hotter than a firecracker one minute, totally over the next—that was a mess. He hoped they could keep their beefs with each other away from their child. Because if they couldn't, if they continued to feel as passionately about each other as they did now, liking each other a little too much one minute, loathing each other the next…

"So if this long-distance, two-parents-who-are-strangers thing doesn't work out," Chance continued, figuring Madison of all people would appreciate his direct approach, "if it turns out it's somehow less confusing for him or her to have one parent, then I promise you I'll do the decent thing and step aside." *I sure as hell won't want to,* Chance added silently, *but I will.* "The bottom line here is we do what is best for our child. Not what is best for me or you," he said firmly. He knew firsthand how complicated life could be. He was determined he would spare their child any hurt, and he would see Madison did, too.

"Why not make it simple then?" Madison challenged, chin lifting, perverse enough to take everything he had said the wrong way. "Step aside right now."

"Before we've even given it a shot?" he countered, mocking her sarcastic tone.

Madison lifted her hands, palms up, on either side of her. "Think of the time it will save!" That said, she spun on her heel and marched toward his pickup.

Chance swore heatedly as he watched her provocatively swaying backside. So much for trying to tell *her* what was on *his* mind. Not about to let her have the last word, now or any time, Chance cut her off before she reached the passenger door. "Don't you think you're overreacting here?" He'd just been trying to cover all possible eventualities. She didn't have to assume it was actually going to come to the worst-case scenario. She needed to be prepared to deal with it, the same way he was prepared to deal with lame horses and droughts and blizzards on the ranch.

Madison whirled. Her green eyes were hot with temper. She poked a finger at his chest. "You're not the only one who suffered through a miserable childhood, Chance Cartwright! I grew up listening to parents make excuses about why they had to keep on making us all miserable," she continued furiously, her hand curling in the sweat-damp fabric of his shirt. "Nothing ever changed. And you know why?'' Using her grip on his shirt, she shook him lightly. "Because neither of them ever wanted things to change!" Releasing her hold, she shoved him away. "I'll be damned if I'm ever going to live that way again. Never mind our baby! Our baby needs a daddy who will love him or her from day one on. No excuses! No halfhearted efforts! Because you're right, Chance. Anything less guarantees only hurt for our baby, and that being the case, why even start down that road?'' Giving him no chance to work in a word edgewise, Madison shoved her hands through her hair. "It's not as if I don't have enough on my plate as it is.'' Grabbing her sunglasses off the top of her head, she angrily waved them around in the air. "Thanks to you and your stubborn refusal to fulfill your duties as spokesperson, I'm about to lose the Ranchero truck account and the vice presidency right along with it.''

Chance heard the fear in her voice. He blocked her way. "Are you telling me your job is in jeopardy?" he demanded roughly. He knew how important her career was to her. This must be killing her.

Madison bit her lower lip and regarded him truculently. "Let's just say when you get yourself let out of your contract, I'll definitely be on my way down the career ladder if not out on the street!'' She stormed past him, vaulted into the pickup and slammed the door behind her.

His feelings in turmoil, Chance circled to the driver's side and climbed in. He let his hands rest on the wheel and stared out the window. Damn it all, his life was spinning out of control and he didn't even know how it had happened. He only knew that from the moment Madison Burnes had made contact with him, his life had never been the same. And now it sure wasn't going to be. He swallowed hard, guilt flooding him anew. All of this was his fault, too. And it was time he did something to rectify it.

As he turned to face her, an unexpected wave of tenderness washed over him. He reached over and took her hand.

"I didn't mean we shouldn't try to be a family for the baby, Madison," he told her gently. "We'll find a way, even if it's unconventional."

But Madison was jerking her hand away from his, shaking her head determinedly. To his dismay, she looked as insecure about being a mother as he felt about being a dad.

"You can't fake a happy family unit, Chance, marriage or no," she said bitterly. "That's one thing I know from experience. A kid will see right through it."

CHAPTER FOUR

"YOU CRAFTY THING, you!" Kit said, sticking her head in Madison's office. "Pretending all was lost! I thought Uncle Ed was going to faint on the spot!"

Madison pushed aside the portfolios of models and actors and rodeo stars she had been sorting through in an attempt to find someone AMV Corporation would accept as a replacement for Chance. All were handsome, all wanted to be the spokesperson, and yet none had that Marlboro man quality Chance had in abundance. None of the men pictured in front of her was right, even if she somehow retooled the ad campaign. With her deadline looming and a secret baby on the way, she did not know what she was going to do. In fact, she could never recall feeling more lost or alone. Maybe it was time for a break. Even a short one. It might clear her head.

Madison sat back in her chair and turned all her attention to Kit's glowing face. "What's going on?" she asked casually.

Kit shook her head and came all the way into the room. "Honestly, Madison! Pretend you don't know!"

Madison shrugged her slender shoulders, aware the waistband of her skirt was already feeling a little snug. "I don't!"

"Pretend Chance Cartwright isn't meeting with Uncle Ed right now!"

Oh, my gosh. Madison leaped from behind her desk. Sped out of her office and dashed down the hall.

"Madison!" Ed Connelly looked up with a smile. "We were just about to come down to see you!"

Madison gulped. She looked at Chance. "Mr. Cartwright."

Chance touched the brim of his hat and moved toward her. She couldn't help but admire the effortless way he moved. It wasn't quite a swagger—that would have been too much trouble. But it was close. Very close. "Miss Burnes."

At the sound of his low, sexy voice, Madison's heart cartwheeled in her chest. Their glances collided, and once she'd looked into his eyes, she couldn't seem to gather the willpower to look away.

Chance clasped her right hand in both of his and shook it warmly. "I was just telling your boss here how much I'm looking forward to working with you on the Ranchero truck account." Chance gave her fingers a final, intimate squeeze. He turned to Ed with an affable grin. "Quite frankly, I'd been having second thoughts. Did I really want to do this? I was ready to pass it up when Miss Burnes came back to Wyoming yesterday to talk to me one last time. And then I realized she was right. This is a once-in-a-lifetime opportunity. And I can't pass it up." Chance inclined his head slightly to the side. "'Course, I've got my conditions," he drawled lazily, "all of which I've already worked out with Ed and the legal department here."

Unwilling to disclose the depth of her ignorance about what Chance was up to, Madison smiled and edged closer. She wanted to be able to discreetly elbow Chance in the ribs and shut him up if it became necessary.

"And?" Madison prompted, noting without wanting to that he had taken extra care with his appearance, shaving closely and scenting his jaw with aftershave. He'd pulled on a mocha suede sport coat along with his usual jeans and boots. And though he wore no tie, he'd put extra starch in his snowy white oxford cloth shirt. In fact, he looked so damn handsome and sexy it was all she could do to keep her mind on the business at hand. "Maybe you'd like to fill me in on what you've decided, too?" Madison finished brightly.

"I will allow my ranch, my horses and myself to be photographed as part of the ad campaign," Chance told her confidently. The beginnings of a satisfied smile tugged at the corners of his lips. "I will not go to trade shows. I'm far too busy training my horses for that. But I do agree to endorse the new Ranchero pickup truck by being photographed using one and accepting one for personal use, as well as half a dozen for the Lost Springs Ranch. Furthermore, all the money earned from my work will go to the ranch."

"We've got a real philanthropist on our hands," Ed said, pleased.

"I just want the money to go where it will do the most good," Chance said matter-of-factly, brushing aside any attempts to make him out to be a saint. "The work Lindsay Duncan and the rest of the staff are doing there is invaluable. I want it to continue in the best way possible."

"That's extremely laudable," Madison said.

Chance nodded, accepting her compliment, then continued brusquely, "I've also stipulated I be allowed to bow out or break the contract at any time should any physical damage be done to either my property or my horses."

"I haven't talked to Ursula Rodriguez yet but I don't see that the manufacturer will have any problem with that," Ed said.

"It all sounds very reasonable." Madison looked at Chance.

"I've also stipulated that I work closely with you during the six weeks it will take to put the ad campaign together," Chance said quietly.

"And to facilitate that, he's offered to let you bunk at his ranch." Ed beamed, pleased.

Madison nodded at her boss, then turned to Chance, her heart beating triple time. She knew Chance's offer wasn't as innocent as it appeared. "That's very generous of you," Madison said huskily, all the while knowing what a bad idea it was. No doubt Chance figured if she bunked there with him, they'd end up making love again.

But Chance was already going on, backing her further into a corner. "It only makes sense," he said practically. "You're going to have to scout locations while you put the storyboards together. There's no sense wasting time, commuting back and forth."

Ed shook hands with Chance. "Good to have you on board." He turned to Madison. "I'm sure you two have a lot to talk about."

Did they ever, a fuming Madison thought. And they couldn't do it in front of Ed.

Fortunately, Ed was already headed to his desk. As Madison discreetly pushed Chance out the door, Ed reached for the phone. "I'll call Ursula," he promised, "and let her know our good news and bring her up to speed."

SMILING AND CHATTING nonsensically about his flight, the weather and his plans for the rest of the day—he had none except a flight home that evening—Madison led the way to her office and ever so gracefully shut the door behind them.

Chance stood for a moment, assessing her private domain. It looked like a haven for a woman who was going places. The walls of her office were lined with awards. One recent advertisement in particular caught his eyes. It was for a popular body soap that had been around for years, but thanks to an inventive new approach had become wildly popular again. It was the sexiest ad he'd ever seen.

Impressed, Chance turned to Madison. "Is that one of yours?"

Madison nodded, making no effort to suppress the satisfaction she felt about a job well done. "It's by far the most successful ad I've ever created, but I'm hoping to surpass it with my work on the Ranchero pickup truck."

Given the cool determination on her face, Chance was willing to bet she would. He turned to the framed ad. There wasn't just sex in the ad, or romance, there was hope. To take a situation that could be irksome at the very least—in this case a man showing up filthy from head to toe—and still turn it into sexy, wonderful fun, required a romantic nature and a sense of humor, at the very least.

The difficulty was that Madison did not approach their personal involvement with the same humor and sunny practicality. Instead, when she viewed the havoc created by their passion, she reacted with fear and wariness.

Reflecting on all that had happened so far between them, Chance could see she was going to be a challenge in every sense of the word. He was responsible for some of it. He never should have made love to her before they got to know each other, no matter how much he wanted her, and he certainly shouldn't have let it end the way he had. That had been wrong, too.

Surveying his expression, Madison frowned. "Enough with the niceties," she barked. And the possibilities of re-kindling the passion between us, Chance thought, imagining he could read her mind. "What's going on here, Cartwright? When I left yesterday you were ready to get yourself fired."

"So I was," Chance agreed, wondering how long it would take to get her in his bed again. Not long, if he had his way. Deciding to get more comfortable, he moved a stack of papers and settled on the edge of her desk, facing her. He shoved his hands in his pockets and stretched his legs in front of him.

Madison remained standing. She drummed her fingers on the edge of the desk. "Does this have anything to do with our, uh—"

"Baby?" Chance asked, wishing he'd reacted better to the news.

Madison gave him a quelling look and propped her hands on her slender hips. "Tell me you didn't," she whispered, aghast.

"Tell anyone?" Chance said, reading her mind as easily as ever. "Nope. Not a soul." Deciding he hadn't annoyed her enough—not nearly enough—he sat in her swivel chair and propped his feet on the edge of her desk. "Did you?"

Madison glared at him and, as if unable to bear his physical nearness even a second longer, folded her arms in front of her and began to pace. "I don't want anyone to know."

Chance sighed and pushed the brim of his hat back with one poke of his index finger. He wished he could replace all her distress over their predicament with joy. "Afraid it will get in the way of your promotion?" he taunted lightly.

"We've got a cardinal rule around here. You don't sleep with anyone you're working with, and if—against all better judgment—you do get romantically involved, it's considered *de rigueur* to take yourself off the project or account and put someone else on in your stead."

"But you're not going to do that," Chance realized unhappily, surprised to find there was a way out for them after all, distressed to learn she wasn't about to take it.

"We're no longer romantically involved, Chance," Madison reminded him haughtily. "Nor are we going to be."

Chance lifted a brow. They'd just see about that. Being here with Madison, seeing her, made him realize how much he wanted to make love to her again. Not just because of the baby. But because she was the sexiest and most exciting, most complex and confusing, downright tantalizing woman he had ever met.

Chance crossed one ankle over the other and folded his hands temple-style over his lap. Realizing he could look at her all day long and never get enough of her, he studied her curiously. "If you have that rule, then why did you get romantically involved with me?" Even if it was for way too short a time. Had she stayed—instead of provoking a fight and rushing off after they had just made love—Chance had the feeling they might have figured out some way to be together and might still be romantically linked to this day, despite the fact they lived in two different states, in two vastly different worlds.

Madison struggled to answer his question as she continued pacing back and forth. "That's something I've been asking myself repeatedly, believe me."

Chance had an idea why. The sizzling passion had caught her as unaware as it had him. Deciding she'd kept her physical distance long enough, he latched onto her wrist, put his feet flat on the floor and pulled her onto his lap.

"I'll be honest with you," he told her, hooking his hands around her waist and holding her when she would have fled. "I don't like you putting your career ahead of our baby. Not at all. But as for the rest, keeping your pregnancy private is fine with me." He ran his hand over her stomach. "I figure we need at least six weeks to get to know each other and figure out how we can best do right by our baby." It wasn't going to be simple, whatever happened. But that was okay. He figured they could handle whatever came up, if they just gave it a little time. And effort.

Madison swallowed and went completely still. He noticed she didn't push his hand away as it rested lightly and protectively over the baby. "That's why you agreed to take part in the ad campaign, isn't it?" she asked, something akin to approval in her misty eyes.

Chance nodded. "We need to spend time together. And not just for the baby, but for us, Madison." He caught her hand and pressed it to his lips. "We have to figure out what's going on between the two of us." Was it desire that made him want to hold her tight and kiss her whenever he was near her? Was it the fact she was carrying their child that made him want to protect and care for her? Or was it something more?

A quick rap was followed by the door opening. By the time Ed Connelly stuck his head in, Madison had leaped off Chance's lap and was standing next to him, looking surprisingly cool and unruffled.

"There you are." Ed smiled at Chance. "Ursula Rodriguez can't wait to meet you. She's headed over here now, then we're all going out to lunch to celebrate. Madison, see if you can get Kit to join us, too, since she'll be managing things at this end for you and backing you up on this account."

Madison smiled. "Will do."

KIT STOPPED BY Madison's office around five that afternoon. With her was a young woman with fiery red hair and freckles whose eagerness to be there was as impossible to overlook as the Texas-shaped silver earrings dangling from her ears or the gum she was surreptitiously chewing. She was dressed in a short circle skirt, snug fitting T-shirt and knit vest. She was wearing black Doc Martens, which had the sturdy look and construction of men's combat boots, and white anklets.

Kit smiled. "Madison, I don't think you've met Shawna Somersby, our new college intern."

Thinking it didn't seem all that long ago that she had been interning at Connelly and Associates, Madison smiled at Shawna and shook her hand. "Welcome aboard."

"Oh, the pleasure's all mine," Shawna said gushing.

"Shawna's going to be working here under my direction for the next few weeks, getting her feet wet, then we're sending her up to Wyoming to assist you once the filming on the Ranchero commercial begins," Kit told Madison.

"Great. I'm sure I'm going to need all the help I can get," Madison said.

Shawna smiled wistfully. "Chance Cartwright looks really cute, too."

Madison wasn't sure it pleased or irked her to know other women found Chance devastatingly attractive.

Kit glanced at the stacks of material around Madison's office. "Packing up?"

Madison nodded. "The travel agency just called with my itinerary. I'm headed for Wyoming next week and I want all this stuff there when I arrive."

Kit assessed the chore in progress. "Looks like you need some boxes here. Shawna, would you run down to the mail room and get a half dozen or so mailing boxes for us, and tell them Madison's going to need an express mail package pickup at around…"

"Six o'clock," Madison said.

"Then you can go on home," Kit told Shawna. "'Cause I know you have those concert tickets for the Dave Matthews Band tonight."

"Thanks, Kit," Shawna said, dashing out to do her bidding.

"She seems nice," Madison remarked after Shawna had zipped in with mailing boxes, tape and address forms, and then sped out on her way to her concert.

"She is. You just have to be careful what you say to her because she's so eager to please."

"Meaning?"

"Meaning don't wish for a cup of Starbucks coffee unless you want her driving off to get you one that instant."

"Oh."

"Yeah. She takes everything pretty literally. But she's a very hard worker and has a lot of initiative, so I think she's going to work out fine. And speaking of fine," Kit said, going over to shut the door to Madison's office so the two of them could have some privacy. "That was some lunch, huh?"

Madison nodded. She told herself it was relief—and not

a tinge of unaccustomed jealousy—she was feeling as she thought back to the AMV exec's reaction to the Ranchero's new spokesperson. "Ursula really went wild over Chance."

"As we both knew she would." Kit helped Madison pack up files to take to Wyoming. "And speaking of Chance Cartwright," Kit continued slyly, "he really seemed to have his eye on you. Every time I turned around, he was studying you or sending you these glances that were almost…tender."

No doubt he'd been thinking of the fact she was now carrying his baby. He couldn't have been thinking about how wonderful it had felt when they made love. Could he? Madison pushed the image of the two of them tangled in his sheets from her mind.

"You're exaggerating," Madison chided as a self-conscious blush heated her cheeks. Just as she was exaggerating the romance of that one desire-filled afternoon in her memories. So what if he had been an incredibly tender and sensual lover? So what if he had made her feel more passion in that one day than she'd ever dreamed of in her lifetime. It didn't mean they were destined to spend the rest of their lives together, did it?

Kit studied her like a mother hen protecting her young. She wasn't buying Madison's denials. Not for one second. "Come on. 'Fess up now. What's going on with the two of you? Why the tension—or whatever it is?"

Madison brushed aside the memories of Chance's kiss as she reached for her Day-Timer. "It's just awkward between us right now," she said finally.

Kit threw up her hands in dismay. "I could see that."

But sort of intimate, too, Madison thought, amazed at how the baby was changing things, bringing them closer together despite themselves.

Aware her best friend was waiting for some explanation, Madison continued honestly, "I never should have bought him at that auction. He's probably still a little peeved about me taking advantage of the situation to talk to him about the account. Especially when I knew from conversations with people in the horse business that he's very much a low-profile guy at heart. I mean, he loves what he does, and he doesn't mind being renowned for his work with horses, but he doesn't have an interest in being recognized by the average person on the street or having his privacy disrupted. I know he really wants to help the orphanage, and the six figures he'll earn for his work will go a long way toward that, so this whole experience is a mixed bag for him, too.''

Madison and Kit continued boxing up things. "Somehow, I had the feeling it was more than that," Kit said finally. "Like maybe he was doing this to please you."

Madison flushed self-consciously. She turned away from Kit's probing gaze and reached for a pen. She began printing the address of Chance's ranch on the first of a stack of shipping labels. "Now you're really reading too much into this."

Kit didn't think so, Madison noted with dismay.

Kit closed a box and taped it shut. "Then why is he demanding that you and you alone oversee the filming of the commercial and stay at his ranch, if not to have time with you?"

"Because he knows how much I want this commercial to happen, and he trusts me to make sure it's done right." And though he hadn't come right out and said as much, Madison sensed he wanted to share in her pregnancy, at least for a little while. Which wasn't all that uncommon. This was his baby, too.

"I still say it's more than that," Kit said persistently.

Madison finished one label and reached for another. "Look, I know living in that all-male household of yours has given you an understanding of men in general that is unparalleled around here. But Chance is different."

"Not that different," disagreed Kit, who was happily

married and the mother of two teenage sons. "Not in my book."

Finished with the shipping labels, Madison paused. "He's an enigma. Remember? That was one of the reasons we wanted him so badly for this account in the first place. In every photo we saw, there seemed to be so much going on behind his eyes."

"There still is." Ever the matchmaker, Kit smiled. "Only now it's all directed at you."

Madison was silent, knowing that was true, to a point. But she was not, she told herself firmly, foolish enough to romanticize this predicament they'd found themselves in any more than she already had done.

"He's probably just thinking about the money he's going to get for the ranch and all the good it's going to do."

Kit nodded. "You've got to say this about him, he's a very decent guy."

Generous to a fault. "Yes. He is." Madison zipped her briefcase. Even though, on a personal level, he was constantly getting under her skin, and on a professional level, he could be very difficult, too.

Finished with the boxes, Madison and Kit opened the door and pushed them into the hall just as Ed walked by, cigar in hand. He looked happier than he had in weeks. "Madison, I'm glad I caught you," he said.

"Chance got off to the airport okay?" Madison asked, glad Ed had offered to drive Chance.

Ed nodded. "He said to tell you he'll pick you up at the Casper airport when you arrive."

Out of the corner of her eye, Madison saw Kit raise a brow. "I'd planned to rent a car," Madison said.

"He said he's got a vehicle you can use out at the ranch. Besides, it'll be a good opportunity for you to smooth things over and get to know him a little better—sell him on this project and remind him what a good thing it is for all of us." Ed used the end of his cigar to punctuate the air as he talked. "I just got off the phone with Ursula Rodriguez. After meeting him in person and seeing how charismatic he is, she's more determined than ever that Chance appear personally at the trade shows along with the Ranchero."

Madison paused, her anxiety returning full blast. "You know that's the one thing Chance said he wouldn't do, Ed!"

Ed remained confident. "I'm sure you'll be able to change his mind. You're going to have plenty of time to work on him."

Madison ran her hands through her hair, pushing it off her face. "And if I can't change his mind?"

Ed sobered abruptly. "Madison, I'm sure I don't have to remind you how much this account means to us."

"No, Ed," Madison replied, feeling herself tense at the thought of the stakes involved, "you don't."

"Not just to the firm, but to you, too," Ed continued earnestly as Kit slipped discreetly from the room and went to tell the mail room Madison's boxes were ready for pickup. "I really want you to have that VP slot. But to get it," Ed warned, "you're going to have to prove that you can do the high-level wheeling and dealing that comes with the territory, no matter how difficult the situation. Am I making myself clear?"

"Perfectly," Madison said. Advertising was a cutthroat business. To succeed she was going to have to play on the team with the big guys.

"Good." Ed slapped her on the back companionably and stuck his cigar between his teeth. "'Cause we're counting on you, Madison. Don't let us down."

THAT, MADISON THOUGHT late the following week as Chance Cartwright strode across the Casper airport to her side, was a feat easier said than done. Even though it was late afternoon, he looked freshly shaved and showered. He wore tight, faded jeans. As he neared her, she could see the crisp black hairs springing from the open collar of his freshly laundered light blue shirt. His curly hair sprung from beneath the brim of his Stetson, and for the first time she could recall, he was wearing sunglasses. He whipped them off and stuck them in his shirt pocket. Before she could stop him, Chance relieved her of her laptop and brief-case. *Cowboys should be illegal,* Madison thought. *Manners, and gorgeous from head to toe, too.*

Madison wished he didn't smell and look so damn good even as she found herself coloring warmly and wishing irrationally for a welcome-back hug. But to her disappointment, he made no effort to wrap his strong arms around her or clasp her against his broad chest. Madison swallowed and reached out to take her belongings back. "Really, you don't have to...I can manage."

"No problem," Chance said, not about to relinquish any-thing. "Besides—" he grinned at her, his teeth a dazzling white against his suntanned face "—you shouldn't be car-rying all that heavy stuff now, should you? Especially in your—"

That did it. Madison quickly went on tiptoe and shushed him with a finger to his lips. "Don't say it." She paused. Her senses swam as she drew her hand away from the soft, warm give of his lips. "But you probably have a point," she murmured, not sure who among the locals cluttering the terminal Chance might know. "I'll just get one of those little carts." The same kind she had gotten for herself at the Dallas airport.

"No need for that." Chance's fingers closed warmly over hers. He forced her to put her dollar bill aside before she could insert it in the machine next to the baggage claim. "I can handle everything. Unless—" The corners of his mouth quirked up in amusement. "How many suitcases did you bring?"

Madison rolled her eyes. She wasn't going to apologize

for the fact she'd need more of a working wardrobe than he would. Looking polished and professional was part of her job. "Two. But they're on wheels."

"No problem, even if they weren't." The mirthful crinkles around his eyes deepened.

"Did all my boxes arrive?" Madison asked, concerned. She wanted to be able to start work right away.

"Days ago," Chance replied, a flash of disapproval in his eyes, as if he already knew she was planning to use her commitment to her work to help keep her on track and the two of them apart.

Acutely aware of his hand on her elbow, Madison followed Chance to the baggage carousel for her flight. They stood together, watching for her bags. "Thanks for picking me up at the airport," Madison said awkwardly when the silence continued to stretch out tensely.

"No problem," Chance said laconically.

Madison rummaged through her pocket for her baggage claim checks. "Although you didn't have to do this," she continued, trying her best to keep things on a businesslike level.

Chance apparently had no such compulsion. He gave her a look that said he couldn't wait to get her back in bed. "Of course I'm going to pick you up," he said softly. His glance slid surreptitiously to her tummy, checking it out. "Under the circumstances."

"Will you stop that?" Madison asked, wishing he didn't look so damn happy about this pregnancy of theirs, now that the news had had time to sink in. The next thing she knew he'd be resting his hand on her stomach, caressing it. "I don't want anyone to know," Madison continued crankily, wishing just the thought of Chance touching her again didn't make her feel so buttery warm inside.

Chance shrugged. "They're going to know soon enough anyway," he pointed out calmly.

Madison flushed and stepped away from the other passengers. She took his hand and tugged him along with her until they were out of earshot of others. "Well, I'm not show—I mean, I don't look—it's not a problem now. So please don't give anything away. At least until we get all the commercials filmed and make everyone happy."

Chance leaned down, standing closer to her than before. Behind them there was a loud click and a whirr as the conveyer belt started up. "Then maybe it won't matter so much anymore?" Chance guessed, equal parts sympathy and disapproval in his eyes.

"I'm hoping." Madison watched the first suitcase glide out. Then another and another. She wished Chance didn't have the power to make her feel so vulnerable. As if she needed to apologize for being career-minded and ambitious. It was her job and her devotion to it that would keep her and her baby safe and warm.

"So how was your flight?" Chance asked, his glance dipping surreptitiously to take in the increasing ripeness of her breasts before settling once again on her face. "Your stomach okay? Sometimes women in your, uh, you know, have a little trouble with, uh, air sickness."

Madison rolled her eyes, wondering if Chance was going to be this oversolicitous the entire pregnancy. Would he want to touch her breasts, cup them with his hands, measure their increasing size? Later, would he be around to help her nurse the baby during the first six weeks, as the doctor had advised her to do?

Madison shut her eyes against the sudden image of her with her baby at her breast and Chance at her side. This was reality here, she reminded herself sternly, not some soft-focus fantasy of parenthood. Besides, right now Chance was focused on morning sickness.

His solicitousness was going to be every bit as irritating to her as his disapproval regarding her ambition. Turning away from the sudden tenderness in his eyes, Madison pointed to the first of her suitcases.

When it came around to them, Chance reached out and grabbed it and lifted it off the conveyer belt. He set it beside her. "Don't tell me. You're an expert on pregnancy, too," she scoffed.

Chance grinned, as he always did, at the first sign of any crankiness from her. No doubt he thought her mood swings were due to her pregnancy.

He shrugged his broad shoulders in a way that made her want to lean into them and draw from his strength. "I don't know about expert," he drawled, looking at her with mock seriousness. "But I've brought a few foals into this world. Does that count?"

Madison refused to laugh at his gentle humor. "Not really, no," she snapped. Realizing she had only been back a few minutes and it was already beginning to feel far too intimate between them, she pointed out her second suitcase and watched him grab it. "And to answer your question, Cartwright, thus far, although I've had my share of queasy moments, I've only actually been sick once. And I don't intend to be sick again," she announced loftily. "Mind over matter, you know."

He grinned at her approvingly. "I like it when you do that, you know," he said, tucking a strand of hair behind her ears.

"What?" Madison flushed despite herself.

"Call me Cartwright." He grinned and shook his head, all the while holding her eyes with his hot blue gaze. "When you say it—" he sighed, yearning openly "—damn, but it sounds sexy."

"It wasn't meant to be." Madison attempted to cool his ardor with an icy glance. A lesser man would have folded. Not Chance. He still looked ready for anything—and she did mean anything. Madison blew out a frustrated breath. She'd been right to think she was going to have her hands full coming here again, even if she hadn't been carrying his child. "Are you ready?" she asked impatiently.

Chance nodded. "Just follow me."

Madison knew what he meant, but she rolled her eyes anyway. "That'll be the day," she muttered, even more cantankerously. Chance laughed, the sweet sexy sound filling the air around them. His mirth was so infectious it was all Madison could do not to chuckle, too. "Just go," she said, hanging on to her straight face with effort.

Grinning, Chance strode toward the exit, carrying everything for her—two big suitcases, a laptop computer and her briefcase. She tagged along beside him, feeling ridiculous with absolutely nothing save the lightweight leather handbag looped over her shoulder. Not that it seemed to bother Chance. He bore the weight of her belongings as if it were a feather.

He strode through the automatic glass doors. They were buffeted by a warm summer wind and clear blue skies overhead as they headed for the battered pickup parked some distance away.

Madison paused. This wasn't what she had expected. "Wasn't the Ranchero delivered to the Double Diamond this morning?"

Chance nodded solemnly. "It got there, all right."

"Then why didn't you drive it?"

A mischievous grin tugged at the corners of his lips. "Because I like driving this one."

Madison arched a disapproving brow. Was he going to be this difficult about everything? "And the seat belt on the passenger side?" she prodded.

"Is still broke. But don't you worry." He gave her a little pat on the small of her spine. "The one in the middle works just fine."

Madison pushed aside the memory of what it had been like to sit so close to him as he drove, his thigh brushing hers with every touch of his foot to the accelerator.

Reluctantly, she allowed him to help her in, but she resisted his assistance with her seat belt, pushing his fingers away. "Look, this is all well and nice, but you can't go on treating me like this," she told him crankily. Their fingertips had barely brushed, and already the skin was tingling all the way up her arm, across her shoulders to her breasts.

Chance shrugged laconically. He fit his key in the ignition, started the truck's motor and slid his sunglasses over his eyes.

He turned to her, smug male possessiveness oozing from every pore. "It's gonna be damn hard to behave otherwise, darlin', considering you have my baby growing inside you."

Madison flushed and drew in a startled breath. "Well, try."

Seeming in no hurry to speed them on their way, he reached over to adjust the air-conditioning. When the cool air was flowing over them both, he leaned back against his seat. "Have you eaten dinner?"

The way he said it, it sounded as if he were proposing a date.

Madison had a fleeting fantasy of what it would be like to be seated across from him in some cozy, candlelit restaurant, his attention focused solely on her. She sighed, knowing it would be a seduction waiting to happen. A seduction she could ill afford. She had work to do. "I packed a lunch to take with me on the plane. I've been munching on it all afternoon—I've found small amounts of food frequently do better for me than big meals."

"So in other words you're not hungry," he said, his disappointment evident.

Madison smiled. "Not at all. Thanks, anyway. But if you're hungry and you want to go out on the town or something after you drop me at the Double Diamond, that's fine. I can probably even get the agency to pick up the bill."

"Thanks." Chance favored her with a smile that let her know he knew exactly what she was doing and wasn't always going to let her get away with it. He put the truck in gear and backed out of the space. "But I can get something at the ranch later."

Damn, Madison thought.

"So how are you doing otherwise?" Chance asked as they bumped along in his old pickup on the two-lane highway leading to his ranch. "Have you been to the doctor?"

Madison nodded. Chance was gazing at her hungrily, as if they hadn't seen each other in ages, when in reality it had just been a week. More disconcerting still was the fact it felt that way to her, too.

"I had an appointment with my obstetrician before I left this morning." That was why she'd had to take an afternoon rather than a morning flight. "He said the baby and I are both doing fine." Madison smiled, thinking how exciting it had been to have her first prenatal visit. "He gave me some vitamins and instructions."

"Good." Chance smiled, then reached over and squeezed her hand.

It was easier sharing the details of her pregnancy with Chance than she'd thought it would be. Madison wasn't quite sure what to make of that.

"Have you told your family you're pregnant?" Chance continued.

"No." Madison reflected on the fact that although her parents were still alive, she was almost as orphaned as Chance. "My parents are abroad."

"How about your siblings?" he pressed, determined to know more. "Have you told them?"

Madison fidgeted in her seat. They were headed for dangerous territory. "Don't have any."

"Me, either." Chance turned the air-conditioning to low. "So where are your parents?" he asked curiously. "I mean, if you wanted to tell them, surely there's a way for you to contact them."

"Yes, of course there is." Madison's shoulders stiffened

under his persistent questioning. "I just choose not to do so."

"You think they'd be upset because we're not married and have no plans to be," Chance guessed, looking as if he were beginning to have second thoughts about the wisdom of that, too.

Madison turned her glance to the cattle grazing in a pasture alongside the road. "That's not it." She sighed. They'd be less apt to lecture her than shake their heads and say, "Now do you understand?" And maybe throw in an "I told you so" for good measure. Right now, Madison did not want to hear it. She didn't want to feel that she was more like her parents than she had ever wanted to be— reckless like her father and with the lowered expectations and cynicism of her mother. But there she was—a product of both.

Chance shot her an odd look, as if he were still trying to figure her out. "Then what is it?"

Madison tried to decide how much to tell him. Generally she made it a rule not to discuss this with anyone. Finally, she answered, "My father is a vice president in a multinational public-relations firm. For the last five years he's been running their London office, so he and my mother have been living over there."

Once again, Chance seemed acutely aware of all she hadn't said. "How do they like it?"

Madison trained her eyes on the granite-topped mountains to the west, rising majestically over the plain. It was disturbing to realize how easily Chance read her thoughts and feelings. No one had ever been able to do that before. She was used to being a closed book to all the men she dated. "They're as happy as they can be anywhere, I suppose," Madison replied, her irritation growing by leaps and bounds.

"Not exactly a ringing endorsement." Chance turned the

truck onto Double Diamond property. It bumped as it went from pavement to gravel.

"You're right," Madison bristled. "It isn't." She glanced in the passenger-side mirror and caught sight of the clouds of dust kicked up behind the truck.

Chance shut off the air conditioner abruptly and opened the window. The scent of new-mown grass filled the air. "That must be tough on you," he said compassionately.

Madison nodded and looked away from the understanding in his blue eyes. She didn't want to think about how the unhappiness of her childhood had colored her views of marriage or the potential for lasting happiness in any man-woman relationship. "It is and it has been." She drew a deep breath, aware that it was making her feel a lot better to unburden herself to Chance, even just a little bit. "In any case, dealing with my folks is one stress I'm better off without just now."

Determined to push the unhappy thoughts from her mind, Madison looked at her surroundings. "Oh, Chance." She caught her breath as she spotted the collection of pink, lavender and red clouds gathering on the horizon just above the snow-topped peaks of the granite mountains. The vibrant green of the cottonwood trees, the thick groves of blue spruce and pastures strewn with wildflowers stood out in stark relief, gilded by the fading light of an absolutely gorgeous sunset. "This is so beautiful," Madison breathed. "Would you mind stopping the truck and letting me get out and take a few pictures?"

Grinning, Chance watched as she grabbed her handbag and took out her camera.

"I can imagine it all now," Madison rushed on enthusiastically. "And it's going to be so wonderful. We'll have a tailgate picnic. You'll be in black tie, of course—"

"You never stop," Chance observed. The way he said it, it didn't sound like a compliment.

"And you'll be accompanied by a beautiful woman."

Ignoring him, Madison pushed open the door and scrambled from the truck. Chance joined her as she began snapping photos. ''We'll get a model, someone who looks good with you.''

Legs braced apart, hands on his hips, Chance turned away. ''Let me know when you're ready to go.'' Demonstrating little interest, he strode off.

Ignoring his surly mood, Madison took pictures until she ran out of film. It wasn't her fault he was bored. But it was her fault that she could readily imagine the two of them sharing a kiss or having a romantic moonlight picnic on this very spot. Which was ridiculous, she scolded herself firmly, because it wasn't going to happen. She wasn't going to let it happen. Not while she was working on the commercial, and not afterward, either. One erroneous bout of lovemaking was enough. They couldn't keep falling in and out of bed with each other. They had to decide what their relationship was and then stick to it. Anything else would be too confusing.

When she had finished, Madison returned to the truck.

''So, what else will you be having me do besides frolic with a picnic basket?'' Chance asked dryly as he drove the short distance to the ranch house.

Madison shrugged. ''A lot of whatever it is you normally do on the ranch with the pickup truck. We'll have to sit down and figure that out.'' She caught the flare of male interest in Chance's eyes.

Determined to waste no time proving to Chance that her six weeks there would be all business, Madison whipped out a notepad and pen. ''For instance, what time do you normally get up and get going around here?'' she asked briskly.

Chance's shoulders stiffened as the talk turned to her business once again. ''Five o'clock.''

She jotted it down, then looked at it. ''You're kidding. Right?'' More a night person than a morning person, Madison couldn't imagine having to get up at the crack of dawn every day.

"No." His voice flowed over her like the warm Wyoming breeze coming in through the open windows of the truck. He slanted her a teasing glance and seemed to be imagining her lazing around in bed well after dawn's first light. "What time do you normally start your day?" he asked.

"I'm in the office around nine or ten. And I usually knock off around nine at night."

Chance nodded. Obviously, Madison thought, that wasn't his timetable. Another big difference between them. Good. She needed to hang on to those. They would serve as reminders why they could never be more than friends, no matter how much chemistry remained between them.

"What time do you usually call it quits for the day?" Madison asked curiously, wondering how difficult it would be to get the two of them in sync.

"Depends. Sundown or a little earlier," Chance said mildly. Which left a lot of time in the evenings for... Madison brought herself up short. She didn't like where her thoughts were leading.

As they entered the ranch house, Madison noted it seemed smaller and cozier than she recalled it. Chance carted her bags upstairs, deposited them in the guest room, then headed downstairs.

Madison followed him to the kitchen. Noting it was a little warm inside the house, she took off the jacket of her linen pantsuit and hung it over the back of a chair. She watched as Chance moved about the kitchen, getting out ingredients for his dinner—a thick sirloin steak, a loaf of crusty sourdough bread, a prepackaged green salad. "Do you ever get lonely out here?" she asked as he opened the bag and deposited the salad in a bowl.

Chance poured ranch dressing over the greens and mixed

it in with a fork. "After living in the dormitory environment of the boys' ranch, the privacy here is heaven."

He opened the oven door and set the dial to broil. "And before that?" Madison asked, watching him move about the kitchen comfortably.

"I grew up in a small apartment with my dad."

"What did he do?" Madison asked, accepting the glass of lemonade Chance gave her.

"He worked at a lumber yard." Chance frowned and twisted the top off a bottle of beer. "I never had so much as a tiny yard to call my own, so to have all this land now—" He shrugged and left the thought hanging.

"It means everything to you."

Chance nodded, the pride at what he'd accomplished evident in his blue eyes.

"As it should," Madison said, admiring what he had built for himself. "It's beautiful out here, Chance," she said softly. "Truly beautiful." Not only was the commercial they filmed here going to be great, but their child would love it here, too, Madison thought.

A comfortable silence fell between them as Chance put the steak on to broil. Madison yawned. For the first time, she noticed how tired she was.

Chance lounged against the counter and inclined his head at her. "You look sleepy."

"I am," Madison admitted, noting there was nothing she'd rather do at the moment than settle somewhere cozy—the sofa or the bed—and snuggle up with him. But that wasn't going to happen. She couldn't let it happen. She and the baby both needed their sleep, even if it was only seven o'clock.

"I'm sorry." Her actions brisk and businesslike, Madison shut her notebook and capped her pen. "I had hoped to do a little work with you tonight and get started on the storyboards for the ad campaign, but I'm so tired after all the traveling, I'm going to have to hit the sack. But I'll tell you what,'' she continued, trying not to notice how disappointed he looked. ''I'll set my alarm for five tomorrow. I'll get up, and if it's okay with you, I'll sort of follow you through your day. Take notes and tons more photos. And then I'll develop the storyboards for the commercial from that.''

Chance nodded, letting her know her agenda was okay with him. ''What's the slogan for the commercials going to be?'' He turned the steak to the other side.

''Ranchero trucks—they work as hard as you do.''

The smile lines on either side of Chance's mouth deepened. ''You think that up?''

Madison nodded, a little surprised at how much his approval meant to her. A cozy silence fell between them as the aroma of sizzling steak filled the air. ''Sure you don't want some dinner before you go up?'' Chance asked, searching her eyes.

Madison, sensing this was more than a dinner invitation, shook her head. ''Thanks, anyway.'' Trying not to see the flare of disappointment in his eyes, she draped her jacket over her arm.

Chance walked her as far as the stairs, caught her hand at the foot of them. ''If you get hungry later—''

''I'll come down and get something,'' Madison promised. She paused again. This was where a good-night kiss should happen between two people who were having a baby together. ''See you in the morning,'' she said, turning away.

Chance gave her hand a final squeeze, then lingered and watched her head up the stairs. ''See you then.''

CHANCE WOKE at four-thirty. He got up, showered, shaved and dressed and put the coffee on. At five, he heard Madison's alarm go off. It rang. And rang. And rang. Fifteen seconds passed. Then thirty. Forty-five. And still not a sound, not a movement from her bedroom upstairs. Heart pounding, he took the steps two at a time.

"Madison?" He rapped on the door.

Again, there was no answer, only the monotonous, jarring ring of her alarm. Why wasn't she waking up? Feeling something was wrong, he shoved open the door. And stopped dead in his tracks at what he saw.

CHAPTER FIVE

TRY AS HE MIGHT, Chance couldn't tear his eyes from the sleeping Madison. Clad only in a white V-neck T-shirt and panties, she was tangled sexily in the covers. Beside her, the alarm went on and on, as shrill and commanding as a civil defense siren in the early morning silence of the ranch.

Chance didn't see how anyone could sleep through that noise, no matter how tired they were. Unless... His stomach tightened as the unthinkable occurred to him. Cursing himself for a fool all the while, he rushed forward. Turned on the bedside lamp with one hand and grabbed her wrist with the other. To his relief, her pulse was strong.

Madison's eyes opened slowly. Spying him standing beside her bed, she smiled dreamily. Rolling onto her side, she cuddled closer and pressed her cheek against the back of his hand. Sighed blissfully. And promptly fell right back asleep.

By now, Chance's lower half was on full alert and aching with the need to possess her. But that was not, he reminded himself firmly, part of their deal. She was here so they could work out an arrangement to share their baby. That was all.

Aware the alarm was still shrieking and that she must truly be exhausted if she could sleep through that *and* his presence in her bedroom, he leaned over the double bed and reached across her. To his chagrin, his fingers fell just short of the shut-off switch.

Her cheek still resting slumberously on his hand, he

pressed his knees against the side of the bed and leaned a little farther. Almost there. Beginning to perspire, so great was his effort not to disturb the sweetly slumbering woman, he pressed his knees even harder into the mattress and gave one last try.

He grinned as his fingers came in contact with the switch. There was a click, then blissful silence. Letting out a short exhalation of relief, Chance began to draw back carefully. And it was then that her eyes opened again and she saw him, arm stretched out over top of her.

She blinked. Blinked again. Fiery temper flashed in her eyes.

"I can explain," Chance said hurriedly.

"I'll just bet you can!" Madison thrust his hand away from her and struggled to a sitting position.

Chance tried not to notice how great she looked in the man's T-shirt and bikini panties, her long bare legs drawn up in front of her, arms clasped around them. Forcing himself to tear his eyes from the tousled silky blond hair and her sleep-flushed face, he explained evenly, "Your alarm went off."

Madison shoved her hand through her hair, pushing it off her face. She glanced at the clock radio beside her bed, then at him. Her lower lip slid out in a pretty pout. "I didn't hear it."

Chance shrugged and crossed his arms in front of him as he continued to reason with her. "I don't know how," he told her dryly. "It was louder than a civil defense siren."

She paused, wet her lips. Recognition came into her eyes. Finally, she seemed to notice he was already up, showered, shaved and ready to take on the day. She was the one still lazing around in bed, despite her claims that she would get up and join him at five. Madison glanced at the clock. It was 5:06. Blushing, she grabbed for the end of the sheet and tugged it nearly to her waist. He could tell she wanted to believe he was not just trying out some new, inventive way to get them in a compromising situation, but she still wasn't completely convinced. He watched her inhale deeply the scent of freshly brewed coffee. Noticed the fact her bedside lamp was on, illuminating the dawn-gray room. She let out a soft sigh. "How long did it go off?" she asked finally.

"Three or four minutes." Chance repressed the urge to take her in his arms and hold her close. "And, given how loud it was, I worried something might be wrong." He grinned, unable to resist teasing her a little. "I came in to check. I thought you might be unconscious. Either that or suddenly deaf."

Madison wrinkled her nose at him. "Hardly."

Unable to take his eyes from her, Chance moved his shoulders in an exaggerated show of modesty. "So I checked for a pulse, and that's when you grabbed me."

Madison's eyes widened. "I grabbed you!" she echoed breathlessly.

"Yes. And put your cheek on my hand." Her temper appealed to him as much as her passion. "I didn't want to wake you. The alarm was still going off. I reached across you, doing my best not to disturb you, and finally shut the damn thing off. I was just trying to get out of here when you woke up."

Apparently realizing he was telling the truth, Madison scowled. "Must have been the absence of sound that disturbed me."

"I guess." Chance paused. More than anything, he wanted her to know she could trust him. Not just to behave, but with her life. "Anyway, I'm sorry," he continued. "I didn't mean to intrude."

Having recovered from the shock of finding him next to her, she sent him an amused look. "Just don't do it again."

"I won't," Chance promised, trying not to notice the

growing voluptuousness of her breasts, "as long as you shut off the alarm, or better yet, don't set it at all."

"Don't be ridiculous." Madison took a deep breath that lifted the soft curves of her breasts all the more. "How else will I get up?"

Needing to think about something besides the imprint of her nipples against the soft cotton of her T-shirt, Chance studied the fatigue on her face and thought about the baby—their baby. "You could just sleep till you wake up."

She arched her silky blond brows in subtle warning, tossed back the covers and, ignoring her sexy dishabille and its effect on him, shot to her feet. "Then I'd never get up."

Aware how happy he was she was carrying his baby, even if the pregnancy had been unplanned, Chance countered with a matter-of-fact tone bound to irk. "You would if you were rested."

"Are you trying to tell me what to do?" Madison stalked past him, seemingly unaware her T-shirt was twisted up in back to reveal her panties and several inches of creamy backside.

Wishing he could do what he felt like doing—which was take her in his arms and kiss her long and hard—Chance shifted position to ease the increasing tightness at the front of his jeans. "Doesn't appear to me to be doing any good if I am," he observed.

Madison tossed her head. Silky blond hair flew in every direction. "You've got that right." She tugged on a thigh-length kimono and belted it around her. She regarded him with a questioning look. "Hope that coffee I smell is decaf."

Chance frowned at his obvious oversight. "Sorry," he reluctantly told her. "But I'll get some."

"Thanks." Madison ran a brush through her hair, then pivoting gracefully, headed for the bathroom they shared. "I'd appreciate it. I'll be down shortly." She tossed the words cavalierly over her shoulder before disappearing behind the door and closing it softly. "And you can show me how your days usually begin on the ranch."

CHANCE WAS AMAZED to find how much he liked having her on his ranch. Generally, he wasn't much for company in the form of overnight guests—never mind ones that planned to stay for days on end, constantly disrupting and interfering with his routine. But he enjoyed preparing breakfast for someone other than himself and had orange juice, cereal, milk and toast waiting for Madison when she strode into the kitchen a few minutes later.

He was pleased to see she had put on a long-sleeved red denim shirt, jeans and boots instead of a business suit. He was less pleased to see she was carrying a steno pad and pen in her hand. Didn't she ever quit, even for a minute? Her hair had been tied at the nape of her neck with a ribbon. She wore no makeup. Without it, she looked surprisingly youthful and innocent in a freshly scrubbed sort of way. He liked that, too, although whether she'd done it because she thought it made her less attractive or because she was starting to let her guard down with him a little bit, he didn't know. In any case, it didn't matter. With clothes, without, makeup on or off, she was as attractive to him as ever. He wondered what she would think if she knew that, but knew better than to tell her.

Together, they sat down to eat.

"So, what do you usually do most mornings after breakfast?" Madison asked in the same brisk, businesslike tone she had used the evening before.

Chance watched her sip her juice and tried not to think how her soft lips had felt ghosting over his skin, or how long it would be before he felt them again. Not long, if he had his way, that was for damn sure. "Depends on whether it's one of the days I have my part-time help here or not." Chance dug into his wheat flakes with gusto and tried not to think about making love to her again. He couldn't afford to rush things here. Rushing things was what had gotten them into so much trouble in the first place.

"The boys from Lost Springs don't come every day?" Madison asked in the soft throaty voice that had so undone him the month before they'd met in person.

Aware she was studying him from beneath that fringe of blond lashes, Chance gulped his coffee. The burning liquid in his throat was nothing compared to the scorching heat in his groin and the warmth gathering in his chest. "They always get Sundays off," he told her, as if that was all he'd been thinking about. "During the summer, they come in the middle of the day, unless I need extra help, but in the school year it's late afternoons only."

Madison sipped her milk. "They won't be in the commercial anyway, so just forget them for a moment. For our purposes, pretend you're running the ranch alone, with no assistance whatsoever." She searched his eyes. "What would you do around here first thing in the morning?"

After making slow, leisurely love to you? Chance wondered silently, easily imagining Madison living here with him—as his woman—even after their baby was born.

Aware she was waiting for his answer, he smiled and said, "I'd go out and feed and water the horses and muck out the stalls. Put the horses in the pastures, and work with the ones on the schedule for that day."

"Would you mind doing that for me this morning?"

"Not at all." He'd be happy to do a lot more for her, too.

Madison jotted a few notes, then looked at him seriously. "Will you mind if I take pictures of you while you're working? It will help me a lot. I can send them back to AMV and Connelly and Associates. It'll help in the preparations. The more that's decided before the director and the crew actually get here, the faster the filming of the commercial will be."

Chance was all for getting them in and out as quickly as

possible. "Fine," he said shortly. As much as he liked having Madison with him, he was not looking forward to filming the damn commercial. On the other hand, it was what had brought him and Madison together again, giving their relationship—whatever it turned out to be—another chance.

Madison made a few more notes while she munched her cereal, then rubbed her forehead as if she had the beginnings of a headache.

"Are you sure you're up to this?" Chance asked gruffly, wishing she'd realize it didn't hurt to give herself a break every now and then.

Madison gave him a look that reminded him to mind his own business. "If I'm tired later, I'll nap. But I'm used to going all day long."

Was she ever, Chance thought hours later. In fact, she was damn near indefatigable, asking questions, making notes, snapping photos of him at every turn. At first he was self-conscious. It felt odd, having her follow him around, peppering him with questions, documenting practically every breath he took. But he got used to it, even if he couldn't stop wanting to kiss and hold and make love to her all over again.

By the time the evening rolled around and the Lost Springs boys had left for the day, it felt as if Madison had been on the ranch with him forever. It was going to be damn lonely if and when she left again. But he didn't want to think about the inevitable. Not while she was here.

"What do you want to do this evening?" he asked after they had both showered and put together a supper of baked chicken, garlic roasted potatoes, green beans and fresh fruit.

Madison shot him an amazed look as she helped carry their food to the table. Her hair was still damp from her shower, her cheeks and nose pink from a day spent in the sun. In deference to the warmth of the summer evening, she had dressed in a snug-fitting red T-shirt and khaki hiking shorts that showed off her deliciously long legs. Her skin was as soft and luminous as her hair, and her bare feet were every bit as sexy as the rest of her, the shapely toenails painted a delicate shell pink. Next to her, dressed in faded jeans, boots and a khaki shirt, Chance felt almost overdressed.

He held out her chair, and Madison slid into it gracefully. She thanked him with a smile, then spread her napkin on her lap. "I'm going to work."

"You've already worked all day," Chance pointed out. Madison had surprised him by being an excellent cook. She almost put his considerable culinary skills to shame.

Madison sipped her milk while he dug into the food with gusto. "There's a lot to do to get this campaign up and rolling in six weeks," she said, taking a delicate bite of chicken.

Chance shrugged and passed her the basket of oven-warmed rolls. He was willing to do whatever it took to protect her and their baby. "We can expand the time." Hell, he'd like to draw out her stay with him.

Madison shook her head. "The client would never allow it." Her eyes flashed a storm warning. "They've got to have the campaign up and running by the end of the summer in order to get ready for the January debut of the Ranchero."

Damn, Chance thought, although he had figured as much. He was going to have to find a way to spend some time with her that was not business-related.

"What are you planning to do?" Madison asked with a cursory smile.

He had hoped to spend time with Madison and get to know her a little better, not just for the baby's sake, but their own. Clearly that was going to have to wait for another day. "Work on the books, I guess," Chance told her indifferently. "Enjoy the sunset." He tried to hide his disappointment that he would probably be enjoying the sunset alone.

CHANCE'S PREDICTION proved accurate. Madison went right back to work as soon as the dishes were finished, and labored through sunset and beyond. Not wanting to disturb her, Chance brought the ranch books up to date, then sat on the front porch, rocking and thinking, wondering how different things might have been between them if only he had waited and gotten to know her before they had made love.

They would have seen each other again beyond that first weekend, he was sure of it. One thing would have led to another. She would have come to his bed at some point, maybe even carried on a hot and heavy love affair until the traveling back and forth between Dallas and Wyoming wore on them, and they broke it off. But it would have been great while it lasted.

But that hadn't happened, and now they were roped into the current situation. Chance knew Madison felt trapped. He could see it in her eyes, and he couldn't blame her. These circumstances were not what either of them wanted. But there was no use crying over a field that was already harvested. What had happened had happened, Chance thought. They were just going to have to deal with it and go on from here as best they both could. And that meant erasing the heartache of the past and giving his child a father and family like he'd never had.

"Chance?" Madison's soft voice cut across his thoughts. She stepped onto the moonlit porch. Except for the radiant glow that seemed to engulf her from head to toe, no one would ever guess she was pregnant. She was all slender curves and indefatigable energy as she paused to slip her feet into a pair of sandals, then crossed the rough-hewn porch to his side. Her smile was warm and welcoming. "I just thought I'd let you know I'm about finished for the evening."

Chance inclined his head at the place next to him on the porch swing. "How's it going?"

"Very well." Madison hesitated only slightly before accepting his tacit invitation and sitting beside him. Leaving his arm stretched along the back, Chance stopped the swing long enough for her to get settled comfortably, then resumed the gentle rocking motion.

"Seeing you in action today really helped me out a lot," Madison continued, crossing her legs, while beside her, he resisted the urge to slip his hand around her shoulder.

Chance had the feeling that, given the choice, she'd say to heck with politeness, forget about enjoying the starlit summer evening and rush off to bed. To prevent that—and assuage his curiosity about just what she'd been laboring so diligently over all these hours—he said, "So, what have you managed to get done so far?"

Madison sighed wearily and let her head fall back against his arm, her blond hair spilling over his forearm and wrist. Chance had the feeling there was a part of her that wanted nothing more at that moment than to curl up in his arms and go to sleep as he held her. "It's all very rough," she warned finally.

Chance understood the need for one's work to be perfect before sharing it. He didn't like showing a horse that was half-trained, either. "I don't mind."

Madison drew another breath and straightened. As she pivoted slightly to face him, her bent knee nudged his jeans-clad thigh. Suddenly, she was all career-driven energy again. "It's all subject to client approval, of course," she said, her low voice vibrating with infectious enthusiasm. "But what I'm proposing we do is go with two sets of ads, geared to different audiences. The first will open with an Old West film of a cowboy and a horse, and then a pioneer family and a wagon team, with a voice-over that says, 'In the past there was only one way to get around.' Then we'll move to the present, with sexy shots of you driving the Ranchero pickup on your ranch, in all kinds of weather, over all kinds of terrain, using it to haul hay and so on during the day, using it at the end of the day to squire a beautiful woman around, and of course for that you'll be in black tie.''

''Of course,'' Chance said dryly, able to envision it all. And even liking the idea, as long as the beautiful woman he was with at the end of the day was Madison. ''I often wear a tuxedo out here on the ranch in the evening,'' he teased.

Madison rolled her eyes, her face illuminated by the soft glow of the citronella candles in the glass lanterns attached to the porch wall. She leaned toward him, tantalizing him with the subtle but unmistakably feminine fragrance of her perfume. ''We're tapping into fantasy here, Chance.''

Chance wished he could tap into *his* fantasy. He'd have her shifted from the other side of the porch swing and on his lap in no time.

Failing to notice what was on his mind, Madison continued telling him her plans. ''The second spot will feature a shot of all your horses, running wild and free in one of the meadows on the ranch, with the mountains in the backdrop. The voice-over will say, 'If you want the very best horses in the country, there's only one place to go.' There'll be more shots of your ranch and your horses and some of the famous people who've bought some of your horses. Then the scene will shift and the voice-over will say, 'If you want the very best trucks...' And they'll show the Ranchero pickup.''

Chance was impressed by what she had done, and he told her so.

Madison flushed happily at his praise. She relaxed against his arm again, and it was all Chance could do not to tangle his hand in her hair and lift her lips to his. He even knew how she'd taste. Like peppermint. And woman.

''If you wouldn't mind, I'd like to scout specific locations for filming tomorrow and choose the horses that are going to be in the commercials.''

The truth was, Chance was happy for any excuse to spend time with her. By now he didn't care what they were doing as long as they were doing it together. "Sounds fine."

"But I'll need you to help me," Madison warned.

Chance had been counting on it. "It'll be my pleasure," he said. Before her stay was up, he planned to become indispensable to her in myriad ways.

"Thanks." Madison sighed and stretched her arms above her head, her shirt pulling against the soft curves of her breasts.

Watching, Chance knew his life had changed the moment Madison walked into it, and no amount of wishing otherwise would ever change it back again. He wasn't going to rest until she was his. And stayed his. No matter how they had to work it out. But to make that happen would take some doing. Fortunately, because he'd agreed to let the Ranchero ads be filmed on the Double Diamond, he had time.

He smiled at her. "Tired?"

"Very." Madison shivered in the cooling night air. "I think I'm going to get a glass of milk and go to bed."

Chance tore his eyes from the evidence of her chilling. "I'll get it for you."

Oblivious to the way her nipples had puckered beneath the fabric of her T-shirt and bra, she put out a hand to stop him. "You don't have to wait on me hand and foot."

I want to, Chance thought, and it surprised him how much. He'd never been anxious to wait on anyone before. Already on his feet, he headed for the door. "It's no trouble. Just sit tight." Besides, maybe walking around would ease some of the pressure at the front of his jeans, he thought.

Disregarding the throbbing in his groin, he poured her a tall glass of icy cold milk, grabbed a soft cotton afghan Lindsay Duncan, his friend at the boys' ranch, had crocheted for him one spring, and headed to the porch swing. He handed her the afghan first, watched while she smiled and thanked him and draped it around her shoulders. When she was comfortably situated, he handed her the milk, then settled beside her, draping his arm across the back of the swing once again.

"Do you always work this hard?" Chance asked, limiting the motion of the swing while she drank.

Madison nodded. "I have since I started in advertising. But I don't mind. I get real pleasure out of the artistic challenge of designing an ad campaign." She paused to put her empty glass down beside the porch swing. Straightening, she settled into the curve of his arm. Chance's foot touched the floor at the same time and angle as hers did, and they resumed swinging.

She looked at him companionably. "You must feel the same way."

Chance nodded. Since he'd left Lost Springs to strike out on his own, this ranch and the building of his business had been his whole life. He looked at her. "I sometimes wish I had a little more free time, though." He wished he had a little more fun and passion and—hell, even the love of a good woman wouldn't be such a bad thing.

"Not me," Madison insisted stubbornly, drawing the afghan around her a little tighter. "I like having a life that's all business, where everything is under control."

Needing everything to run strictly according to plan was like asking for a ticket to disaster, Chance thought, because life was unpredictable. The more you counted on something, the more likely you were to be disappointed. He did not want to see Madison disappointed.

"Meaning if you had more of a personal life, your life would no longer be under control?" Chance taunted lightly.

Madison narrowed her eyes. "I find it's a lot harder to plan and anticipate in my personal life than in the professional arena." She sighed. "This unexpected pregnancy is a case in point. I really want this baby but—'' she smiled ruefully ''—the circumstances under which he or she was conceived and the timing could have been a little better.''

Chance knew their pregnancy had caught her as unaware as it had him, but she seemed to be taking it in stride, and he admired her for her resilience even as he worried about their future. If anything was bound to be unpredictable, not to run strictly according to plan, it was life with two unmarried parents and a baby. And damn it all, if there was anything he wanted their baby to have, it was a happy, secure home and two parents who loved him.

''What are you going to do about mixing motherhood with business?'' Chance asked, unable to mask his concern.

''I don't know.'' Madison's teeth worried her lower lip, and she steadfastly refused to meet his eyes. ''I haven't had time to figure it out.''

Chance watched her train her eyes on the starry night sky. ''Will the company let you take a maternity leave if you want one?''

''By law, they have to.''

''You know what I mean,'' Chance said impatiently. ''Will you be penalized in terms of opportunity and assignments if you have a child?'' He had friends whose wives had been forced to go back to work much earlier than they wanted to for fear of permanently losing their place on the fast track. It wasn't supposed to happen that way, of course. But behind the scenes, in subtle, unspoken ways, it often did. Chance didn't want to see that happen to Madison. He didn't want to see her pressured by the people she worked for.

Madison frowned. He felt her tense, and at the rhythmic prodding of her foot, the motion of the swing picked up. ''Most of the women at the agency haven't scaled back much, either during or after their pregnancies. In fact, most are back at their jobs within six weeks of the birth of their

babies, if not before,'' she told Chance with a faintly troubled sigh.

She paused briefly, as if searching for some inner reserve
of strength. ''I'm sure I'll be able to do that, too,'' she said
finally, ''and be a great single mom and very loving mother
to boot.'' Her chin set determinedly. ''It's just going to take
more organization on my part, more efficiency.''

Chance wasn't sure who she was trying to convince—
herself or him.

''I'm going to have to get a nanny and a housekeeper to
help me, of course,'' Madison continued resolutely. ''But
with the jump in salary that comes with the VP slot combined with my savings, I think we'll manage just fine.''

Chance didn't want to think about his baby—their
baby—being raised by strangers. But he also knew, at this
point, anyway, it wasn't his decision to make.

Fortunately, he had time to convince her that no job was
more important than their child.

The rocking motion of the swing, combined with the
milk she'd drunk and the blanket she had wrapped around
her, had combined to make her very sleepy, Chance noted.
He slowed the sweetly lulling motion of the swing. ''Ready
to go up?''

Madison nodded. She accepted his hand and got gracefully to her feet. Clutching the afghan around her, she tilted
her face to his. She looked very vulnerable. Very much in
need. Of him. He was determined to be there for her, financially and otherwise.

''Thanks for being so decent about all this,'' she said.
''For not trying to take my baby away from me.'' Her low
voice trembled. ''Other men might not have been so understanding about my career and how much it means to
me.''

Knowing how he had practically sold his soul to get her
on his ranch with him for the next six weeks or longer,
Chance did not feel so honorable. Yet he also knew there

was nothing he wouldn't do or sacrifice to keep Madison and their baby safe and warm and happy. The question was, when the time came...would she let him?

MADISON STOOD outside the corral, watching as Chance ran his hands over Shiloh's withers and down his neck. Slowly, he moved his hands across the big black stallion's flanks, down his belly. Talking softly to the beautiful horse all the while, he picked up each of Shiloh's hooves, holding them off the ground a second or two before moving on to rub his hands over each fetlock and knee. Only when Shiloh was in a state of complete relaxation did he go about saddling him up.

Still murmuring calm but firm reassurances, Chance swung himself into the saddle. For a moment, Madison thought Shiloh might rear, but the moment passed and the big black stallion—who just two months before had been one of the wildest, most fearful animals Madison had ever seen—stood quietly, accepting Chance's weight and then his direction, walking around the perimeter of the pen, first one way, then the other. He slipped easily and dutifully into a trot, then a canter, then back to a trot again, and eventually a walk.

"Amazing," Madison said an hour later, when Chance took a break from the training session and strode over to join her.

"He's coming along, isn't he?" Chance grinned.

"So much so that we'd like to use him in the Ranchero commercial," Madison said. Ignoring Chance's frown, she clasped her notebook and camera to her chest and rushed on. "I've talked to Ed Connelly, Ursula Rodriguez at AMV and Vince Smith, the commercial's director. They all want to use close-ups of you working with Shiloh in the ads."

Chance shook his head. "Shiloh's not ready—"

"He doesn't have to be perfect. In fact, if he were to act

up a bit and you were to calm him while the cameras are rolling, it'd be great.''

Again, Chance shook his head. "You can have your pick of the horses here." And there were plenty, Madison knew. Tennessee walking horses, Morgans, Westphalians, palominos, quarter horses, thoroughbreds, Kentucky saddlers and Arabs. "But not Shiloh," Chance reiterated firmly.

"Why not?" Madison demanded impatiently.

Chance shrugged. "He's still skittish enough as it is without adding too many people and cameras to the mix."

"Then we could film the two of you from a distance."

"No," Chance said flatly, beginning to look a little irritated by her persistence. "You can have your pick of the others. You can even film them all at once if you want. But not Shiloh."

Madison frowned, unable to understand why he was being so stubborn about this. Surely he wasn't afraid of being embarrassed by a horse that wasn't totally reliable just yet, was he? Madison pressed her lips together tightly. She'd never liked hearing the word no. She didn't like hearing it now. "I wanted to show you taming something wild."

Chance grinned and his blue eyes lit up. "I could always work on you."

Glad no one else was around to hear that, Madison blushed and gave him a playful sock in the ribs. "I'm serious, Chance."

"So am I." Chance tugged the brim of his hat over his eyes. "The only wild filly I'm training for the benefit of your film crews is going to be you."

That said, he chucked her under the chin and walked off to resume training Shiloh.

"HOW ARE things going?" Ed asked Madison a couple of weeks later.

Madison, cell phone in hand, looked at the list of potential problems, which seemed to be growing by the minute.

The commercial's director hadn't arrived, and he was already being temperamental in his demands, asking for five-star hotel accommodations when there were none in the area. Shawna Somersby, the new intern, had thus far, despite her eagerness, botched up more things than she had gotten right. And roughly one-third of their usual film crew was not available, which meant they were going to be working with a crew that might or might not be completely in sync. "Pretty well."

"Only pretty well?"

Madison sighed, wishing she didn't have to break any bad news to her boss. "He's cooperative, but only to a point."

"What doesn't he want to do?"

Meet with Wardrobe. Wear makeup. Do anything at all to prepare for his role in the filming. But those were things that could be easily fixed, once Madison went into full persuasive mode. The last difficulty was not going to be so easy to explain, particularly when—thanks to her constant photo and video taking—everyone had already seen the pictures of the big black stallion and gone every bit as wild over Shiloh as Madison had.

Nevertheless, she had to prepare Ed, and the others, for the disappointment. "Chance is refusing to let us film him training one of his wilder horses."

"We're not talking about that beautiful black stallion, are we?"

"Afraid so."

Ed released a string of swear words. "Why the hell not?" he demanded.

Seated at the kitchen table, Madison sipped milk on the rocks and watched Chance work with Shiloh in the distance. "Chance thinks it would be dangerous," she said wearily.

"Is it?" Ed said.

Madison frowned and tried not to think of the headache

gathering behind her eyes as she watched Chance and Shiloh move as one, whirling and backing and sidestepping around the corral as if in some incredible outdoor ballet.

She tried not to think about the fluid way Chance worked a horse, with hands and feet and legs. Day by day, hour by hour, horse and man were connecting, heart and body and soul. And Chance wasn't going to stop till the job was done. Till the horse that he'd rescued had recovered completely. It was Madison's view that Chance was closer to achieving that goal than he was ready to admit.

"I can't see how it'd be one bit dangerous as long as we stayed on the other side of the pasture and did the actual filming from a distance," Madison replied in frustration.

There was a brief silence on the other end of the telephone line. "He won't hear of that, either?" Ed snapped unhappily.

"Not so far," Madison admitted reluctantly as an unfamiliar sports car whipped up the lane, stopping just short of the pasture where Chance was working Shiloh. "But I'm working on him," she promised. The same way Chance was working on Shiloh.

Madison watched as Chance dismounted, left Shiloh on the other side of the pasture fence and headed for the sports car.

"Well, keep it up," Ed advised Madison grumpily. "We want film of something with real derring-do and wild-west sex appeal when it comes to the horses, not something any grandma could do."

Knowing an order when she heard one, Madison shut her eyes and did her best to suppress a sigh. "I got you."

She glanced out the window, then blinked. And blinked again. Was that Rona Fitzgerald, the hottest TV actress going today? she wondered in absolute amazement. It sure as heck looked like the popular star climbing out of the low-slung sports car, and she was smiling and dashing toward Chance exuberantly.

Madison's mouth dropped into a round O of surprise as she watched Chance embrace Rona, lift her off her feet and swing her around in a semicircle.

Madison's research had told her Chance's love affair with Rona was over and had been for quite a while now. Had something happened to change that?

CHAPTER SIX

CHANCE AND RONA were still laughing and smiling and holding each other at arm's length as Madison strode into the yard, notepad in hand. "Are you who I think you are?" Madison smiled, extending a hand.

The blond actress, her long and shimmering Goldilocks hair falling in wild curls nearly to her waist, reluctantly let go of Chance. Turning her gorgeous face to Madison, she smiled and shook her hand. "Rona Fitzgerald, in the flesh."

"Madison Burnes."

Rona turned to Chance, who was standing with his back against the pasture fence. "I agreed to endorse the Ranchero pickup truck. Madison is here to work on the ad campaign," he explained.

Rona, who was clad in custom-made Western clothes similar to the ones she wore on her TV show, arched a brow at Chance. "That doesn't sound like you."

"The proceeds are going to charity," Madison said.

Rona grinned. "Now *that* sounds like you."

"Did you need anything?" Chance asked Madison. His low voice gave nothing away. There was not so much as a hint of intimacy in his blue eyes. Madison should have been happy—they had agreed to keep their affair secret. So why did she suddenly want Chance to claim her?

"No." Madison smiled again. "I just came out to say hello." She turned as if to go back in the house.

Chance looked at Rona, his expression a mixture of business and pleasure. "Ready to go?" he asked her.

Madison told herself that was *not* jealousy she was feeling. She'd never been jealous of another woman in her life. She wasn't about to start now.

"Absolutely." Rona gave Chance the dazzling smile that had won her the hearts of millions. Her eyes sparkled warmly. "Where do you want me to park my car?"

"Same place as usual," Chance said, regarding Rona with the affection of an old and trusted friend. "Down behind the barns."

Her slender hips swaying seductively, Rona sashayed to her sports car. Chance strode toward the still-saddled Shiloh, who was snorting and lightly pawing the ground, demanding some attention, too.

Madison made her way back to the house. Her slender shoulders self-consciously stiff, she let herself inside and headed for the folding table in the corner of the living room where Chance had let her set up her belongings. Minutes later, she saw Chance ride out with Rona. He was on a big bay. She was riding a beautiful palomino. Madison had only to look at the elegant way Rona Fitzgerald sat a horse to know that—unlike Madison—she was as expert a rider as Chance. But then why not, Madison thought resentfully. For the past five years Rona had spent innumerable hours on horseback, filming her TV show.

Besides, it was none of her business even if the two were more than friends, she told herself firmly. It wasn't as if she and Chance had promised each other anything. They had a baby on the way, one they hadn't planned but had agreed to share. Beyond that...

Madison sighed.

So what if the incredible, overwhelming attraction she felt for him from the first was still there in spades? So what if he still desired her? In the end, that didn't make any difference. It didn't do any good to wonder where they would be now if she hadn't needed him for the ad or if things would be different if they had met some other way besides the bachelor auction. There was no way to know if he would even have sought her out again by agreeing to do the ad had she not been carrying his baby. Not that this should have mattered. She had known when she left his ranch the first time that he was definitely not the man for her!

She had to concentrate on her work, Madison told herself sternly. Once the campaign was in place, everything else would work out, too. She would see to it.

Madison was still at it when Chance and Rona rode up hours later. Their boisterous laughter floated in through the windows.

"I can't thank you enough, Chance!" Rona declared. "Same time tomorrow?"

Looking every bit as happy and relaxed as his riding partner, Chance tipped his hat. "Sounds good to me."

Madison glanced up in time to see Chance giving Rona a hug. She kissed his cheek, got in her little sports car and drove off. Aware she wished she had been the one spending the day riding with Chance, that she had been the one on the receiving end of his quick, warm hug, Madison went back to her drawing.

Chance took both horses and headed toward the barn. It was another half hour before he came in. He was hot and sweaty, and his handsome face bore the flush of summer sun, his body the scent of horse and man. Despite all that, he looked happy and relaxed. In comparison, Madison felt the way she'd always felt when working too hard without a break—tired and deprived.

"How's it going?" Chance asked casually. Not waiting for her reply, he tossed his hat on the rack and strode past her into the kitchen. For several seconds, Madison stared at his retreating back. Finally, she rose and headed toward the kitchen. She lounged in the doorway, arms folded, ankles crossed. In deference to the setting and the fact that none of her business associates or film crew had arrived yet, she was wearing jeans and a shirt, too, though unlike Rona's, hers were of the store-bought variety and not custom-made.

Madison raised her voice to be heard above the running water. "I said, it's going well."

Unmindful of her presence, Chance leaned over the kitchen sink. He had already dispensed with his shirt and lathered up to his elbows. He looked sexy and at ease. As she studied him, her heart turned flip-flops in her chest.

Chance shot her a look over his broad, deeply suntanned shoulder, scanning her from head to toe in a thorough, breath-stealing appraisal before turning to the chore at hand. "You don't look particularly satisfied," he drawled.

That's because she wasn't, Madison thought irritably. It had been hard keeping her mind on the storyboards she had been sketching. It was even harder trying to keep from acting on the powerful desire she still felt for Chance. Whenever she was near him, it was all she could do to keep from losing sight of her professionalism, throwing herself in his arms and kissing him madly. It had been so easy to make love with him. And still would be. The hard part had been walking away. And Madison wasn't used to that, any more than she was used to the powerful, highly irrational surge of jealousy in her gut. She was an independent career woman, for heaven's sake. A woman with no strings and no ties. Her world did not rise and fall on the actions of any man. Except maybe Chance.

"So," Madison said eventually, figuring she might as well find out right now exactly how much trouble she was in before she did something ludicrous, like falling head over heels in love with him. "You and Rona are still friends?"

"Yeah, we are." Leaning forward, Chance rinsed his arms, one at a time, in the sink.

Madison was frustrated that he wasn't more forthcoming. That he was forcing her to spell it out even when he had to know darn well exactly what it was she wanted to know. She bit her lip. "There's no easy way to say this."

"There isn't?" he teased.

Madison felt heat climb from her chest into her neck. "Are the two of you still involved?"

Chance shut off the water with a snap. His expression inscrutable, he grabbed a dish towel from the rack and, turning to face her, dried his dripping arms.

She could tell by the look on his face that he considered whatever it was that was going on between him and Rona to be nothing and wanted her to leave it, but she couldn't. She knew what a virile, passionate man Chance was. She knew how much he enjoyed making love. She had to know what she was dealing with even if it hurt, so she could get out now while the getting was still good.

"What is this?" he demanded, his eyebrows rising sharply. "The third degree?"

"First, second, whatever," Madison quipped with a nonchalant attitude she couldn't begin to feel. "I was just curious since she's coming back tomorrow and everything. I wouldn't want to be in your way or, uh, interrupt anything."

"You wouldn't."

Okay, so she was lying through her teeth.

"Live and let live. That's my credo," Madison said breezily.

Chance rubbed his jaw and continued to look at her thoughtfully for a long minute. "That's probably a good attitude to have since you and I aren't having an affair and, according to you, anyway, never will again."

Madison skipped over that, deciding it was something she definitely did not want to comment on, no matter how sarcastic he was being.

Chance thrust the towel aside and leaned against the

counter, his arms folded. "I can see this is still worrying you," he said dryly. "So if it will set your mind at ease, Rona is seriously involved with the producer of her TV show."

Madison tried to ignore the velvety mat of black hair covering his wide, muscular chest and the flatness of his abdomen above his tight-fitting jeans. Her throat unbearably dry, she kept her eyes leveled squarely on his and pushed on with her inquisition. "Oh."

"Jealous?" Chance taunted, holding her gaze.

If you're making love to someone else right now? Hell yes, Madison thought. But there was no way she was telling him that. "I just thought I should know what was going on, for the sake of the baby," she fibbed.

Chance gave her a look that let her know she wasn't fooling him one bit.

"The fact you and I are having a baby wouldn't keep me from making love to Rona, if that was what I wanted, Madison. I could easily be a dad and have a woman in my life, too."

"Be blunt, why don't you?" Madison said, then could have shot herself the second the words were out.

Aware she had revealed far more about her feelings than she was comfortable doing, Madison picked up her camera and strode from the house. Head held high, she darted down the steps, across the yard. All too aware that Chance was right behind her, moving at a typical leisurely pace, Madison began taking pictures of the stables, the ranch house and the tree-shaded lane leading up to it.

"Don't you have anything to say to that?" Chance taunted lazily. "Any rules or regulations to set down?"

Madison caught sight of his bare chest and the sexual promise in his eyes. A river of warmth rippled through her. "There's nothing to say." She aimed her camera at the pasture where Shiloh was contentedly munching on sweet green grass. Making sure that Chance wasn't anywhere in the frame, she focused and snapped the shot. "Except that I have a ton of work left to do. The director wants at least five or six more rolls of film taken of the inside of the stable."

"Why not get a professional to do it?"

"No time. Vince wants the film at his lab in New York— where he's currently working—for developing before ten tomorrow morning. So I've got to get them taken in the next hour if I want to meet the express mail deadline for shipments going out tonight."

Ignoring what she had just told him, Chance clamped his hands on her shoulders and swung her around to face him. "Why are you being like this?" he demanded in obvious frustration.

"Like what?" Madison challenged, knowing she was spoiling for an argument even if she didn't quite know why.

"Icy." Chance sized her up relentlessly. "Remote."

Madison returned the favor, giving him her haughtiest ice queen glare, the one that had sent men running for as long as she could remember. "How would you expect me to react?" she asked. "You and I have to work together and pretend to all the world like nothing's happened, when you and I both know I'm carrying our baby inside me. As if that alone isn't hard enough, you bring your old lover here and go off alone with her for hours." Yes, she had had a miserable afternoon, and so what?

Chance smiled at the mention of their baby and frowned when she referred to Rona. He ran a hand through his hair, shoving the unruly black locks off his forehead. He turned his glance away, then back, his blue eyes laser-bright. "Rona doesn't get much time off and she loves to ride," Chance explained, as if she were yanking the words from him one by one. "Not in bits and pieces like she does on the show, but in the open countryside. For the record—" his voice dropped another gruff, warning notch "—she comes here anytime she wants. And when she does, I usually drop everything and go off with her.''

Madison's spine stiffened. She was shocked at how possessive she felt toward Chance, and at the same time unwilling to admit how much the idea of Chance being at another woman's beck and call hurt. Was this how it had been for her mother all those years? She didn't want to think about any of this, but Chance's actions, the unexpected events of the afternoon had brought it all back anyway, with startling force.

"So what do you want here, Chance, a permission slip? You've already made it quite clear we've got no claim on each other.''

"Do you want that to change?''

"Oh, for heaven's sake, Cartwright, I'm no idiot.''

He glared at her in utter frustration, as aware as she was that she hadn't exactly come right out and answered his question. Ignoring her sarcasm, he regarded her resentfully. "I've done nothing to make you distrust me.''

So, he didn't like having a leash on him, either. "Then you have my apologies.'' Madison shrugged uncaringly as the sun beat down on them.

"And yet you do distrust me,'' Chance persisted.

Try all men. "It's nothing personal.'' Madison's hands clenched her camera as she struggled to retain the cool sophistication that had become her trademark.

Chance swore profusely, this time loud enough for her to hear. "And that's supposed to make me feel better?'' he demanded roughly.

Unfortunately, he wasn't the only one feeling rattled and uncertain. Which just went to show, Madison thought, how emotional this pregnancy had made her. She sighed with world-weary resignation and did her best to get a grip and shut him out once again. "Look, Chance, if I appear jaded and cynical—''

"You do.''

Why wouldn't he just let this go? Angry at how quick this footloose and fancy-free cowboy was to criticize, Madison answered in the most even voice she could manage. "Let's just say I've seen and heard it all before." She pushed the words through her teeth.

Chance studied her relentlessly. "From whom?"

You really do not want to know. "My father."

"What does he have to do with Rona buying another horse from me today?"

As that news sunk in, Madison muttered a single, succinct expletive. If Chance had set out to deliberately punch holes in her composure and get her where she was most vulnerable, he had certainly succeeded. She had just made a complete and utter fool of herself. And it all could have been avoided had Chance mentioned the fact Rona was there to buy a horse.

She turned away, aware she could cheerfully deck him at that moment. "Just drop it, Chance. Okay? None of this has anything to do with anything."

He grabbed her by the arms and swung her to face him. "Tell me."

Feeling she'd already told him too much, Madison went utterly still.

Chance dropped his hold on her, stepped back. "Did your father cheat on your mother?"

"All the time. He's still doing it. All right? Are you satisfied?"

Pain twisting her heart, Madison spun away from him and stalked to the stables. Stepped inside the cool light. The horses were all outside for the day. The cement-floored building had been hosed down earlier with a mixture of disinfectant and water by the part-time help. Fresh straw had been laid down and the automatic feed buckets filled. The wide doors were open at each end, creating a welcome breeze that swept through the wood-paneled building. As she lifted the camera to her face, Madison forced herself to think about her work. She knew Vince Smith, the director, was going to love this place. There was a lot about it to love.

Chance hovered just to the left of her as she snapped photo after photo of the interior of a spacious wooden stall. He leaned against a beam, his arms folded casually. He smelled of soap and sun-warmed skin. He wasn't saying anything. But he wasn't leaving her alone, either.

Madison knew her father's unfaithfulness had bred in her a distrust of all men. Madison remembered without wanting to all the times she had stumbled on her father cozying up to other women while her mother pretended not to see what was going on right in front of her.

The worst time had been at a party her parents had been hosting. She'd been ten, and they were living in Paris. She hadn't understood much of what the woman in the wine cellar had been saying to her father, but once Madison caught sight of the two of them, their faces alternately white then red as they hastily tried to adjust their clothing, she'd understood enough.

Madison had known even then her mother deserved better. Just as she had eventually come to realize that her mother was as much to blame as her father for allowing it to keep happening without doing anything. It was so much simpler to be married to your work.

Standing in the center aisle of the stable, Madison focused her lens on the barn doors at the far end.

Chance moved to block her. He stood in front of her, legs braced. He seemed to understand that some hurts were deep enough to defy logic. "You want to know about my relationship with Rona, I'll tell you about it," he said gently.

Madison averted her eyes from a bare chest so fine it could have graced the cover of *Playgirl* magazine. She wanted to tell him it wasn't necessary—he didn't have to explain—but the truth was she wanted to know. She wanted some reassurance that she wasn't just another in a long string of talented, successful women who had wandered in and out of Chance's life.

Keeping his eyes locked on hers, he continued, "Our affair began six years ago, Madison. Rona was getting ready to film the pilot for *Woman of the West*. She didn't know how to ride, and she knew if she couldn't ace that, she'd be replaced—pronto."

Unable to turn away, Madison shoved a hand through her hair. "The producers didn't know she couldn't?"

Chance shrugged his broad shoulders restlessly. "She'd lied to them to get the job. And she came to me because she had heard I had a way with horses. She was hoping I could teach her the way, too." His blue eyes darkened. "I understood that kind of desperation."

Chance ducked into the tack room and came out with a crumpled but clean blue chambray shirt in hand. He slipped it on but didn't bother to button it or tuck it in. "I'd started this ranch from nothing, and if I had a penny for every time I had severely overestimated my—let's just say resources to the banks, I'd be a very rich man. So I taught her to ride in an intensive two weeks, and even lent her a horse to take with her, a sweet gentle mare to ride during the filming of the pilot. She told me later it was her way with the horse that got her the job. So when she came back to thank me and pay the first of many installments on that horse, we let her gratitude and my loneliness lead us into bed. Eventually we realized the love we felt for each other was not the kind that endures. Besides horses and the sex, we had nothing. And after a while, well, nothing can get to feeling pretty empty to the point that it's almost worse than being alone. So we both moved on."

Moved on, Madison thought. Was that what she and Chance were eventually going to have to do, too? she wondered uneasily as she thanked Chance politely for clarifying things for her and got right back to work. And if so, why was she finding even the thought of it so hard?

BY THE TIME Madison finished taking photos of the interior and then the exterior of the stables, plus all the surrounding area, Chance was showered, shaved and sitting inside doing the books on his computer. Madison had only to look at the set expression on his face to see how much she had hurt him. She turned away from him and once again buried herself in the safety and security of her work. She knew he didn't deserve it. Not at all. Because her misgivings about herself and her ability to sustain a relationship with a man, to keep him interested and faithful over the long haul, had nothing to do with Chance.

Madison could see Chance making a fabulous husband someday, settling down right here on the ranch, maybe even raising a family. She just wasn't sure she could ever be a *wife*.

That would most likely mean giving up her career, Madison thought, as she prepared an express mail package for the director, enclosed the film she had taken, then walked over to Chance. He paused as her shadow fell over him. "Do you have professional photos of your horses I could send to my bosses?"

Chance rose and wordlessly went to his file cabinet. Five minutes later, he had assembled eight-by-ten glossies of all the horses he had for sale. He handed them over.

Judging by his expression—which had never been less welcoming—Madison figured she'd better warm up to that apology she owed him, rather than just jump right in. She fit the pictures in the cardboard mailer along with the film and sealed it. Glancing at her watch, she figured she had better get going if she wanted to make it into town in time.

Several hours later, she was back and Chance was still sitting in the same place. To her disappointment, he looked just as surly and unapproachable as he had when she'd left.

How long was this mood of his going to continue? And why did she care so much, anyway? Madison chastised herself sternly.

Grateful for the occupation of her work, Madison told him, "I was thinking about the commercial on the drive back—"

Chance gave her a smile that did not reach his eyes. "What a surprise."

She paused and cleared her throat. So he wasn't going to make this easy for her. So what? She had lived through worse. What was important was establishing some sort of renewed peace between them. And the best way to do that was to get them talking to each other again, even if it was just about business. She leaned against the corner of his file cabinet, jerked in a deep breath and continued pleasantly. "Maybe we could do a far-off shot of all your horses, running in a meadow or something like that, with you on horseback, riding with them."

Chance narrowed his eyes on her. "Maybe we could at that," he agreed reluctantly after an exceptionally long pause. "But only if the cameras were well outside the pasture fence."

"I'd see to it," Madison promised, wondering even as she spoke how someone as passionate and exciting as Chance could also be, at heart, so solid and dependable.

"Although," Chance continued matter-of-factly, almost as if she hadn't spoken, "I'm not sure how appealing fenced-in horses would be for an ad, even if you had a cowboy riding among them."

He was right on the mark about that, Madison thought, admiring his vision. Fenced-in anything didn't hold a candle to wild and free.

Unable to resist, she edged closer, inhaling the brisk, spicy scent of his cologne. "We could use digital cameras and cut the fence out of the shot with computers. The important thing would be to have the mountains in the backdrop.''

Chance leaned back in his swivel chair, his disappointment in her obvious. He propped his feet on the edge of his desktop, cocked his head and gave her a thorough onceover. ''Is this Madison the woman talking or Madison the account exec talking?''

There was no need for him to be so rude when she was trying to make up with him. Madison's shoulders stiffened. ''What do you mean?'' She hated the way he was looking at her—like she was a lost cause.

Chance reached over, his hand brushing her linen-clad thigh, and turned on his printer. As it sputtered to life, he leaned back, lifted a hand to his jaw and rubbed the angled contours with a slow deliberation she found extremely annoying. He completed an even more thorough survey of her face. ''I mean, are you being nice to me all of a sudden because you feel bad about the way you acted earlier this afternoon—first jealous, then bitchy, then aloof?'' he queried softly. His blue eyes glinted with a cynicism that stung. ''Or because you don't want me getting difficult on you again?''

IT WAS EASY for Chance to see his words had hit her like a sucker punch to the gut. And though he'd never meant to hurt her, he couldn't exactly say they were undeserved, either. He didn't care if this pregnancy had turned her into a bundle of hormones. Madison Burnes needed to learn to put *people* before business every time. It was the only way to be truly successful, no matter what line of work you were in.

''I'm sorry.'' Madison swallowed as Chance retrieved the pages spitting out of his printer. Clearly, Chance thought bitterly, she'd had time to reconsider her actions on the drive to and from town in the Double Diamond pickup truck he'd loaned her.

Madison lifted her head proudly. "If I've been prickly it's because I've been embarrassed. I knew all along I had no right to wonder about the specifics of your personal life."

"Why? Because it might help us to get closer?"

"Your private life is your business," Madison continued.

"You can say that again," Chance said gruffly, tossing the printed pages into a file on his desk, leaning forward and shutting the printer off with a decisive snap.

He hadn't had to answer to anyone about anything since he'd left Lost Springs Ranch, and he didn't intend to start again now. He was his own boss. He lived his own life. And that was just the way he liked it. So why did he suddenly want Madison to understand and approve of him? It didn't make sense.

Madison twisted her hands in front of her. Swallowed again. Persisted with typical Madison determination. "It's just—seeing you with Rona, knowing you're the father of my baby—it struck a nerve with me. It shouldn't have, but it did."

Chance stood and closed in on Madison deliberately, not stopping until only a scant two inches remained between them. He stood with legs braced apart and gazed at her like a hawk eyeing his prey. He wanted her to continue telling him what was on her mind, and in her heart, but only of her own volition.

Her voice turned even quieter. "Knowing you'd once had a sexual relationship with her struck another one."

Chance wasn't going to apologize for that, any more than he expected her to apologize for any relationships she had been in. Reaching out to others was—and always would be—a very important part of one's life. Even if you weren't very good at it in the long run.

Chance hooked his thumbs through his belt loops and shrugged. She desperately needed reassurance for reasons that had nothing to do with him, and damned if he didn't find himself wanting to give it to her anyway. Maybe it was because he understood how much higher the stakes were now that their baby was involved. They couldn't afford to let anything, past or present, get in the way. "I imagine we both have people in our pasts who ultimately were wrong for us," he told her warily.

Madison nodded, but to his frustration did not elaborate about her past love life.

Silence stretched between them, more uncomfortable than ever, broken only by the sounds of the birds singing and the wind rustling through the leaves on the cottonwood trees. For a moment he thought she was going to shut him out again, as she always did whenever he started to get too close. Then with a sigh of resignation, she clasped her hands in front of her and glanced away. "I don't want my child to grow up in the kind of family I grew up in."

Neither did he, from the sound of things, Chance thought.

Knowing a loving touch could gentle even the wildest filly, Chance touched her face with the callused roughness of his palm, cupping her chin in his hand, moving his thumb across the trembling softness of her lower lip. "So we'll find a way to do better."

"How, Chance?" Madison turned away just as he had the sharp suspicion she really wanted him to kiss her. Misery radiating from every inch of her, she began to pace. "How can we do that with both of us doing our own thing, seeing other people whenever we feel like it?"

Chance was beginning to see where this was going.

Madison would never admit it, but despite the fact that neither of them was the marrying kind, marriage—the safety of it, the commitment of it—was what Madison needed. An affair, with all the loopholes and easy outs, would never cut it for her. Never give her the security she deserved. The question was, did he have it in him to give her what she needed? And maintain his own life-style and independence, too? Could he give her what she needed without sacrificing his own dreams?

Oblivious to his thoughts, Madison continued with her usual practical take on things. "We won't be married, of course—"

"Of course not," Chance cut in dryly, glad to see he and Madison were on the same page, after all.

"But if we're raising a child together, it will sort of seem like it to our child. And the older our child gets, the more he or she is going to be aware of our relationship." She knotted her hands together in frustration. "I don't want our child to see us get involved with person after person after person. It would be...confusing."

"And then some," Chance agreed with mock solemnness, wondering where in heck Madison was going with this. Clearly, she had some objective in mind. "So what are you suggesting we do?" Chance squinted at her, trying to read her mind, not to mention what was in her heart. "That we both swear off sex until our kid is grown up?" That was ludicrous!

"Of course not." As Madison faced him, bright color stained her cheeks. She laid a hand against her breasts. "I would never ask you to deny your...your needs in that respect any more than I would want to deny mine for the rest of my life!"

"Then..." Chance left the question hanging.

"I was wondering. As long as you're not emotionally involved with anyone else, and neither am I—" Madison hesitated, her lower lip trembling. "Maybe we could agree to sleep just with each other."

A RIVETING SILENCE fell between them that had Madison's heart doing flip-flops in her chest and all her nerves jangling. She could see his shock doing battle with his interest. No doubt about it, she thought as his sexy smile widened, he loved her proposed arrangement. "Hmm. Steady sex without the wedding rings or any of the other attendant hassles," Chance declared finally with a long sigh of anticipation.

Madison shrugged, aware the idea wasn't as ludicrous as he was making it sound, even if saying it out loud had made her feel all hot and flustered. She and Chance were both very passionate people who currently had no outlet for their passion. "We made love before without being in love."

"Which is how we ended up in this situation," Chance pointed out, obviously not nearly as anxious to jump into bed with her again as she was to jump into bed with him.

Desperate to restore some normalcy to the situation, Madison ignored the heat washing over her breasts and thighs and gave him a carefully friendly smile. "I just thought it would make things simpler." Chance wouldn't be deprived of something he might otherwise feel driven to get. She wouldn't have to feel jealous. Neither of them would have to be frustrated or lonely. Plus, pregnancy had left her feeling sexier than she had expected. She went to bed every night remembering what it had been like to lie in his arms and woke up every morning desperate to do so again. Only her stubborn wish to keep their relationship simple and uncomplicated had kept her from giving in to that desire thus far. But now that she knew there was nothing simple about sharing a child, anyway...

"What about the business aspect of all this?" Chance folded his arms across his chest and lounged in front of the huge fieldstone fireplace. "I thought you were concerned about mixing business and pleasure," he reminded her, looking determined to break down every barrier she'd put up around her heart.

"I still am," Madison said, as she fought to control the situation the only way she could—with a bunch of new rules and an entirely new contract. But she could see he wasn't concerned. Never had been. Never would be. Maybe because sex with her and their business together always remained totally separate in his mind. But then he was self-employed, Madison reminded herself hotly, even as she yearned for the freedom he already enjoyed. If she alone could decide what was proper and what was not, she'd already be sleeping with him. And why not? She'd proved she was capable of successfully doing business that involved him, regardless of the fact they'd tumbled recklessly into bed and were now having a child because of it.

"So?" Chance prodded, lifting a brow.

But there were still ad agency rules to follow, Madison realized, disappointed. "So we'd wait until after the ads were finished, my business here at the ranch over, and then pick up where we left off, so to speak."

Something sexy and dangerous glimmered in his eyes. "Sort of an ongoing hit-and-run proposition, so to speak," he mocked dryly.

She could see, even though he didn't want to be, he was interested in her matter-of-fact proposition.

Unable to help herself, Madison flushed. "It's only going to be another month or so, Chance." One that would seem an eternity to her, but would pass nevertheless.

"Even so—" Chance paused and shook his head. And Madison knew with a surge of disappointment what he was going to say even before he spoke.

"Sleeping with each other whenever the spirit moved us would only make things more complicated," Chance said abruptly, the muscles in his jaw tightening in a way that let Madison know she'd struck a nerve with her unexpected proposition.

In for a penny, in for a pound. She was not going to give up yet. "How do you figure that?"

"Suppose we're sleeping together, and then one of us does meet the love of our lives, then what?" Chance asked, carefully studying her face for her reaction.

Maybe I already have met the love of my life, Madison thought. Shocked at the possibility, she pushed the unwanted thought away. Cooler heads prevailed, she reminded herself. And with so much at stake, she couldn't afford to go around falling in love with anyone, not even Chance Cartwright. "First of all, that's not going to happen." Chance was not going to fall in love with someone else.

"But if it did," Chance persisted, beginning to smile, as if he were seeing things she didn't want him to see.

Madison flushed self-consciously.

"Then what?" Chance persisted.

Still holding Chance's gaze, she lifted her shoulders carelessly, let them fall. She was not going to let him goad her into blurting out anything foolish, like the fact that she might just might be starting to fall in love with him a tiny little bit.

"Then we renegotiate our contract with each other, I guess," Madison told him carelessly, as even more warmth crept into her cheeks.

Chance tilted his head to the side. His gaze lazily tracked the shape of her lips, her breasts, before returning to her eyes. "You don't think that will be messy?"

Madison tingled everywhere his eyes had touched and everywhere they hadn't. "I think we're both very good businesspeople, Chance. I think we can handle anything we set our minds to handle." *Including and especially each other.*

Chance frowned, and for a second she could have sworn he was teasing her. "I don't know, Madison. My understanding of these things is they just happen. It isn't like you can pick a date or place and say, 'Hmm, I think I'll meet someone and fall in love today.' When something like that hits you—and it doesn't hit often—it hits with the swiftness of a lightning bolt. You're powerless under the spell."

Madison studied him even as she listened to the reverence in his voice and the mingled emotions of awe and yearning in his deep blue eyes. She had to hand it to him—he really sounded like he knew what he was talking about. "That's just it, Chance. I don't want to be powerless."

Maybe if she took these feelings she had for Chance and dealt with them openly and honestly, she wouldn't be caught unaware by the desire. Or blindsided by it. The reality was, it was going to be very hard to share a baby with him and not eventually make love with him again. That being the case, why not accept the inevitability of the situation and work out the ground rules for any further love-making in advance? Heck, maybe if they made love a few more times, she would eventually get him—and their passion—out of her system. Because passion alone could not last forever. Her father and mother and darn near every other married couple she knew had told her that.

Chance regarded her. "I can't say I'm not tempted to haul you into my arms right now and make love to you all over again."

Madison heard the *but* in his voice and tensed, unable to contain her hurt. He wanted her, but only on his terms. Not hers.

"Nor am I ruling it out permanently," he continued, "'Cause heaven knows I still want you." He gently rubbed her cheek with the pad of his thumb, then dropped his head to hers and kissed her gently, evocatively. "More than I would ever have believed possible."

Then we have something in common, Madison thought determinedly as she wreathed her arms about him and responded to the sweet and tender kiss, *because I want you, too, more than I ever would have thought possible.* Just thinking about being with him again made her feel all hot and bothered inside. And she'd been thinking about it a lot, alone in her bed at night.

Regret colored his low tone as he lifted his lips from hers and dropped his hand from her face. "But we shouldn't jump into bed again without at least establishing friendship first.''

Sensing the hot-blooded argument on the tip of her tongue, he cut her off firmly. ''I've been this route before, Madison. I've learned the hard way that sex without love eventually leads you down a road you don't want to be on.''

Like this one? Madison thought bitterly, her insides still tingling from the tantalizingly brief contact. What was he trying to do to her? Show her how hard it would be to leave him when her time in Wyoming was up? Because if so, it was working.

''That might not be a problem if it weren't for the baby you're carrying,'' Chance continued soberly, ''but we have to do what's right in the long run for all three of us. And that means getting to know each other a lot better before we decide we want to pick up where we left off.''

His words made sense. They were even chivalrous to a fault. They just weren't what she wanted to hear.

''You're right, of course,'' Madison said stiffly, unable to help but feel rejected by his considerate concern for her well-being and that of their baby. ''We should be friends,'' she said hoarsely. A wave of despair crashed through her as she realized how completely her efforts to protect herself and their baby had failed. ''Making love again would just get in the way of that,'' she agreed numbly. No matter how pleasurable it was. How comforting.

Chance touched her shoulder. His restraint didn't seem to be costing him as much as it was costing her. ''I didn't mean to hurt your feelings—''

''You haven't.'' Madison forced a bright smile completely at odds with her inner turmoil. She'd put her pride on the line, her entire heart, by unburdening herself to him, and he hadn't understood a thing! He'd thought—erroneously—that her proposal was all about sex, from beginning to end, when it was really about so much more. It had been about hope and their future and finding a way to build something that would last by first and foremost using what they already had going for them—a mutual concern for their baby and physical passion. She'd been hoping the rest would follow as long as they promised to keep other potential sexual partners or romantic rivals out of their lives and were faithful to each other. But Chance hadn't gotten it. Nor had he understood what it had done to her pride just making such an offer! She wasn't sure he ever would, she realized miserably, given the fact she was the only one in the room who secretly suspected she had already been hit with the lightning bolt called love.

"Madison—"

At the entreaty in his low voice, it was all Madison could do not to groan. Now he was going to be polite. She couldn't bear it if he was polite and chivalrous, too. It would have been a lot easier on her if he had been mean or rude as he turned her down. Her heart aching, Madison shook her head at Chance and turned away. They'd discussed enough for one day. Much more and she'd be totally destroyed.

Giving him no chance to stop her, she grabbed her cell phone and headed for the stairs. "If you'll excuse me," she said, mocking his politeness to a T, "I've got some phone calls to make."

This relationship b.s. was for the birds.

Business, she could handle.

As promised, Rona returned first thing the next morning. She had with her a certified check for Chance, her producer boyfriend and a groom, who would be helping transport her new horse to her California ranch. After the financial transaction was complete, the necessary papers signed, the two men went off with Chance to back the pickup truck to the barn and load the beautiful palomino into the trailer Rona had brought along.

Madison was still stinging from Chance's velvet-glove rejection but also felt bad about the way she had initially misjudged Rona. She stepped outside to talk to Rona, who was standing in the yard watching the men.

"Chance showed us his new Ranchero," Rona said, inclining her head at the truck Chance had received as a sweetener from AMV and had not yet bothered to drive, at least not that Madison had seen.

"It's a great pickup truck." Rona sighed admiringly. "I'd like to have one." She turned to Madison. "When will they be coming out?"

"They'll be at trade shows late this fall, and then introduced to the open market sometime early next year, probably during the football playoffs or on Super Bowl Sunday," Madison said with a smile, more relaxed now that she'd decided to concentrate on business instead of Chance. To aid that endeavor she'd decided to look the part and had put on a smart linen pantsuit that morning instead of the jeans and cotton shirts she had been wearing since arriving at the ranch.

Rona opened the driver's door and slipped behind the wheel. "Does that mean the commercials Chance is going to be in will run during the big games?"

Thinking the interior might be a little warm because the vehicle had been sitting in the sun, Madison went around and opened the door on the other side, too. "Most likely the commercials will run during the big football games since most pickups are bought by men."

Rona grinned as she smoothed her delicate-looking hands over the steering wheel. "That could change if and when women see someone like Chance behind the wheel, you know. They may want a little of the fantasy for themselves, if you get my drift."

Given how charismatically handsome Chance was, Madison knew that was true. Just as she knew she was no longer in the running for his mate on any level.

"His sex appeal is precisely why we wanted him for the commercial," Madison said, glad she could think about Chance as a commodity again, instead of a potential love interest. "If anyone can sell a new environmentally friendly pickup truck to the families of America, it's a gotta-do-right guy like Chance."

Rona glanced down, checking the position of the accelerator and brake. "I'm surprised you were able to talk him into doing the ads even if his remuneration is going to charity." Still gripping the wheel, Rona sat all the way back against the seat and sent Madison a knowing look. "He doesn't even like having his picture taken for fun."

"So I've noticed," Madison said dryly, watching as Rona checked out her own appearance—which was letter-perfect—in the rearview mirror. The only time Madison could photograph him well was when he didn't know she was snapping his picture. "But I think he'll live through it," she predicted optimistically. "The actual filming of the commercial is only going to take a couple of weeks, depending on how much the weather cooperates and how long it takes our director to get what he wants when it comes to the cinematography. Unfortunately, Vince is very, um..."

"Temperamental?" Rona guessed.

Unable to help herself, Madison grimaced. Vince had already been a handful, and he hadn't even arrived yet. She could only imagine how demanding he would be when he started the filming. Worse, Chance was not the kind of guy to put up with any prima donna antics from anyone.

"I'm sure it will all work out fabulously in the end," Rona predicted.

"I hope so," Madison murmured. She was beginning to get a little nervous about it, and the two very different men hadn't even met.

"Trust me." Rona shut the glove compartment with a snap and turned her attention to the adjustable seat, moving it up, forward and back. "There isn't an artist of any kind on this earth who isn't just a little driven and protective of their work," she continued knowledgeably. "And that goes for Chance and his horses, too. You just have to know how to meet them on their terms, understand what they want from you and then give it to them as best you can. It doesn't mean you can't have any input into the process—you just have to allow them theirs. I tried to explain all that to Chance yesterday when we were out riding and he was complaining about having to go through this."

"He's looking forward to it that much, hmm?" Madison was happy for Rona's input, but stung to discover Chance had confided his private frustrations and fears about the work ahead of them to Rona and not her. Rona wasn't even involved in this!

"Not to worry." Rona reassured her brightly. Finally having the driver's seat the way she wanted it, she smiled and looked forward, once again gripping the wheel. "I told him it'd all be over before he knew it. Now me," Rona continued, pretending for a moment she was actually driving as she smoothly worked the conversation around to her favorite subject. "I love doing commercials...."

"So what's going on between you and Madison Burnes?" Lindsay Duncan asked Chance several days later. She had brought a couple of the younger boys from Lost Springs over to ride two of Chance's premium horses. It was an honor bestowed on the younger boys only after lots of hard work and good behavior, and one the kids really looked forward to. She and Chance followed on the trail behind them.

More interested in his supervisory duties than discussing his personal life, which appeared to be in one hell of a mess at the moment, Chance lifted one hand from the reins and cupped it around his mouth. "Tucker! Randy! Don't get so far ahead! Not more than fifty yards. And stick to the trail!"

The two boys swung around in the saddle and waved giddy acknowledgment at Chance, signaling they intended to follow his instructions.

Lindsay spurred her horse—a spirited Appaloosa—to keep up with Chance. "You're not answering my question, pal."

Chance shot Lindsay a look from beneath the brim of his hat. "That's 'cause I don't know what you mean."

Lindsay squinted against the early morning sun. "Then let me refresh your memory. Your charity auction date with her ended two months ago, and now here she is living with you at your ranch, getting ready to film you in your first ever commercial endorsement. Don't tell me there's nothing going on, cowboy. Particularly when she looks at you that way."

Knowing exactly what his friend meant but deciding to play dumb anyway, Chance asked, "What way?"

Not about to let him off the hook easily, Lindsay quirked a brow. "Like she loves you and despises you all at once."

Chance tugged the brim of his hat even lower, letting it shadow his face from his old friend's probing gaze. He hadn't bothered to shave for a couple days, and the stubble on his face itched like the devil. "Getting a little carried away with the romantic imaginings, aren't you?"

"I don't think so. But if you don't want to talk about it—"

"I don't."

"Okay. I'll change the subject."

"Much obliged, ma'am, if you would."

"How's Shiloh coming along?"

"We're getting there. Making progress day by day. But we're still a long way from being able to trust each other completely."

Lindsay clicked her heels and urged her horse to pick up the pace. "That's not surprising, is it? Given what a hard start Shiloh had in this life." She shook her head. "I can't tell you how upset everyone at the ranch was when we saw how Shiloh had been mistreated. If you hadn't come along to rescue him—well, we all know he wouldn't have had a chance in this world to end up in a good home. You really are to be commended for taking him on.''

"It's not that big a deal, Lindsay," Chance said, beginning to get embarrassed.

"Yeah, it is," Lindsay persisted, as proudly as if she really were his sister, instead of a self-appointed one. "You've got a way with horses—especially the damaged ones—that is par to none. I wish I had half your skill when it comes to training horses."

Chance shrugged and transferred his reins to his other hand. He wished he had half that skill in his relationship with Madison. "What I do here isn't all that different from what you do over at the ranch. The kids there know you're not going to give up on them, no matter what. It's the same here with my horses. Sometimes you go back a step, skip around, try different things, see what works and what doesn't. But you never give up on them."

Chance rode ahead and cut Tucker and Randy off at the next pass, directing them to an easier trail. Groaning their disappointment, the ten-year-olds did as he said, albeit somewhat reluctantly.

Noting the kids were safe, Chance looked at Lindsay and continued, "Bottom line, the horse has to know you'll stay, even when sorely tested. He's got to know your love and gentleness can be depended upon, that you won't ever hurt him or betray him. The horse has got to know you're there to love and protect him, come what may. Once he does, once he believes it in his heart, then the horse is yours for life."

Lindsay grinned. "Now if you could use those same principles on women," she teased as the boys rode ahead, turning from the craggy peaks of the mountains and into a field dotted with dazzling wildflowers.

Heaven knew he was trying, Chance thought. Unfortunately his plan to try to get closer to Madison before they hopped back into bed was not turning out the way he had hoped. Every new nugget of factual information he was able to coax out of Madison left him feeling more frustrated and no closer to her than he'd been when they'd started their quest to become friends. It was as if Madison were telling him all the basic facts about herself—where she went to college, how she got her start at the agency—while still maintaining a wall around her heart.

Chance knew he couldn't give up—that was what he and his dad had done, and they had never broken through the barriers that separated them, never been really close. He didn't want the same thing to happen with him and Madison. He wanted them to be as close as two people could be, and not just for the sake of the baby. They had found something special in each other, something unique. And one day he'd get her to admit that, too. He just had to keep plugging away, trying different things. Go back a step, if necessary. Go forward. Skip around.

Because it wasn't just sex drawing them together. Simple sex left you feeling empty—sated but empty. What they had shared had left him wanting more—and not just sex. It wasn't just the baby drawing them close, either, as Madison would have them believe. A baby only went so far toward bringing people together.

The attraction he and Madison had for each other was something special.

Something people spent a lifetime looking for.

Chance wasn't giving that up, and he wasn't going to let *her* give it up, either.

Meantime, the clock was ticking and time was running out. Another three weeks or so and Madison would be headed right back to Dallas.

He couldn't let that happen before he had done everything he could to win her heart.

CHAPTER SEVEN

"FIRST AND FOREMOST," Kit said to Madison when she called early Monday morning from Dallas, "have you gotten Chance Cartwright to agree to appear at the trade shows when the Ranchero is introduced?"

Madison, who'd been up for hours preparing for the film crew currently en route from town to the ranch, cast a glance at Chance, who was supervising the moving of all of his horses to pastures away from the house. The horses weren't needed for today's shooting schedule, and although Chance hadn't come right out and said as much, Madison could tell he was relieved to have them out of harm's way.

She turned from the sight of the Lost Springs boys, who'd been promised they could watch Chance's first day of commercial filming provided they were quiet and well-behaved. "I haven't brought it up," Madison told Kit finally.

"We know you're going to have trouble getting him to agree to it," Kit said.

"And then some," Madison muttered. "But don't worry. I'll figure out a way." Somehow.

"Well, you better get to it as quickly as you can because you're running out of time. The public relations people at AMV are putting together a schedule of events for Chance and the new pickup truck as we speak, and they're going to want to get his verbal okay and start making travel reservations by the end of the week."

"All right. I'll take care of it," Madison promised. She

didn't know how, with her and Chance barely speaking to each other, but she would.

Kit went on to discuss several other matters of importance, then said, "As you know, Shawna Somersby was sent up to assist you."

"She arrived last night with the rest of the crew, didn't she?"

"Right. She's still a little overeager," Kit cautioned.

Meaning, Madison thought, Shawna's lack of experience had caused a few problems in Dallas.

"But I've been working with her here and she should be a lot of help as a runner. And I'll be here, handling things on this end."

"Thanks, Kit. And thanks for sending Shawna up to help out, too." With all she was going to have to juggle, Madison needed someone at her beck and call. It would help to have Shawna there.

"No problem."

No sooner had Madison hung up with Kit than a convoy of trucks, vans and cars rolled in, kicking up clouds of dust on the gravel lane leading to the ranch house. A tractor trailer truck, bearing every color and variety of the new Ranchero pickup, brought up the rear. Madison grabbed her clipboard, cell phone and pen and strode out to meet them. It was early morning, but the day already looked to be a blistering one.

Chance intercepted Madison in the yard. "Overdoing it a tad, aren't they?" he observed dryly, inclining his head at the number of vehicles jockeying for parking spaces along the lane while the catering truck quickly set up in the shade. Technicians piled out onto the grass, looking eager to get started, while Ed Connelly and Ursula Rodriguez, who were both going to be on hand during the entire shoot, tumbled out of a big red Suburban and conferred briefly in the shade.

"It can seem a little overwhelming, I know," Madison

soothed, knowing this was just the beginning. The confusion was bound to get a lot worse before they finished.

"And then some," Chance muttered unhappily, glancing at the damage being done to the neatly manicured grass around the ranch house. He looked her straight in the eye. "When you said a commercial, I figured one camera, a couple of trucks, a few people, not this onslaught."

Madison clutched her clipboard to her chest as a long black limousine drove through the crush. "I'm sorry I didn't make that clear."

Chance took off his hat and rubbed the perspiration from his brow. "Anything else you forgot to tell me?"

Actually, yes, Madison wanted to say. But now was not the time to tell him he was also expected to do several months of trade shows promoting the Ranchero. Her conscience prickling, she looked past Chance and saw Vince Smith, the director, coming toward them. Breathing a sigh of relief and hoping she would feel better once they got going, she said, "There's Vince now." He looked as eager to get started as the rest of them.

LOOKING SMART and professional in a white linen pantsuit and expensive low-heeled shoes, Madison threaded through the grips and technicians and made her way to Chance's side. She had her sunglasses perched on top of her head and a clipboard clutched against the lusciously soft swell of her breasts. Just watching the graceful, fluid way she moved made the blood pool in the lower half of his body. Never mind the enticing, pouty curve of her lips, just begging to be kissed, Chance thought, or the windblown disarray of her hair, begging to be coaxed into place by his fingertips. As she stopped just short of him it was all he could do not to haul her into his arms and kiss her soundly until she forgot all about business and thought only about being with him again in the way they were meant to be together.

Oblivious to the sensual direction of his thoughts, Madison was all business as she began to speak. "We're going to start with the hayloft scene and try to get that done this morning."

Chance knew what he wanted to do in a loft with Madison. It wasn't film a commercial with twenty-five people looking on.

Struggling to contain his spiraling emotions, half from temper, half desire, Chance glanced at the boys from Lost Springs. They were lined up at the catering truck, enjoying the free treats Madison and her boss had generously allowed them. At least someone was having a good time today, he thought disparagingly. With effort, he reminded himself what his work here would mean to the kids at the ranch. It was a lot of money he was earning, and it was all for them. That being the case, he figured he could find a way to deal with it.

Chance looked at Madison. Damned if she wasn't the prettiest woman he'd ever seen. And, at the moment, the bossiest. "Refresh my memory."

"We went over this yesterday," Madison reminded him.

Chance tried his best to recall what she had said about the loft. Something about the horses, and taking care of them. Oh, yeah. He brightened as it all came flooding back. "I'm supposed to pitch hay out of the top of the barn and into the bed of my pickup, which will be parked below."

Madison smiled and drew such a deep breath her breasts rose—and fell—seductively. "Right." Her smile widened at his newfound cooperation. She gazed at him as if she'd just discovered something wonderful. "It shouldn't take more than the morning," Madison reassured him enthusiastically.

Chance started to nod, feeling a little besotted just looking into her eyes, then stopped as her words sunk in. "What do you mean the morning?" he demanded impatiently. No one had said anything about him having to do this in slow motion. "The commercial is only going to last thirty seconds," he reminded her brusquely. "With all the action scenes you have planned, the shot of me tossing hay out of the barn won't take more than a second or two."

"But it has to be precisely the right shot."

Chance shrugged, unable to see what all the tension and hysteria were about as grips and technicians ran here and there while Vince shouted directions to one and all. If he ran his horse ranch the way the director ran the set, they'd never get anything done. "So set it up right in the first place. And then we'll only have to do it once," Chance advised.

Madison's lips compressed. Her green eyes glowed with new temper as she slapped her clipboard against her side. Clearly, she did not want his advice about this. "You just do your job, Chance. I'll do mine."

"Right."

To Chance's frustration, despite all the people running to and fro, it was noon before they had the cameras and lighting set up and the pickup truck positioned below the loft doors of the hay barn. His frustration level mounting—there were so many things he'd rather be doing than standing around cooling his heels while Vince and the set designer tried to decide if he wanted the hay bales two inches to the right or two inches to the left—Chance said, "About ready to get started here?"

Madison took his arm and steered him over to a canvas chair set up in front of a trailer. "Another fifteen minutes. But you're right." She signaled for a young woman with a large carrying case similar to a fishing tackle box. "It is time to get you made up."

Chance cringed at the orangey-looking cup of goop and sponge the makeup person held out. "You're kidding, right?"

"Without a thin layer of pancake and powder, you'll look like Casper the Ghost on film," Madison said.

"Which isn't exactly the look we're going for," Ursula said, coming up to join them. She looked at Madison. "We're doing this first shot without the shirt, right?"

Chance cringed as a very thin layer of goop was smeared across his face and neck.

"Cartwright's jeans need to be more worn," Vince shouted over his shoulder.

"I think the boots need to go," the wardrobe lady said, shaking her head at Chance's scuffed and serviceable brown boots. "They're not individual enough. Maybe something two-toned or—"

"The clothes are mine," Chance interjected gruffly, not about to be made over into something he wasn't. "This is what I'm wearing. What I always wear. And the shirt stays on."

To his chagrin, Madison merely gave him a cool look that seemed to say, "We'll see."

"Let's just get started," Madison told Vince as the two of them exchanged understanding looks that said they, at least, were of one mind. "Do a few preliminary shots and see what we come up with. Then we'll make changes."

"Sounds good to me," Ed Connelly said, coming to join the group.

Chance leaped up. He was beginning to see how hard this was going to be. He didn't like it. Not one bit. He strode to the barn, headed into the shady interior, which was a good ten degrees cooler than the sunny barnyard, and climbed to the loft. For the next hour, he tossed bales of hay into the bed of the truck. The instructions he received were relentless.

"Smile more!"

"Not that much!"

"How about taking off the shirt? At least undo a few buttons."

"Could you make it look a little more physically demanding?"

Figuring the more he cooperated with them, the sooner it would all be over, Chance did his best to follow directions. But when they started replacing the first pickup truck with another color, and then a third, he lost all patience.

Wordlessly, he climbed down from the loft.

Madison met him inside the barn.

"What do you think you're doing?" she demanded, for once looking every bit as hot and tired and irritable as he felt.

Chance took her elbow and steered her aside. "This is ridiculous."

Madison didn't think so. "It's advertising." She sounded as if she were speaking to someone with limited intelligence. "It has to be perfect."

Chance clenched his jaw and struggled to hold on to his soaring temper. "At this rate, we'll never get done," he pointed out succinctly.

New color swept into Madison's cheeks. "I warned you it would take several weeks of shooting."

He'd thought they would have time to spend together. Not this. All work and no play with way too many people around. "You didn't tell me I'd be tossing hay out of the barn for hours on end!"

"It'll go easier once you get the hang of it."

Chance didn't think so. In fact, he was not cut out for this at all. "Maybe you need an actor here to play my part." Maybe he could just get money for Lost Springs by letting them use his land and his horses.

Ursula joined them. Chance wasn't surprised to see that the AMV executive looked every bit as unhappy as he felt. "An actor won't do it, Mr. Cartwright," Ursula told him, looking sleek and polished in her Armani pantsuit despite the increasing humidity. "We want you in these commercials. So unless you want to be in breach of contract—"

Madison held up her hand, effectively silencing Ursula. She turned to Chance. Sweat had broken out on her brow, above her upper lip, on her neck. She looked pale but determined as she slipped off her linen jacket and reached for a bottle of water. "You're getting paid handsomely for this, Chance." Madison took a long sip of water, wiped her forehead with the back of her arm. "The money you turn over to the boys' ranch will mean a lot to them. Try to remember that," she told him stonily.

He was trying. Unfortunately, it didn't make it any easier, and he was too honest to pretend otherwise. "I don't have the patience for this," he told her frankly. Even if he did admire hers.

Madison patted his arm reassuringly. "It'll come."

Like heck it would, Chance thought as Vince joined them. Vince gestured at the sheen of perspiration on Chance's face. "Nice touch. I like it." He looked Chance up and down in an insultingly thorough manner, then turned to Madison for her reaction.

"I think we should do some close-ups and play that up, too," Madison said, in complete agreement with Vince.

So now what, he was supposed to sweat on command, too? Chance wondered as he saw Madison wipe her forehead with the back of her hand yet again.

He was about to suggest she sit down when the color left Madison's face. Chance saw her sway. He rushed forward and barely had time to catch her before she collapsed.

"YOU FAINTED."

Madison moaned. A glance around showed her to be sprawled on the sofa in Chance's living room. Someone had put a cold, damp cloth across her forehead and another on the back of her neck. She felt about as dizzy and miserable as it was possible to feel.

"What happened?" Shawna Somersby leaned over Madison, her youthful face deeply concerned.

"I don't know." Madison released a shaky breath as she

let the freckle-faced intern help her up. "I must be coming down with something," she fibbed. Like Chance's baby.

"I heard there's a twenty-four-hour virus going around," Chance said gravely.

Just that quickly, everyone in the circle around her—everyone but Chance—backed quickly away from Madison.

"You poor dear," Ursula said from a distance. Madison couldn't be sure, but she thought Ursula was holding her breath, probably to avoid inhaling any germs.

"We've done enough for today anyway," Ed announced, backing toward the door.

"Do you want me to try to get you an appointment in town with a doctor?" Shawna asked helpfully.

Kit had been right, Madison thought, Shawna was showing a lot of initiative. She'd also had a very good idea.

"Actually, I can handle that since I'm familiar with the doctors here," Chance said. He looked at Madison. "I'll drive you."

"Good idea," everyone concluded.

Minutes later, the crew had packed up and headed to the various motels where they were staying. As soon as they'd gone, Chance called the local obstetrician to arrange for an emergency appointment, then came to where Madison was sitting on the sofa. She still felt shaky. "Thanks for not giving my pregnancy away," she said.

One hand on the small of her back, the other wrapped around her hand and the glass, Chance helped her take a small sip of water. Then another. "They're going to know sooner or later."

"I'd prefer it be later," Madison said, sitting perfectly still. "We have enough to worry about just putting this ad campaign together."

Chance left her to change his shirt and scrub the pancake makeup from his face. When he returned, he took her hands in his and knelt in front of her. He wanted to tell her this job was too much for a woman in her condition. It made him angry to see her working so hard when he knew she didn't have to. He had enough money to take care of both her and the baby for the rest of their lives and never deprive them of a thing. But he also knew Madison would be lost without her work. In her job, she was confident and capable. There was no sign of the vulnerability and uncertainty she felt in her personal life. As much as he wanted to protect her, he couldn't take that away from her. It would be up to the doctor to decide what she could reasonably handle and what she couldn't. He only hoped she would be honest about the kind of stress and pressure she was under.

He studied her face for a long moment, then asked gently, "You feel like you can walk to the truck?"

"Sure," Madison said, but no sooner had she gotten to her feet than her knees turned to jelly. Chance caught her before she could fall and swept her into his arms. His chest was warm and strong and comforting. She felt safer than she had in a long time.

"Maybe you could do something like this in the commercial, too," Madison said as he carried her to the new Ranchero he'd been given. The air-conditioning was already on, and it was blessedly cool inside. He settled her in the deeply cushioned passenger seat, reached across her to fasten her seat belt and then, ever so gently, adjusted the seat to recline. "You know," Madison continued, albeit a little shakily, forcing her thoughts to business and away from the luxury of what it might be like to depend on Chance permanently, "it would make a great shot if you were to romantically sweep a woman up in your arms and carry her out to your new truck."

"Only if it's you I'm carrying," Chance said, looking at her tenderly.

A thrill went through Madison at the heartfelt concern in his eyes and the low, throaty possessiveness in his voice. If she didn't know better she would swear he'd fallen head over heels in love with her. "People would talk," she said softly.

Chance straightened. He looked her in the eye and gave her a grin as wide as all Texas. He braced his hands on his waist. "Let 'em."

Madison was mulling over the new feelings of love and tenderness welling inside her, when he slid behind the wheel. Was it the baby, the fact of being pregnant, that was causing all of this? Or was it Chance? Had she really fallen this deeply in love with him? Shaken by the realization, Madison turned her attention to the brand-new pickup truck she was sitting in.

"You're finally driving your new truck," she marveled.

Chance shrugged. "I figured it'd be best for you and the baby."

Obviously doing his best to keep the ride as smooth as possible, he turned the new pickup truck for town. He slanted a look at her face. "You still feeling sick or are you just worried?"

A little of both, Madison thought, but not wanting him to worry—she was doing enough for them both—she swallowed and said simply, "I'm just not used to fainting." Normally she was healthy as a horse. To find herself collapsing with no warning was unsettling, to say the least. It made her want to depend on Chance, rely on his strong arms, and stronger will, forever.

"Just close your eyes and rest," Chance said, reaching over to squeeze her hand.

Madison did, and by the time they'd completed the nearly two-hour drive into town, she felt much better.

"I'm going in with you," Chance announced as he parked in front of the clinic doors.

"Really, it's—it's not necessary," Madison said. To her surprise, the rest had done her good, and she felt almost normal again. Ready to take on the world. Or at least this doctor's visit.

Chance looked at her. "You're sure?"

"Positive." In fact, she felt so good it seemed silly to be seeing the doctor. But for the baby's sake she had to be sure everything was okay.

Chance hopped out and circled around to her side. He opened the door and chivalrously helped her from the cab. One arm around her waist, he escorted her to the front double doors of the clinic. "I'll wait for you in the waiting room then."

When Madison emerged some thirty minutes later, Chance was sitting on a sofa. He had several kids clustered around him while he read from a battered copy of *Goldilocks and the Three Bears*. They were all snuggled up against him, looks of utter contentment on their young faces. A mixture of tenderness and yearning swept over Madison as she watched.

"That your husband?" the young receptionist asked, shooting an admiring glance at Chance that had as much to do with his reading technique and his way with kids as his sexy good looks. "He's going to make some daddy."

Madison smiled and didn't tell the receptionist she and Chance weren't married. "He is very good with children, isn't he?" she remarked softly, shooting Chance another sidelong smile as she paid the bill. So good, in fact, she felt a pang that their child wouldn't have him around nightly to read to him. But that was just the way things were, Madison reassured herself bluntly, telling herself she was and always had been a very practical person. They would find a way to work things out.

"So how are you?" Chance said as he escorted her to the Ranchero.

"Fine." Madison blew out a relieved sigh. "The doctor said it was perfectly normal. There's a tendency to fainting at any period in the pregnancy and it's likely to occur if I get up too suddenly or stand for prolonged periods."

"Which is what you were doing this afternoon," Chance surmised protectively. "Standing for too long."

Madison nodded. "Right. So I'll just have to make it a point to sit down a lot more. And take a break at the first sign of faintness."

"I'm glad you and the baby are okay," he told her softly, looking into her face.

Madison reached over and squeezed his hand. "Me, too."

THE REST OF THE WEEK was as busy as Monday had been. The crew rolled in around nine in the morning. Filming started around noon and continued until suppertime. Chance spent all of Tuesday driving up to a pasture filled with horses and hopping out of the truck. Again and again and again. Wednesday, he loaded a gleaming leather saddle into the bed of the pickup. Again and again and again. Thursday, he hitched a horse trailer to the back of his pickup. More than two dozen times—until every aspect of his "look" and "action" and "expressions" was deemed perfect by an increasingly demanding Vince. On Friday they wanted to film him loading a horse into the trailer hitched to the Ranchero pickup. And it was there, finally, that Chance balked again. Big-time.

"I'm not confusing this horse by making her go in and out of the trailer a hundred times in one afternoon," Chance exploded in exasperation after the third take.

Vince whipped off his sunglasses. "We have to get this right!" he snapped. "And I'm not stopping until we do!"

"Then start filming more accurately to begin with." Chance snapped right back, whipping his hat off and slapping it against his thigh.

Ever the peacemaker, Madison, who'd been sitting in a canvas chair beneath a shade tree, jumped to her feet and darted between Chance and the director before punches could fly. She spread her hands beseechingly and gave

Chance one of her most officious looks. "Mr. Cartwright! Please—"

Chance was in no mood to be humored as if he were the prima donna when the well-being of one of his prize horses was at stake. "Don't you Mr. Cartwright me!" he snarled.

Cool as could be, Madison turned to the director. "Mr. Cartwright may have a point, Vince," she said smoothly. "If the horse gets confused or begins to balk, we're not going to have much of a shot, anyway."

"Balking might be good," Ursula Rodriguez interrupted practically. "It'd be more action-oriented." She gave an elegant little shrug as everyone turned to look at her. "It would give Chance an opportunity to show how well he handles these animals."

Chance's nostrils flared as the reason for his concern was ignored and Madison hurried to intervene. "It's been a long week." And Chance had been, in her opinion, more than patient, given what he'd had to put up with, especially considering he was not a professional.

"You can say that again!" Chance snarled bad-temperedly.

"Madison, may I see you a moment?" Ed Connelly said. He wiped his head with a handkerchief.

Madison nodded. "Everyone else take ten—make that fifteen!"

As everyone scattered, Madison met Ed on the shade of the front porch. "We're not going to get anywhere with Chance this afternoon, are we?" her boss asked in obvious frustration.

"It would not appear so," Madison said as she watched Chance lead his horse to the barn to cool down. "But not to worry. We can shoot the mountains this afternoon, start again tomorrow. Vince has been wanting to take a crew up there, anyway, to try to capture a sunset at close range on the digital camera."

"Fine," Ed said. "But when tomorrow morning comes,

Madison, I want Chance Cartwright to cooperate fully, not just for a few hours, but for the rest of the shoot.''

Aware her heart was racing, Madison drew a breath. ''Ed, you're looking for guarantees and—''

''You're darn right I'm looking for guarantees!'' Ed exploded, apparently at the end of his rope, too. ''And any vice president worth her salt would be able to give them to me. So you do what you have to do, Madison,'' he stormed, unaware, as Madison was, that Chance was headed their way. ''You let that cowboy have the afternoon off, and then you take him out tonight for a nice steak and a shot or two of bourbon and a fine cigar or whatever the heck else it takes to smooth off the rough edges.'' Ed continued instructing Madison furiously. ''But come what may, he better be in a frame to cooperate fully first thing tomorrow morning. Or it's your head on the chopping block.''

HOURS LATER, Madison settled back in her comfy chair at the country inn and sipped her glass of milk on the rocks. Aware this was one of the tensest business dinners she had ever conducted in her life, she tilted her head to slant Chance a pleasantly obsequious look. ''How's your steak? Is it okay?'' When Chance offered no immediate response, Madison pushed on. ''Is it big enough?''

Chance clamped the unlit cigar between his teeth. ''You tell me,'' he drawled, giving her the once-over. ''Is it?''

Madison didn't see how it couldn't be. His steak was the biggest one on the menu, the sixteen-ounce porterhouse, prepared perfectly, if she did say so herself. In fact, her chicken was magnificent, too, not that she'd been able to enjoy it with Chance being the most ungracious, untalkative dinner companion on record. ''We can get you something else if you prefer,'' she continued.

Chance quirked a brow and idly tapped his cigar against the rim of his plate. ''Actually, now that you mention it, maybe I would prefer the panfried rainbow trout with cole-slaw.''

Madison blinked, not sure if he was serious. "That's, um, not served here," she said delicately.

"Hmm." Chance shrugged and looked at her as if he expected her to solve the problem.

"But maybe I can go and see what the chef can do."

"Why don't you do that," Chance said, clamping down on the end of his unlit cigar.

Jerk, Madison thought as she excused herself. She went in search of the hostess, who, after hearing Madison's plight and learning how much Madison and Connelly and Associates were prepared to pay to keep their star happy, was only too eager to take Madison to see the chef. Madison returned a good fifteen minutes later to see Chance had demolished much of his steak. And passed entirely on his bourbon.

"All set," Madison announced happily as she eased into her chair and spread her linen napkin across her lap. "Your panfried rainbow trout and coleslaw will be here momentarily. The chef even decided to throw in an order of fries and hush puppies with it," she added happily.

Chance sipped his ice water lazily and favored her with a decidedly edgy smile. "I've decided I don't want it."

He didn't want it. Madison quelled the urge to bash him over the head with her dinner plate, to heck with her half-eaten roast chicken and steamed vegetables. She sipped her milk. "The chef's feelings will be hurt." He had gone to a great deal of trouble to manage this, arranging for another employee to rush over to the nearest grocery and back in record time for the necessary ingredients.

"Then you eat it," Chance said.

Madison held on to her temper with effort. Ed Connelly didn't know what he had been asking of her when he had ordered Madison to take Chance out and smooth over the rough edges. The man's edges were rough, all right, but after the week they'd all had, smoothing them over was the impossible dream. And then some.

"Fine." Madison smiled at him, unperturbed. "I'll have them wrap it up when it's ready and we'll take it with us." She'd just triple the tip and explain to Ed later. Still, it was rude of Chance, putting others out this way, and she didn't like it.

An hour and a half later, they arrived at the ranch. Not waiting for Chance to help her out of his pickup, Madison grabbed the sack containing Chance's dinner and climbed from the truck, stumbling slightly when her skirt hitched halfway up her thighs in the process. No doubt about it, she thought, the short skirts she favored were definitely not made for climbing in and out of pickup trucks.

Chance rescued the dinner and caught her by the arm, all in one smooth motion. "You should have waited and let me help you," he growled.

For Madison, the tersely voiced order and involuntary chivalry—after an evening of complete and utter rudeness—were the last straw. "Oh, go jump in a lake!" she snapped. Jerking free of him, she headed for the door.

Chance followed her laconically up the front steps, his one deliberately lazy stride matching her every two. He put out a hand to stop her from opening the front door. "What did you say?"

Madison whirled on him, her temper brimming over at last. She wanted him to gather her close, let her rest her head on his shoulder. "I said go jump in a lake." She forced the words through gritted teeth.

Chance braced a shoulder against the frame. "Not exactly the words I would have expected you to use on a recalcitrant prima donna you're trying to cool down."

Madison tossed her head. How amazing, to find out at this stage of her life, that she went for the exasperating type. "Prima donna is right!" she retorted, aware the men on the shoot weren't the only ones perilously close to losing their tempers.

"Aha!" Chance's brows rose in mock indignation. He leaned closer, his expression reckless, relentless. "Then you don't deny you were trying to get me back in line."

Knowing he'd expect the opposite, Madison moved in closer, not stopping until they stood toe to toe and nose to nose. "You know darn well those were my orders!" she murmured, goading him with a way too innocent smile.

Chance's blue eyes darkened to the deep, fathomless blue of a mountain lake. He backed her against the front door and braced a hand on either side of her, effectively caging her in front of him. "And you were only too happy to carry them out."

Madison's heartbeat speeded to triple time. "It is my job," she returned sweetly.

"Well—" Chance scowled, leaning back abruptly and letting her go "—don't try manipulating me."

Trying not to feel bereft that their little set-to had ended without so much as a near kiss, Madison frowned as she watched him unlock the front door and usher her inside. "You are a royal pain in the butt, you know that, Cartwright?"

"Why?" Chance shut the door after them and ripped off his tan corduroy sport coat and Stetson, both of which he tossed onto the sofa. He lifted a skeptical brow as he worked at the knot of his tie. "Because I don't want you simultaneously clenching your teeth and giving me fake smiles out of some…business obligation?"

Madison liked the way he looked, with his hair all rumpled and the blush of sun highlighting the ruggedly handsome features of his face. Deciding he wasn't the only one who could get comfortable for the rest of this discussion, she took off the pale blue suit jacket that went with her short, sleeveless sheath dress and kicked off her heels. "It's part of my job to make sure everything goes smoothly and that all tempers stay in check, and I am not—I repeat *not*—going to apologize for it.''

''I gathered that much,'' he said dryly.

Aware of the avalanche of longing roiling inside her, Madison replied, ''Fine.''

He caught her wrist and stopped her from climbing more than one step of the stairs. Using his grip on her wrist, he brought her around to face him.

''I still prefer outright honesty to artificial sweetness every time.''

Madison tried not to notice that standing one step up like that almost put her at the same height as Chance. ''Fine!'' She glared at him and leaned closer. ''You want honesty?'' Because it was either kiss him or kill him, Madison flattened both her hands across his chest. ''I'll give you honesty, cowboy!'' She tapped his warm, strong chest for emphasis. ''You have been acting like a number-one jerk all week long and making a difficult job all the harder with your continual impatience.''

Chance leaned closer until his face filled her vision and his warm breath caressed her face. ''Let me get this straight. You think I'm out of line because I don't like wasting time?''

''Vince's work is wonderful because he is such a perfectionist.''

Chance yawned with comic exaggeration. Seeing he had annoyed her, which was obviously his goal, Madison noted, he grinned even more. ''It still looks like a giant waste of money to me,'' Chance drawled.

''This is a hugely expensive account they are launching. The AMV Corporation wants this pickup truck to be around for years. They also want to get a lot more than just one commercial out of the film they're using here. They're hoping to have at least five or six different spots, maybe more, that will be shown all over the world. So, yes, they are taking their time about it, and making sure it is done right.

And they don't want to have to come back here to film later. So if they do each shot two or three dozen times in order to make sure they've gotten precisely what they need, then so be it. It's better than having them come back again.''

Chance was silent.

She could see she had gotten through to him a little. She could also see he was still angry and overemotional and frustrated beyond belief. As was she. Largely because the two of them hadn't had a moment alone all week. When the crew wasn't here, she had been on the phone with them, or falling into bed at night exhausted, only to get up the next morning and start all over again. Meanwhile, Chance had been stripped of his privacy and reduced to a commodity. And that did not sit well with him, either. Who could blame them for being out of sorts after five days of nonstop pressure?

Madison swallowed as guilt flooded her anew. At least she had known what to expect. Chance hadn't.

Just as he didn't know about the trade shows he was supposed to appear at, either, Madison thought. Wondering how and when she would broach that subject, she ran her fingers through her hair. "Look…" She sighed wearily, leaning against the banister and meeting his eyes. "I'm sorry if this has been rough on you. And I do appreciate what you're doing." Her voice dropped a notch. "For the kids at the boys' ranch. For me and my career—"

"Don't kid yourself," Chance said.

Without warning, his arms were around her.

"Kid myself about what?" Madison gasped.

Chance smiled as he tilted his head and slanted his lips over hers. "I'm doing this for me, too."

MADISON WAS PREPARED for the kiss—she wasn't prepared for the kiss's impact on her. It rippled through her in great undulating waves until she wanted to touch him everywhere, kiss him everywhere, and never stop. She ached with the comfort of his hand in her hair, his warm, strong body pressed against hers. And as he continued to kiss her and hold her, something inside her melted, and the barriers around her heart, everything that had been keeping them apart, fell away. As all the passionate feelings they had for each other came pouring out, Madison realized she wanted to make love to Chance again more than anything.

"Your bed or mine this time?" Chance whispered, the shuddering beat of his heart giving him away.

If only it were that simple, Madison thought as her hands curled in the front of his shirt and she rested her head on his chest. Still trying to catch her breath and calm the quivering ache deep inside her, she closed her eyes. "We can't do this," she murmured in a welter of yearning and regret.

It was the wrong tack to take. His eyes, already smoldering, turned to blue fire as he stroked his hands through her hair and continued to hold her close. He pressed kisses on the top of her head. Hooking his thumbs beneath her chin, he made his way down the side of her face, his warm breath ghosting over her skin as he caressed, kissed and explored. "Why not?" he whispered seductively, his breath hot and sweet against her skin.

"Because." Madison's breath hitched and caught. This was the sexy, reckless, relentless Chance, the Chance she'd not been able to resist. "As you said…" She trembled all the more as his hands cupped the undersides of her breasts. Her head fell back in abandon, and she shook from head to toe. "We're already having enough trouble trying to work together."

She felt, rather than saw, his smile. "Did I say that?" he murmured as his hands slid lower and his palms rounded her hips, bringing her against him.

"Yes." Figuring a simple kiss couldn't hurt much of anything, Madison kissed him back the way she wanted to kiss him, wantonly and slowly, before their mutual need to dictate the terms of the relationship had gotten in the way. "You did."

Chance sighed and nibbled along her jaw as his hands fitted her even more expertly against him. "What else did I say?"

Madison shuddered at the heat and pressure of him where he pressed against her, hip to hip. Her eyes drifted to his, and she looked at him through a thick screen of lashes. He looked wonderful, handsome and sexy. Smug male confidence exuded from him in mesmerizing waves. "Something about us needing to be friends first." She paused to kiss his neck, amazed at how hot and quick and urgent the need for him could be. Sighing, she stopped kissing him and drew back long enough to look into his deep blue eyes. "And because," she whispered softly, honestly, "this pregnancy has me feeling so mixed up about everything right now." One minute she wanted him, the next...well, the next she wanted him, too, she thought, vexed. She never seemed to stop wanting him, hadn't from the first. She just wasn't sure it was wise to want him so.

Chance's expression gentled. "I don't pretend I've got absolutely everything worked out yet, Madison, although I'm getting there. But I'm clear on this. A baby needs a family. And I need you."

"Oh, Chance," Madison whispered, emotion welling up from deep inside her.

"I've never felt as strongly or passionately about a woman as I do about you. And that," he said huskily, lifting her hand and kissing the inside of her wrist, "was true before I ever knew you were carrying our child."

Madison's heart soared at the news. A slow, sweet smile blossomed on his face. And what she saw in his eyes was the same wellspring of desire she felt.

"What I'm feeling for you is not going to go away," Chance told her softly and surely, "any more than what you are feeling for me is going to go away." That said, Chance swept her into his arms and carried her up the stairs.

He dropped her—ever so gently—onto the rumpled covers of his bed. He came down beside her and took her mouth in a harsh, groaning union that wrapped them in each other's arms. "I guess," Madison breathed as he reached for the back zipper on her dress, "this means we're done talking about this."

Chance eased the zipper down and peeled away the dress. He kissed her bare shoulder, then the curve of her breast, before settling on the rosy peak and suckling it gently. "We've already done too much talking, Madison," Chance whispered as he filled his hands with her breasts and kissed them through the lace of her bra, teasing and caressing them until her nipples tightened into rosy buds of pleasure. "What we need to do right now is love each other. Just love each other," he told her huskily as he slipped between her legs. And with hands and lips and mouth, he set about doing just that, stroking her sensuously with his tongue, cupping her femininity with his hand. He kissed her with a wildness that was thrilling, positioning her against him in a way that banished any doubt about his need for her.

Her hands, her lips were just as darting and playful, just as thorough and erotic. They studied each other. Explored lightly and provocatively. And learned each other anew. Over and over they kissed and caressed, touched and loved, until nothing mattered except getting closer, taking their passion to completion, giving and receiving all. He lifted her up. She took him inside her. And then they were one, moving swiftly, passionately. Celebrating with every stroke the moment and the wonder that they'd found each other at all. Moving inexorably toward completion, they celebrated the new life they had created in the first and only other time they had been together. Then at last, both arced into the bliss that had eluded them for so long.

AFTERWARD, Madison and Chance remained locked in each other's arms. Madison had never anticipated such a feeling of belonging, of overwhelming contentment. Lying there, wrapped in his arms, her head pressed against the solid warmth of his chest, she felt as if she had come home at long last.

It was, she thought, the best she had felt in weeks. There was only one problem, Madison realized eventually, and her tummy seconded the notion, sending up a comically loud growl.

"Hungry?" Chance teased, stroking loving hands down her spine.

"Well…" Madison drew a breath and sat up. She propped a leg beneath the sheet and rested her elbow on her bent knee. "I didn't eat much dinner."

"Fortunately, that can be remedied." Chance kissed the end of her nose and bounded from the bed. He grabbed the pair of jeans he'd had on earlier in the day and slid his legs into them. "I'll be right back."

Chance returned five minutes later with a tray. On it were two glasses of milk and two sets of silverware, as well as the panfried trout dinner, warmed, and the container of tangy coleslaw. The chef had also added, unbeknownst to Madison, a generous slice of his chocolate-almond mousse cake.

Madison was sitting propped up in bed, the sheet drawn to her waist. She'd slipped on the shirt Chance had worn to dinner. It was deliciously scented with his cologne and the fragrance that was uniquely him. She'd left it unbuttoned, figuring it was only going to be undone minutes later. Obviously thinking the same way, he'd only fastened half of his button fly. Knowing he was planning to make love with her again, as soon as their bodies were fed, rested and ready, added an undeniable sensuality to the moment.

Looking at the delicious meal spread out before them, Madison said, "Looks like the chef outdid himself."

Chance forked a golden brown hush puppy and lifted it to her lips. "My steak dinner was great, by the way."

"I knew it." Madison used her fingers to feed him a bite of tender succulent fish.

Chance spread butter on a roll for them and fed Madison a bite of that. "I don't eat out that often. It's easier to fix something here than drive into town and back."

"Do you miss being able to go to a restaurant whenever you feel like it?" Wondering what it would be like to live here permanently, Madison sipped her milk and sat back against the pillows. She studied Chance, who looked incredibly sexy and handsome clad in just his blue jeans. Her spirits rose as she realized he was as happy and content as she was.

Chance shook his head. His dark hair was agreeably rumpled from their lovemaking. "Before I went to the ranch, fast food and diner food were all I had," he confessed. "My dad never learned to cook—after my mom died, he didn't have any interest. Then when he died and I went to Lost Springs, we ate in the ranch dining hall most of the time. So I've had it both ways. A steady diet of restaurant food and a steady diet of home cooking—which is what the ranch served."

Madison grinned as the two of them demolished what was left of the tangy green coleslaw. "Which do you prefer?"

"Home cooking." Chance licked his fingers, then teasingly began working on hers. "Definitely. What about you?"

Madison's toes curled as he kissed the salty crumbs from her fingertips. "I guess I had a pretty good combination. My mother was a homemaker, and she excelled at it, took all sorts of gourmet cooking classes. And because we lived in cities—Dallas, Houston, Phoenix, New York, London and Paris—and there were abundant fine restaurants, we ate out a lot."

"What about now?"

"Although I can cook at least a few things, thanks to my mom, I eat out most of the time, or order in. I work so much I don't have time to do anything else."

Madison dug into the dessert, closing her eyes in ecstasy as the rich chocolate melted on her tongue. She fed Chance one spoonful, then another and another. "I've seen other women do it, be homemakers and love it—especially if their marriage is a really good one—but I don't think I really need to be married. What about you?" She studied the cocky, know-it-all curve of his lips. "Could you give all this up for marriage?"

Chance shook his head. "I've worked too hard and too long to attain it." His eyes glowed with a new, ardent light and his grin widened as he removed the tray from her lap and set it aside. Tugging her into his arms, he regarded her with lazy enjoyment. "So I guess that means only one thing." Tunneling his hands in her hair, he slanted his mouth over hers. "We better enjoy this while you're here," he murmured, as they began to kiss with sweeping intensity. "Because you won't be here for long."

It wasn't exactly the solution either of them had been hoping for, but at the moment, Madison knew, it would do. It would have to.

CHAPTER EIGHT

MADISON GLANCED OUT the window in time to see Chance—who had been working with Shiloh in the corral since shortly after dawn—climb onto the temperamental stallion's back. Instead of bucking or fighting, the stallion bore Chance's weight stoically. Head held high, Shiloh pranced around the corral like a show horse before a race. Once, twice, three times. After a few more rounds, Chance slipped off Shiloh's back and unlocked the corral gate. He led a surprisingly docile Shiloh through it, then climbed on and headed out.

Madison glanced at her watch. The crews were due any minute, but she didn't blame Chance for wanting to reward Shiloh's hard-won progress with a taste of freedom. It was the first time Shiloh had been out of a fenced-in area since he had arrived at Chance's ranch.

Meanwhile, Madison thought, she had problems of her own. She had broken her cardinal rule once again of not getting involved with anyone she was working with and let fantasy become reality last night by making love with Chance, not just once, but again and again and again.

And yet despite the conflict, despite her nagging conscience, she was happier than she had been in weeks. She felt close to Chance. At peace. Optimistic about the future. And those were things she hadn't felt since she didn't remember when. If the two of them could continue this way indefinitely, she thought wistfully. If they could continue to be together without putting any undue pressures or restrictions or conventional expectations like marriage on their relationship, she could see them being happy forever. But with a baby on the way, change was ahead of them.

The waistbands on all Madison's clothes were beginning to feel snug. Although she could wait on the maternity clothes for another month or two, she was going to have to go up another size in regular clothes, and soon! She didn't want anyone noticing her pregnancy yet. Madison frowned, looking down at her to-do list for the day. She had to stop thinking about Chance and the baby and how happy she was to have both in her life. She had enough on her hands trying to put the Ranchero ads together for the AMV Corporation.

Seconds later, the caravan of trucks and cars began filing in the lane, kicking up gravel dust. Madison grabbed her clipboard full of notes on the day's planned activities and headed down the stairs. By the time she had stepped onto the porch, Chance was riding up on Shiloh. His tall, strong body framed against the golden glow of the morning sun, he rode through the meadow with the mountains rising majestically in the distance.

Watching how he sat a horse—his body straight and tall in the saddle, his gloved hands easy on the reins—Madison couldn't help but be impressed. He was so handsome and so kind and so wonderful. The quintessential cowboy, she thought, as Chance urged Shiloh into a trot and cantered toward them. And he was all hers, at least for the moment.

"Damn, but that man can ride," Shawna remarked as she joined Madison on the low-roofed porch.

"What an incredibly magnificent horse," Ed added, shaking his head in admiration as Chance dismounted and put Shiloh in the adjacent corral.

Ursula couldn't take her eyes off the black stallion. "We should use that horse in the ads."

Madison put up a hand stop-sign fashion. "That won't

be possible," she said firmly, immediately taking Chance's side.

"I'd like to know why not," Ursula retorted, looking peeved.

"Because Shiloh's barely trained," Chance responded, whipping off his leather gloves and coming to join them. He was happy Madison was supporting him. It meant a lot.

Ursula's lips tightened. It was clear she felt Chance was being contrary again. "He looked fine to me."

"Looks, as we all know, can be deceiving," Chance replied, folding his arms as if for battle.

"Chance is right," Madison said quickly, stepping between them and doing her best to make peace before an argument broke out. "Shiloh is just now getting trained. He would be unreliable, at best. It isn't worth the risk."

Ursula's frown deepened.

Madison's boss sent a conciliatory look at the AMV Corporation exec then turned to Madison. "May I see you a moment? Privately?"

Uh-oh, Madison thought, *here it comes.*

Chance brushed by them, heading for the front door. "I'm going up to get a shower," he said.

"No. Don't. Stay just as you are," Ursula interjected.

Vince Smith joined them. "I agree," he said.

"I thought we were going to try and match Chance to one of the models and film the black tie scenes today," Madison said.

"Right now I want some shots of Chance just as he is," Vince stated.

Chance rolled his eyes at the absurdity of it all, at least from his point of view, but gave up on the idea of a shower—momentarily, anyway. He stalked to the garden hose, turned it on and drank deeply from the water pouring out of the end.

Meanwhile, Ed steered Madison to a corner of the yard. "May I remind you that this is one of the largest accounts our agency has ever had? Thus far, given Chance Cartwright's uncooperative attitude, it hasn't been going all that smoothly. So if Ursula and/or the AMV Corporation want that particular horse to be used—''

''I know what you're saying.'' Madison put up her clipboard to cut short the lecture. ''And normally I would agree with you and just do what the client wants, even if we had to discard the film later because it wasn't right for the commercial. Unfortunately, we can't do that here. Shiloh may have responded to Chance's gentle touch, but he's still prone to some pretty drastic mood swings. He'll be totally calm one minute, completely wild the next. We can't possibly use him in any of the commercials. There are, however, many other horses here that are equally beautiful that Chance has given us full permission to use.''

''Any other big black stallions?''

''Well, no, but they are docile and completely reliable when it comes to following Chance's direction.'' She had seen him working with them over the last few weeks.

Ed grimaced and turned his glance to the activity going on around them as the film crew set up their equipment. ''I have a feeling 'docile' is not what Ursula wants here.''

''Just trust me on this, okay?'' Madison said, as determined to protect Chance's interests as she was to finish the commercial. ''AMV is going to be happy with the finished Ranchero ads.'' She paused and met her boss's assessing gaze, her stubborn determination evident. ''I haven't let you down yet, have I?''

Ed didn't reply. He didn't have to. They both knew she hadn't.

And wouldn't, Madison thought. Not if she had anything at all to say about it.

''VINCE IS RIGHT—it's like trying to pair a swimsuit with combat boots and a gun.'' Madison shook her head. ''It isn't going to work no matter how we pretty things up.''

"I agree." Ed Connelly sighed. They had spent hours attempting to pair Chance with one of the half-dozen models the Dallas agency had sent. "The look just isn't right."

And with the dinner hour nearing, Madison thought, glancing at her watch, there wasn't much hope they would get the shots accomplished on schedule.

"There's no chemistry between any of them," Ursula complained.

Madison knew that, and she couldn't help but be secretly pleased.

"Even when he's trying to look interested, Chance comes off as barely engaged," Ed observed.

"You'd think he would cotton to one of them," Shawna said wistfully. "I mean, you gotta admit—" she leaned close, confiding "—these ladies are no slouches in the looks department, and we've got a good variety, too. Two blondes. Two brunettes. And two redheads. All with figures and faces to die for."

"There's just no faking chemistry. Either you've got it or you don't," Vince said, frowning.

"That's true," Ursula remarked as she sat in one of the canvas folding chairs. "The only woman I've seen Chance warm up to the whole time we've been here is Madison."

Abruptly, all eyes turned to Madison. Embarrassed, she tried not to flush. "I've worked hard to develop a rapport with him," she explained.

"Then why not use it?" Ursula said practically. "Let's pair Madison with Chance on film and see what happens. She's certainly pretty enough. And, as Madison said, they've already established a rapport."

Madison gulped. "I couldn't possibly." Carrying on with Chance in private was one thing. She had begun to see that as inevitable. But having it known, or even suspected, would put her in a league with her father, whose affairs with colleagues had been and were still the cause of a lot of gossip. Madison did not want to go down that road.

"Sure you can," Ed said, smiling his encouragement. He stood and beckoned the wardrobe mistress with a crook of his finger. "Get Madison gussied up. We're going to try filming her."

Thirty minutes later, Madison was dressed in a sleeveless white evening gown, her hair swept into a sophisticated French twist, tendrils escaping down her neck.

Chance strode onto the front porch, a fistful of wildflowers clutched in his hand. He swept off his hat—just as the director had ordered—as he neared her.

"Looking good," Chance whispered as he approached her on cue.

Nothing they were saying to each other was going to be on the commercial, of course. They were just supposed to be seen smiling and speaking to each other, as a man and a woman would on a real date.

Madison smiled and tried not to feel self-conscious. Or let herself be reminded that the first time they'd met he had presented her with a bunch of flowers, too. "Looking good, yourself." She tried to keep her actions loose and natural and found it wasn't as easy as it looked.

As scripted, Chance offered her his arm. "Ready for an evening of fun?"

Madison hooked her arm through his. "As soon as this is over?" She held his gaze, aware she could cheerfully drown in the sexy twinkle of his gorgeous eyes, even if it hadn't been in the script. She took the flowers from him and briefly buried her face in them. "You bet!"

Chance leaned down and kissed her just above the ear. "So how does it feel to be on camera?" he murmured.

Madison hugged him, also as scripted. "Horribly uncomfortable," she said, holding his eyes in the flirtatious manner in which they'd been directed. It was wonderful, being with Chance. And it continued being wonderful as they went through the paces of their "date" in the new Ranchero pickup truck. And for the first time since filming had begun, Chance didn't seem to mind doing something over and over and over again.

Finally, they were near the end.

Vince relayed rapid instructions. "Okay, the date's over, so help her down from the cab—that's it—very gently. Set her down in front of you and hold her there. Now slide your arm around her waist, Chance—perfect! Escort her toward the front porch. When you're almost there, take her in your arms and kiss her!"

Madison blushed as she and Chance came to the obliged halt in front of the steps and turned slowly, inevitably, toward each other. "You wouldn't," she murmured sweetly beneath her breath, tipping her head to his.

"Watch."

The next thing she knew, Chance had swept her into his arms. His mouth came down on hers. He kissed her with all the sweetness and tenderness and passion she could have wished for. And then kept kissing her and kissing her, until finally the crew started chuckling and Vince yelled, "Cut!" He strode to Chance and slapped him on the shoulder. "Finally! Something you can get into."

Chance chuckled. For once, he and Vince had not locked horns. "I could kiss Madison anytime," Chance drawled.

"So noted," Ursula Rodriguez said dryly. The AMV exec looked happy, too.

Madison, blushing, tried to restore order to her hair, even as she ignored the thoughtful looks her boss was sending her way. "I think that's enough for today, don't you, folks?"

Vince nodded, clearly more pleased than he had been since starting the shoot. "We got everything we needed here today. And then some."

"STOP GRINNING," Madison said to Chance as they watched the last of the cars, trucks and vans turn onto the highway. They headed into the house, and Chance led her upstairs to change out of the formal wear—which would be turned over to wardrobe in the morning.

"Can't help it," Chance drawled, looking as unable to stop thinking about the kisses as she was.

Madison knew what he meant about feeling powerless. She had never blushed so much in one day in her entire life. That bothered her. A lot. It wasn't like her to wear her heart on her sleeve. She had a business reputation and an air of utter professionalism to maintain. Even in situations like this. Especially in situations like this. "What we were doing out there was just—" Madison paused as she searched for an appropriate word "—playacting."

Chance quirked a disbelieving brow and continued to look at her steadily as he shrugged out of the tuxedo jacket. "Except you're no actor." He loosened the knot of his bow tie and took the onyx tuxedo studs out of his shirt. "And neither am I."

"So the...attraction—" Madison began when a search for a better word failed her.

"—and the passion—" Chance interrupted with a very satisfied, very male grin. He watched as she took her earrings off, one by one.

"—we've been feeling for each other showed through," Madison concluded, kicking off her shoes. "It doesn't mean we can't go back to business as usual tomorrow."

Chance removed his suspenders and dropped them over the back of the chair. "With you calling the shots and me following orders," he guessed. Shirt undone, he headed toward her.

Her heart pounding, Madison struggled against giving herself up to the inevitable. "Right."

A skeptical look on his face, he braced a shoulder against the wall. The sexy sparkle was still in his eyes, but along with it was something stronger, deeper, more tempting than simple desire.

"You don't think we can do that?" Madison asked, aware her blood was racing.

Chance shook his head slowly, his heated gaze caressing her from head to toe. "When you kissed me back the way you did today?" he murmured softly. "Quite frankly, no."

Madison swallowed, aware she wanted nothing more at that moment than for him to take her in his arms and kiss her long and hard, and then make love to her, not just once, but as he had the night before, again and again and again. She knew he would, too; she just didn't know when.

Aware he was making her feel far too vulnerable, she turned so he could unzip her evening gown. "As great as all this is, it's just passion, Chance," she murmured. Maybe if she said it enough she would believe it. And anyway, as much as she wanted him, Madison reassured herself firmly, as much as she cared about him, she was still a strong, independent woman who could handle anything that came her way.

Chance drew her zipper down, not discouraged in the least by her practical words. "Just passion," he echoed, sliding his hands inside the fabric of her dress, running his lips along the nape of her neck, down her spine.

Madison shut her eyes. She thought of the past and warned herself not to get caught in the trap of expecting—of wanting—too much. But with Chance it was so easy to do. She could look in his eyes, drown in his kisses and easily imagine a thousand and one sunsets. And sunrises. All spent together. But what if it didn't happen? What if the newness and excitement faded, and a month—a year—down the road he no longer wanted her? What would she do? How would she cope then? Already she could hardly imagine her life without him.

She swallowed and turned away, aware she had ventured into dangerous territory. And that her heart and her future, as well as her baby's, were on the line. She struggled for a casual tone. "I've been down this road before." She slipped out of her dress and hung it on a hanger. Clad in her undergarments, she walked to the garment bag.

Struggling to understand, Chance sat on the edge of the bed. "Made love with someone you're working with?"

"No." Madison hung up her dress and reached for her robe. She belted it on over the lace and silk teddy. "Had a love affair based on physical attraction." Not trusting herself to sit on the bed next to Chance, she leaned against the bureau. "It was great while it lasted," she fibbed, knowing full well that her first and only experimental love affair, embarked upon while she was in college, was nothing at all like this. "And then it ended." Leaving her feeling lonelier and more disillusioned than she had been before it started.

"Let me guess." Chance braced his hands on either side of him, giving her a look that let her know no matter what she did or said, he wasn't going to go away. "The two of you remained friends."

"No. We completely lost touch." A fact for which Madison was eminently grateful. She couldn't think about that time without feeling foolish. Duped, somehow. As if her life had been cheapened by it instead of enriched, as all the magazine articles had promised it would be.

Chance was enjoying their intimate talk. These were the kind of things he needed to know about her if he was ever really and truly going to understand her. He leaned across the small space between them, grabbed her wrist and tugged her over to sit beside him on the bed. "And that didn't break your heart?"

"Actually," Madison said, choosing her words with care, "it was a relief."

"How so?" Chance asked, carefully folding his clothes.

Madison hadn't felt anything back then. She'd thought making love would have changed things between them, brought the missing spark and pizzazz to their relationship. Instead, the lackluster lovemaking had made the loneliness all the worse. "Because technically, Brad and I were right for each other." Madison studied their linked hands and tried to figure out a way to explain all she had felt. "We had the same type of backgrounds, the same career goals, the same interests. But emotionally we were all wrong." She paused and shook her head. "In the end, we just didn't click the way we should have. I was never able to read his mind. He was never able to read mine. So when Brad graduated from college and went off to take a job in Santa Barbara and I stayed in Texas, it just seemed like the time to say goodbye."

"And you're comparing what we have to what you had with this Brad guy?" Chance held tight to her fingers when she pulled away.

"Don't you see?" Madison confessed on a tortured breath, all her insecurity coming to the fore. "If that ended eventually, then this will, too. Because you and I have *nothing* in common, Chance." Frustration turned the corners of her mouth down. "I'm a city girl who lives and dies by her career. You're a rancher. I'm in Texas. You're in Wyoming."

"All I see is that I want you and you want me." Chance wrapped his arms around her waist and lifted her onto the warmth and security of his lap.

Madison barely repressed a moan. She wished like hell he would stop trying to make everything so easy and simple when it clearly wasn't. "Chance—"

Chance tunneled one hand through her hair, tilting her face to his. He had to get her to trust him, heart and soul, if he ever wanted to get her to commit to him for more than a moment. "This doesn't have to end, Madison." He rubbed his thumb across her lips, tracing the soft bow. "Not when the filming is over," he promised. He lowered his lips to hers and touched them lightly, evocatively with his. He drew back and finished speaking with a curious gruffness to his voice. "Not even after the baby comes, if we don't want it to end.'' They could have the rest of their lives together, if only she would give them a chance.

Hope sprang inside Madison, but with it came caution and the need to be honest—even if it hurt. She tried not to think about how nice it would be to just kiss him again and not talk about all this. But the businesswoman in her—the part that wanted everything spelled out plainly in direct terms—wouldn't let her.

She smiled at him ruefully. ''You say that now.'' Maybe he even believed it. ''But you aren't going to want me when I'm out to here—'' Madison put a palm out to indicate the swollen belly that came with the later stages of pregnancy. ''And I have stretch marks and heaven only knows what else.'' She sighed. She didn't want to fall in love with him. Didn't want to be that vulnerable. But she already knew in her heart it was too late. She did love him, heart and soul, and always would.

Chance grinned. ''You're wrong about that, Madison,'' he drawled, and he covered her mouth in a kiss that was as demanding as it was tender, then untied her belt and opened her robe. He slid his hands inside, tracing the lace-edged silk of her teddy. ''I'm going to want you for the rest of my life.'' He bent his head and kissed her again, until passion swept through her and her body arched and her hands clung. He kissed her until she lost what was left of her restraint and abandoned herself to the pleasure of the moment. Her pulse jumped as he eased the ribbon-thin straps of her teddy over her shoulders and exposed the uppermost curves of her breasts to his rapacious view. He bent and brushed light butterfly kisses across her skin. A soft moan—or was it really a sigh of surrender?—shuddered through her as he lowered her slowly to the bed. ''But I can see bein' the city girl slash career woman you are that you're having a hard time believin' a slow old cowpoke like me could be forever faithful to anything but his horse. So I guess I'll just have to prove it to you....''

Madison laughed softly and tried to pull away, but he held fast. "Chance—"

He responded by closing his lips over hers and lightly tracing the curve of her lips with his tongue. "Hmm?" Still kissing her, he shackled both her hands in one of his and peeled the teddy to her waist.

"I don't think—"

"Yes," he said, chuckling softly, and Madison knew he was reading the soft acquiescence of her body, knowing it spoke volumes louder than the trembling indecision of her words. His kiss grew warmer, more insistent, melting her resistance. "You do, Madison. We both do."

He kneaded her breasts with his hands, tenderly caressing the plump mounds as a thousand feelings swept over her. His thumbs stroked the dusky centers, discovering the new voluptuousness her pregnancy had wrought.

His hands slid lower, sending tiny featherings of yearning shimmering along her nerves. Still kissing her rapaciously, he pushed the teddy past her hips, letting it slide down to just above her knees. Giving her no chance to kick free of the restraining silk, he dropped to the floor in front of her, cupping one hand behind her, easing his other between her thighs.

He smiled as she gasped and whispered his name. He loved her with his hands and his mouth until every sensation she had ever known or imagined was funneled toward the center of her being and desire exploded inside her. He held her till the shuddering stopped, then moved back to the bed. Trembling, Madison looked into his face, a bit embarrassed at the way she had raced ahead. She'd never been selfish. She didn't want to start now. "I wanted—"

Grinning, he curved his fingers around her breasts and aroused her with a magical touch. "I know," he murmured. "And I'll catch up. I promise," he teased. "Even without a horse to ride on. But not," he said, a decidedly wicked gleam in his eyes as he divested her of the teddy, leaving her thigh-high stockings on, ''just yet.''

He swept her into his arms and lifted her from the end of the bed to the pillows. He drew back the spread. His eyes holding hers all the while, he lowered her to the rumpled cotton sheets.

Madison rose to her knees. Moving to the edge of the mattress, she knelt in front of him. ''You're very bad. You know that, don't you?''

''Why, yes, ma'am.'' Chance pretended to poke back a hat. ''Fact is, you inspire me.''

And he inspired her, Madison thought with a lusty sigh. She met and held his eyes. ''Let me.'' Her fingers trembled as she spread the edges of his pleated white tuxedo shirt. Marveling at the pleasure just looking at him brought her, she smoothed her palms across the warm, bunched muscles of his chest, delighting in the tightness of his flat nipples and the velvety softness of his skin.

''With pleasure, darlin'.''

Chance tensed with delight as she tugged off his shirt and kissed and kneaded her way across his shoulders. Making love with Madison was an incredibly intense experience. Having her want him as much as she apparently did took it to another level. He shuddered with delight as she forged a wanton path through the mat of crisp hair that formed a velvety arrow to his waist. Heat pooled in his groin, intensifying in a low, rhythmic ache.

''Uh-oh—''

''What?'' Madison asked, feigning innocence.

''You could be getting ahead of me.''

He groaned as her nimble fingers found him. ''Madison,'' he warned, his hands tangling in her hair. If she was going to go this slowly, she might not be the only one who couldn't wait.

''Just a minute, you slow ol' cowpoke,'' she teased him naughtily. ''I've got to see where this leads.''

Cummerbund, trousers, jockey shorts—all fell victim to her gentle ministrations. Hands gripping his thighs, she dropped to the floor in front of him and loved him with her mouth. Thoroughly. Languidly. Until the touch of lips on flesh was electric and he, too, thought he would die from the pleasure of it. Shuddering with the effort it was costing him to restrain his desire, he scooped her up and shifted her beneath him. His hands swept down her body. To their mutual pleasure, he found her even more wet and welcoming than before.

"Oh, Chance, I want you," Madison whispered, parting her thighs. *Not just now, but forever.*

"I know." His body trembling, Chance lowered himself over her. "I want you, too," he whispered, knowing that right here, right now, was everything he had ever dreamed of. He just had to find a way not to let it slip out of his grasp, he thought, as he kissed her long and hard and deep. "More than you could ever know."

Madison bent her knees. Her back arching in anticipation of their joining, she closed her hands around his velvety hardness and guided him closer. "Now."

"Like this?" He lifted her and touched her with the tip of his manhood in the most intimate way.

"Yes," Madison gasped as he braced himself above her, his hardness a wonderful counterpoint to her softness, his strength to her vulnerability. "Just like this."

With one bold but gentle thrust he sheathed himself in her satiny warmth, then stroked, tantalized, took. Until for the first and only time in his life, he felt he'd given a part of himself that could never be reclaimed.

HOURS LATER, Madison cuddled against Chance in drowsy contentment, her arms and legs tangled with his, her head resting on the hair-whorled warmth of his chest. In the two hours that had passed, they'd made love three times—first playfully and passionately, then softly, with exquisite tenderness. The third time had been excruciatingly slow and abandoned. Each time the wonder and excitement they shared were surpassed only by a feeling of safety and contentment. Madison knew—even if she didn't want to admit it—that Chance was right. She was going to want him for the rest of her life. And he was going to want her. Nothing, and no one, not even the demands of their careers, the separateness of their daily lives, would change that. The only question was, where did they go from here? And how much longer before they had to decide?

"HEY THERE! Mr. Cartwright!" Shawna Somersby waved her arms wildly and trotted after him, the soles of her clunky Doc Martens making clouds of dust as she raced across the yard to catch up with him near the stables.

"I told you," Chance said to the summer intern who had been following Madison around doing her bidding, "you can call me Chance."

"Okay," Shawna said eagerly. "Chance." She took a deep breath as she opened the manila folder in her hand. "Have you seen Madison?"

"She's inside the house, talking to Vince, Ursula and Ed."

Shawna nodded. She rustled through the papers in the file. "I'll just go ahead and give you your copy now."

"My copy of what?" Chance asked.

Usually they just told him what to do—he didn't have to read the choreographed descriptions of the scenes they were filming.

"Your schedule of events." Smiling efficiently, Shawna produced a stack of papers held together with a clip.

Chance's brow furrowed as he struggled to figure out what she was talking about. What events? "For the filming?" he asked, putting down the feed bucket in his hand and taking the papers she gave him.

Shawna shook her head. "For the promotion."

"What promotion?" Chance echoed. He gave her a blank look and waited for her to clue him in.

Shawna smiled at him with brisk efficiency. "You know. The list of trade shows you'll be appearing at next fall." She pointed at the neatly typed pages in his hand. "As you can see, it's mostly weekends—Friday through Sunday—that you'll be appearing along with the Ranchero trucks."

She was speaking as if it were a done deal. His mood grim, Chance thumbed through the pages. "I never agreed to this."

Shawna paled. "Sure you did," the young intern retorted, beginning to look a little panicked. "Madison told everyone she'd take care of it."

Chance stared at Shawna, unable to recall when he'd felt so damn duped.

Flushing, Shawna studied Chance. "You're telling me that Madison didn't discuss this with you?"

"Not yet." Chance clamped his lips together. He felt as if he was going to explode. He had to fight to stay in control as he folded the pages and shoved them in the back pocket of his jeans. "But we're going to—ASAP."

Chance strode in the direction of the house. Everyone was filing out after the impromptu meeting. Madison was taking up the rear with Ed Connelly. She looked pretty and at ease.

Ignoring Madison's boss, Chance advanced on her purposefully and cut her off at the steps. A thick silence fell over the group as he tipped his hat back and blocked her way. "I want a word with you," he growled. "Now."

MADISON HAD NO IDEA what burr had gotten under his saddle, but she was not about to be treated like the woman who had wronged him in front of her co-workers.

Ignoring the gaping looks of the others, she said as smoothly as possible, "In a minute."

"Now, Miss Burnes."

Madison could only stare, stunned, at the hard lines bracketing either side of Chance's mouth.

"She'll be with the rest of you shortly," Chance said over his shoulder, effectively dismissing the others.

He took her by the arm and escorted her into the house. He shut the door behind them, then leaned against the jamb, crossing his arms.

Madison had no earthly idea what was going on, but she felt she had suffered enough drama for one morning. "Do you mind telling me what's going on?" she asked icily.

Chance narrowed his eyes at her. "Funny, I think that's my line."

Madison had never been the target of such undisguised fury. She rested her hips against the back of the sofa and struggled to remain calm. "What are you talking about?"

Chance whipped some papers from his back pocket and shoved them at her.

Madison shot him another peeved look, then glanced down. The second she realized what it was he had, she felt all the blood drain from her face. She let out a low string of swear words.

"My thoughts exactly," Chance said, sneering. "When were you planning to tell me?"

"I—" Madison's voice was barely above a whisper. "This wasn't supposed to happen." Dread slithered down her spine.

Chance quirked a disbelieving brow. He drew so close his arm brushed hers. She could smell the fury on him as surely as the spicy fragrance of his aftershave. His lips were pale with suppressed rage. "I wasn't supposed to be told yet? Or the events weren't supposed to be scheduled?"

Madison pressed a trembling hand to her forehead. Drawing a steadying breath, she mustered all her courage and looked him squarely in the eye. "Of course the trade shows are scheduled. Those shows happen every year, and the AMV Corporation, along with every other car and truck manufacturer in the United States, puts in an appearance.''

He gazed at her, but his eyes revealed none of his thoughts. ''So it's just me who wasn't to be told,'' he said in a sarcastic tone that held an edge of menace. Chance braced a hand on either side of her and leaned in close, trapping her between the back of the sofa and him. ''Tell me, Madison, when was going to be a good time to lay all this on me?'' he said, the heat of his palms burning into her sides. ''After we made love again?''

He was standing so close she had to tilt her head to see his face. Feeling as if all the air had been sucked from her lungs, Madison glared at him. She was willing to discuss this calmly. She was not willing to trade accusations. She flattened her hands on his chest and shoved. He went exactly nowhere. Expecting to be able to move him when he didn't want to be moved in the slightest was like asking an ant to shift a tractor trailer.

Refusing to back down even if she couldn't manage to put any more physical distance between them, Madison clenched her teeth and instructed calmly, ''Stop it.''

Chance clamped his hands around her wrists and forced them to her sides.

''Why? That's the truth, isn't it?'' His eyes raked her with contempt, and the menace in his soft drawl made her want to cringe. ''You thought I'd be easier to manipulate after we hit the hay.''

If only it were that simple, Madison thought miserably, all too aware there were a lot of people outside waiting on the two of them, wondering just what in Sam Hill was up between them. She decided it was better not to discuss sleeping together under the circumstances. ''You're not an easy man to deal with, Chance Cartwright. Never have been and never will be.''

Chance glanced at the papers she held in one fist. ''So you're denying you had any knowledge of this?'' he said.

Madison gulped. Like it or not, it was time to tell the truth. Even if it infuriated the heck out of him. "I knew they wanted you to do it."

"And you were supposed to talk me into it, right?"

She regarded his handsome features warily. "That was the plan."

"Only you hadn't gotten around to it yet," Chance guessed.

That part was her fault, Madison knew. She lifted her shoulders in a delicate little shrug. "I knew it was going to be difficult."

"But you were determined to do it anyway—when the time was right."

"That's my job!"

"I see. Is that why you went all out in the lovemaking department, then, to help facilitate your plan? Make things a little easier to schmooze me? I mean, it was obvious the bourbon, a good cigar and steak dinner routine didn't work!"

"You know I'm not like that!" Madison retorted.

His expression said he knew nothing of the sort. Chance studied her until she felt sure her legs would no longer hold her. "You know I don't want to do this."

Madison nodded. "Yes." He had said as much in Dallas when he agreed to do the commercials.

"Are you going to tell the AMV Corporation that? And get this killed?"

Madison hesitated. Now came the tricky part. "No," she said finally. "I'm not."

"Why not?"

"Because it's my job to see that the client is happy. And this is what the client wants. Personal appearances from you on behalf of the truck. A testimonial, if you will, of how great a vehicle you think it will be for ranching, pleasure, work, you name it." There, she'd said it, she'd made the pitch.

Chance let her go as swiftly as if she had burned him. He backed away from her. "You don't see anything wrong with this picture?"

"I'm sorry you found out this way." And that was the honest truth.

He studied her, then asked in a tone that warned of simmering anger, "How would I have found out, if it had been up to you?"

"I would have talked to you about it over lunch or dinner, probably in a day or so."

"I see." Chance whirled away from her and stalked out of the house. He headed down the steps, marched across the yard and into the stable. Holding up a hand that instructed others to back off and not interrupt, Madison dashed after him.

By the time she caught up with him he was busy tossing a saddle on Shiloh. "What are you doing?" Madison demanded.

Wordlessly, Chance took Madison by the shoulders and guided her into the tack room, well out of harm's way. He stalked across the aisle, grabbed the reins and led Shiloh out of the stall and through the stables.

"Where are you going?" Madison asked, not sure whether to cry or stamp her foot, knowing she wanted to do both.

"As far away from you as possible!" Chance said. As soon as he'd cleared the barn, he swung himself into the saddle and took off. Seconds later, he was cantering across the meadow. Ursula and Ed came storming to Madison's side.

"What the heck is going on?" Ed demanded, incensed. Within seconds, Vince Smith and his entire entourage had joined them. "We're supposed to start filming here in five minutes!" Ed said.

"I know," Madison replied.

"What did you say to him?" Ursula demanded.

"Obviously not enough," Madison muttered.

CHANCE HEARD the Ranchero's engine coming up behind him. He turned, incensed to see Madison driving along the adjacent ranch road. He turned Shiloh toward the mountains. She followed, taking the four-wheel drive off-road.

Swearing profusely, Chance brought his horse to a stop and waited for her to catch up. When she did, he dismounted, leaving the increasingly reliable black stallion a good fifteen feet away from the Ranchero. He jammed his hat lower across his brow and strode toward her. "What in blue blazes do you think you're doing now?" he demanded angrily. He didn't know whether to shake her or kiss her. He knew he wanted to do both.

Madison shut off the ignition and got out of the cab. She glided toward him, her actions as graceful and elegant as his were quick and deliberate. "I'm here to talk some sense into you."

Chance struggled for patience. "We've said everything we have to say to each other."

"No, Chance—" Madison held her head proudly as her green eyes found and held his "—we haven't. I'm sorry." She put up a delicate hand before he could interrupt. Her pretty chin lifted another notch. "I never meant for you to find out about the trade shows this way." As she continued to look at him, a faint smile curved lips that were soft as silk. "I'm not going to say I wouldn't have tried my damnedest to talk you into it," she admitted wryly, with the kind of honesty and directness she had wanted from him all along, "but I never would have gone behind your back and arranged for you to make personal appearances at the trade shows without consulting you first."

Chance braced one leather-gloved hand on his waist. He drew a long breath. "Then why did you?"

"I didn't."

A pulse throbbed in his neck. He wanted to curse her as

pungently as he was cursing himself. He had known from the start that taking this commercial on was a mistake, but he'd done it because he wanted to be close to her and because he wanted Lost Springs to have more money than he could afford to give.

Chance looked away a long moment and shook his head. He was no fool. Never had been. Yet the way she still had him wanting to believe was damn near amazing. Or maybe just downright foolish, he thought self-effacingly.

"This is your account," Chance pointed out evenly. "That memo Shawna gave me had your name on it. How did that happen if you had nothing to do with it?"

"I don't know," Madison returned evenly, still holding her ground. "But I'm going to find out."

Chance grimaced and turned away. "You do that."

Madison dashed after him, stumbling on the uneven ground.

He reached out to steady her. As always, he liked the feel of her soft, feminine form in his hands a little too much for his own good.

"Chance, I'm not going back until we've worked this out," she insisted stubbornly, leaning into, instead of away from, his touch.

Reluctantly, he let her go. "Like heck you're not," he growled, and strode toward the cab. He reached in, got the ignition keys and pocketed them. Then he picked up the cell phone on the dash and handed it to her. "Call someone and have them come here and get you," he ordered gruffly, knowing if he stayed much longer he was going to end up kissing her. That had been their downfall from the start.

She gaped at him. "You're not going to leave me stranded!" Her posture was stiff and defensive.

"I'm not going to let you follow me off-road, either," Chance replied roughly as he gave her one last quelling look. "It's too dangerous for you and the baby. Meanwhile,

I need some time alone.'' And whether she liked it or not, he was taking it.

Madison swallowed. ''How much?'' Her eyes were awash with regret and frustration.

As much as he damn well needed, Chance thought. Ignoring her beseeching look, he pivoted away from her. ''I'll let you know.''

CHAPTER NINE

"I DON'T UNDERSTAND how this happened," Madison said, holding the crumpled papers Chance had given her.

"It's my fault," Shawna said, trying not to cry. "The day you got sick? The publicist from AMV called, wanting to talk to you. She'd been unable to get ahold of Kit in Dallas—I guess Kit had the afternoon off to do something with her sons. Anyway, the publicist said she had lined everything up, and they wanted to make sure that you and Chance had plenty of time to plan for the scheduled events. I told her that I'd make sure you and Chance both got a copy of the schedule as soon as she sent it to us. So when it came in this morning's mail pouch, I just took it right over to Chance." The young intern's lower lip trembled. "I didn't know he didn't know yet. I thought—the way you two were getting along—that everything was fine! It was all arranged." Shawna twisted her hands. "Nobody told me there was a problem."

"It's okay, Shawna," Madison said gently, putting a hand up to stop the flow of distressed words. "I know you didn't mean to do anything wrong. But from now on, please, clear everything with me first before you ask Chance anything."

"I will. I promise." Shawna wiped her eyes with a tissue. "I really am sorry."

"I know you are." Having made her own share of mistakes at the intern level, Madison patted Shawna's shoulder gently as more tears splashed down the young woman's face. "It's okay. It will work out."

Ed and Ursula, seeing Madison, walked over. Ed looked straight at Shawna, murmured a word of comfort to the young intern, then sent her on her way before he turned to Madison. "Get everything straightened out with Chance?"

Madison drew a deep breath. "I'm working on it."

Ursula, who was no doubt thinking about what this was costing the AMV Corporation, compressed her lips disapprovingly. "I expected you to bring Chance back with you."

So had Madison. She met Ursula's gaze equably. "He needed some time to think."

"How much time?" Ursula bit the words out.

Madison gulped. With the whole crew standing around waiting, she couldn't afford to fudge. "I don't know." She turned and looked at Ed beseechingly. "Maybe we should talk to Vince and get some more film of the ranch and the horses without Chance while we're waiting."

"This is a complete waste of time," Ursula fumed, looking angrier by the second. "And on my company's dollar!"

"Connelly and Associates will absorb the expenses if the day turns out to be fruitless. I don't think it will," Ed said smoothly.

"After all," Madison improvised, "we don't have Chance but we still have the pastures and the house and the stables and all those beautiful new Ranchero trucks. We can shoot plenty of film of the trucks today. And without Chance here to get in the way, it might even go better than usual."

Ursula could not argue with that. "Fine," she snapped, putting a hand to her perfectly coiffed jet black hair. "But if this happens again—" She looked at Madison warningly.

"It won't," Madison reassured her smoothly.

"See that it doesn't. Because to my way of thinking, if

you can't handle the talent, you've got no business handling the account!'' Ursula stalked off to speak to Vince.

Madison turned to her boss.

''I agree with her,'' Ed said shortly. ''You need to get this fixed. Pronto! Before the client walks.''

Ed stormed after Ursula. A trembling Shawna brought Madison a cup of fresh lemonade from the catering truck. ''Are they very mad?'' she asked nervously.

''Very. As they should be,'' Madison said glumly. Feeling as if she were going to collapse if she didn't sit down, she went on the porch and sat on the swing.

''Are you feeling fluish again?'' Shawna asked.

Madison shook her head. Just sick at heart.

''I'm just frustrated, that's all.'' Madison sipped a little of the icy lemonade, all too aware of the gathering heat. Judging by the temperature and the amount of humidity in the air, it was going to be another scorcher.

Looking a little more composed, Shawna perched on the porch railing opposite her. ''With Chance?'' she asked.

''With everything.'' Madison sighed as she looked at the activity going on in the yard. Vince was pointing and gesturing to the crew. The grips and technicians were positioning lights and Ranchero pickups in front of the stables.

''Can I ask you something?'' Shawna asked after a moment.

Madison nodded.

''Is it always so, well, tense around here?''

Madison looked at Shawna, knowing she should be honest about what lay ahead of the industrious young intern if she chose this line of work. ''Yeah, I'm afraid it is,'' Madison said bluntly. ''Advertising is a cutthroat business to begin with. And when you work for a big, important agency like Connelly and Associates, where large amounts of money are at stake, you have to be prepared to face a lot of pressure on a daily—hourly—basis from your bosses and your clients.''

Madison stretched her legs in front of her, knowing for the baby's sake she had to take a fifteen-minute break in the shade or risk fainting again. "As for what happened this morning," she continued, taking another sip of her drink, "Ed and Ursula were right to be peeved with me." Madison scanned the horizon for any sight of Chance and Shiloh, but to her disappointment saw none.

She sighed. "I should have taken care of the trade show thing days ago." And would have, she amended silently, if she hadn't been pregnant with Chance's baby. And attracted to him. And wary of rocking the boat. And distracted from her work. And so many other things. "But I didn't, and—well..." Madison turned to Shawna with a self-deprecating shrug. "You can see what happened this morning as a result."

"But that was my fault!" Shawna protested.

Not entirely, Madison thought grimly. "It could easily have come from someone else. I knew what was expected of me. In fact, I had a conversation with Kit about this a few days ago." And then promptly forgot all about it. "The bottom line is I didn't deliver." And that was a first. In the past, Madison hadn't let anything get in the way of her work. Because it was her work—and her success at it— that had sustained her. But now, without even realizing it, her priorities were shifting. Becoming more personal. Less business-oriented.

"But you're still going to be the next vice president at the agency, aren't you?" Shawna asked anxiously. She leaned forward and laid a hand across her heart. "I mean, my goof won't prevent that from happening for you, will it?"

For one fleeting moment, Madison wasn't even sure if she wanted the vice presidency. At least not the way she had before she'd gotten involved with Chance. Getting the position would mean devoting one hundred percent of her time to business, so that things like this did not occur. Be-

ing a VP would mean her life was going to be one long
stress-filled day after another, Madison realized wearily,
rubbing the tension headache starting in her temples. And
so was her baby's.

"Madison? Are you okay? Should I get you something
else? Some orange juice, maybe, instead of lemonade? Or
some aspirin?"

"I'm fine." Madison said, holding up her hand. For her
baby's sake, she had to be. She just needed to stay on track,
that was all.

Her priorities and her thinking straight once again, Madison stood. Chance might not be back yet, but she knew
what she had to do, what she should have done all along.
Her movements brisk and decisive, Madison turned to
Shawna. "Would you do me a favor and ask Ed and Ursula
to meet with me inside the ranch house ASAP? I've got
something important I need to go over with them."

HOURS LATER, Madison was curled up on the porch swing,
a light summer sweater thrown across her shoulders to ward
off the evening chill, when she saw Chance ride across the
pasture. Her heart beating rapidly, she pushed wearily to
her feet and headed for the stables. By the time she got
there, Chance was standing in the aisle, caring for Shiloh.

His back to her, he routinely went about the task of un-
saddling his horse and putting him away for the night. "If
you're expecting me to say I'm wrong about the trade
shows, you're going to be waiting a long time," he said
gruffly, rubbing the big black stallion down before he led
him into his stall. Chance added water and feed, then shut
the door.

He turned to Madison, his hot glance skimming her face.
He slipped his hands into the back pockets of his dusty
jeans. He was sunburned and sweaty, but not nearly as exhausted as she would have been had she been out riding
the range most of the day. "If you expect me to say I was

wrong about taking off like that, in a fit of temper, you'd be right.'' Chance grabbed the saddle, blanket, bridle, reins and saddlebag he'd hung over the stall door and headed for the tack room, where he routinely went about putting those away, too. "I should have stayed. But if I had, there's no telling what I might have said, I was so ticked off. And that being the case, I decided to head out."

Madison lounged in the doorway of the tack room, determined to finish this discussion, whether he wanted to or not. "I'm sorry."

He looked at her, some of the anger gone, all his disappointment still intact.

"And you don't have to worry about the trade shows anymore," Madison continued, trying not to react to the simmering contempt she saw in his eyes. "I had a meeting with Ed and Ursula. They agreed to back off about that. Permanently."

Finally, she'd said something that registered. "How did you manage that?" Chance washed up at the sink.

Madison watched as he blotted his sinewy forearms and hands with a towel, then hung it on the rack. "I told them it would be a lot more effective if they allowed you to be a gorgeous man of mystery in the commercials. The focus needs to be on the product, not you and your horses. Besides, when it comes to public speaking, it's possible you could bomb at trade shows. It'd be so much better to have a public-relations professional do that for us."

"And they agreed?"

"Once they thought about it? Absolutely." Now she just had to come up with a dynamite pitch person that the AMV Corporation would love more than Chance—not an easy task.

He swept off his hat, raked his hand through his hair and settled the hat on his head. "Thanks for taking care of that."

I only wish I'd done it sooner, Madison thought. Then

they could have averted all this. "You're welcome," she said simply.

Without warning, Chance began to relax. "I'm sorry I blew up at you." He shook his head and crossed to her side, took her elbow and switched off the light.

As he guided her toward the end of the stable, then into the dusky light, Madison realized with relief that everything was going to be all right. She'd made a mistake. He'd been ticked off at her, and justifiably so. She'd taken action to correct the situation. And now he'd forgiven her. And was—judging from the look on his face—willing to let it all go.

Knowing they had that in them—the potential to disagree heatedly without their relationship falling apart completely—was more comforting than she could have imagined.

"This whole business of having so many people constantly underfoot is beginning to get to me." Chance's voice was more relaxed as they crossed the yard to the front porch.

"I understand." Madison sighed. Another gorgeous sunset of red, pink, lavender and purple streaked the smoky blue-gray of the evening sky. Birds sang. And the soft scent of sage hung in the air as a breeze whisked away what remained of the day's heat and humidity. Madison shook her head. "When the whole crew is here, cell phones going off everywhere, Vince shouting directions that almost no one understands, everyone running to and fro and getting crabby as can be, it's as if I brought Dallas with me."

"You say that as if you don't like Dallas." Chance took her hand and led her up the steps.

Madison paused at the edge of the porch. She tilted her face to his as she confessed, "I have to admit I've liked working on the creative aspects of the project—which are always my favorite part, anyway—out here on the ranch in an environment of peace and quiet."

"Have you ever thought of living and working anywhere but Dallas?" Chance asked. He settled on the porch railing. Taking her hands, he drew her to his side.

Madison perched on the railing, too. "After the day I had today, it has occurred to me to try and do something less stressful," Madison quipped. But she also knew her work was a very big part of who she was. "Besides," she said lightly, looking at their tightly twined fingers and trying to ignore the growing knot of emotion in her throat, "you wouldn't find me anywhere near as attractive if I weren't a successful career woman."

"Don't bet on that." Chance favored her with a sexy grin. "It's you I'm attracted to, Madison, not your job title. You're more than the sum of your work and you always will be."

Madison let out a short, bleak laugh. "I wish I could believe that," she said bitterly, shaking her head, "but I grew up seeing for myself that, when put to the test, men react otherwise."

Chance used his leverage on her hand to tug her into the open V of his legs so she was settled on his thigh. Madison tried not to think how good—how warm and strong and solid—his leg felt beneath her hips.

"My mother stopped working soon after my parents married, to have me." Madison's lips took a downward curve. "Their marriage was never the same after that." She had seen the same phenomenon in other marriages, too. The wife became less glamorous and interesting. The husband either strayed or turned to his guy friends for company.

Chance studied her from beneath the brim of his hat. "You blame yourself, too, don't you?"

Madison shrugged and turned her eyes toward the shadowy mountains in the distance. Once again, Chance saw what few others did. "Maybe if I hadn't been there, my mother would have been able to keep working and have a career." Madison swallowed hard around the growing knot of emotion in her throat. "Maybe then my father would have remained in love with her."

"And maybe if your mother had built some fabulous career for herself, their relationship still would have lost its luster," Chance countered practically.

If only I could believe that, Madison thought. *If only I could believe in the happily ever after.*

He studied her, his expression tender. "You don't believe that?"

"I don't know." Madison shrugged, all her troubled thoughts coming to the fore. "Maybe I would if my father hadn't always cheated on my mother with other career women. Don't you see? He never became involved with any housewives—no matter how sexy or witty or wonderful they were. He always went after colleagues, women he worked with."

Laying his hand on her wrist for emphasis, Chance grimaced and said, "Did you ever think that was probably just due to proximity?"

Madison drew a deep breath and let it out slowly. "That plus excitement. I heard him tell my mother once that these women had minds. Lives apart from him and from me."

"Madison, the one thing you could never be is dull," Chance said firmly as he wrapped his arms around her. He bent to kiss her forehead. "Work or no work, you are the most exciting, most unpredictable, most headstrong and determined woman I have ever met."

Madison felt the tingle of his lips on her skin from the point of contact to her toes. She looked at him, her heart already beginning to race. "And you like that?"

"Oh, yeah," Chance said softly, sexily. "I like that a lot."

Just when she thought he was going to kiss her, he pulled back. "But we've got a problem here."

Madison went very still.

"Look at me." He brushed his hand down his dusty

sweat-stained form. "And look at you." He gestured at her impeccably pulled-together appearance. "Looking at the two of us, I'm reminded of a soap commercial you put together. You know, the one where the guy comes in like this, and his woman takes him in hand."

His woman. Madison liked the sound of that.

"You're suggesting?"

Chance grinned. "That you lead me to the shower. And help me wash all this grit off. You bet."

Madison's heart was racing. Her body humming with anticipation, she stood up. "I think I can do that," she teased.

Chance tossed his hat. It landed on the swing. "It'd certainly make my fantasy come true."

Short minutes later, the two of them were in the shower, stripped to the skin, standing under the warm, invigorating spray. He held her fast against him, making her feel the heat, the need. His hands slid down the curve of her back to her buttocks. Murmuring her name, he kissed her. Hot, openmouthed kisses. Nuzzling kisses. Sexy kisses. Tender kisses. Again and again and again. And taking him by the shoulders, she kissed him back, kissed him until they were breathless. Wanting—even if it wasn't exactly in their bargain—some guarantee that what they had was strong enough to last a lifetime. Wanting some kind of a commitment, if not in any legal sense, then one in body and soul.

And as he backed her against the cool tile wall, kissing her thoroughly all the while, Madison noted that Chance seemed to want the same from her, even if he didn't come right out and say it, either. Knowing what it was to want, to need, to feel so damn lonely inside you could cry, she indulged him in turn—making no secret of the fact that blood rushed hot and needy through her veins or that she enjoyed soaping him as much as he enjoyed soaping her. Making no secret of the fact that they'd barely started and already her body was treacherously ready for him, treacherously wet and waiting.

And still he made her wait. Eyes dark with yearning, he bent his head and kissed her again, kissed her hard. She wrapped her arms around him, urging him on, engulfing him with tenderness, giving her all. The insides of her thighs clasped the outsides of his, and as his hands swept between them, exploring and caressing, she let him have his way. She loved the feel of him, the scent of him, the way he strove—almost continually—to possess her and stamp her as his. She loved the way he anchored his hands around her hips and lifted her against the wall. And then he was inside her, slowly, inexorably taking her, claiming her as his and his alone. Even if he didn't say the words, she felt them in the way he loved her, the way he gave her pleasure even as he sought his own. So what if they weren't exactly in love with each other, Madison thought defiantly as a tidal wave of pleasure swept through her, overwhelming her. They had this. And each other. And a child on the way. For now, maybe forever, it was enough, she told herself firmly. It had to be.

URSULA, ED AND MADISON stood beneath the tent, watching Chance barrel out of the cab of a mud-splattered Ranchero pickup truck and into the pouring rain, where he stood grimly sizing up a section of downed fence and several trees that looked to have been blown over by a fierce storm. He was clad in a yellow slicker that covered him from shoulders to mid-calf, Stetson, boots, jeans and plain white shirt. As scripted, Chance jumped into his Ranchero with the agility of a professional stuntman. Turning it swiftly, he raced across a bumpy pasture to a nearby stream. Braking, he parked and jumped out again. Working with the speed of a rodeo cowboy, he tied a rope to the trailer hitch and fastened it around his waist, then waded knee-deep into a rushing stream.

"Cut!" Vince yelled.

"That was great, Chance!" Ed called. Ursula nodded.

"Think you can do it one more time?" Vince shouted.

Chance turned, gave the thumbs-up sign and headed to the Ranchero while the rest of them huddled beneath the tent, protected from the pouring rain.

"Explain to me again how all this is going to work," Ursula said.

Madison smiled, happy to comply. "The scenes we shot with the digital camera earlier today—of Chance leading one of his mares and her colts in out of the rain—are going to be edited in, via computer, to this footage in the finished commercial. It will look as if Chance is actually rescuing the mare and the colt from the stream."

"Just like in a movie," Ursula murmured, pleased.

"Just like in a four-star movie," Madison agreed, knowing this commercial was going to be as exciting as any action-adventure movie when it was finished. Ranchero truck sales would probably explode.

"Chance is outdoing himself today," Ed murmured, pleased.

"He has been a really good sport," Madison agreed. They'd done this take alone sixteen times. Yet Chance approached it tirelessly and in good humor.

She had to admire him for that even as she wondered if his happiness—and hers—had anything to do with their tender, passionate lovemaking the night before. She hoped so. She wanted their relationship to be as good for him as it was for her and their baby, because only then would they stand a chance for real, lifelong happiness.

By the time they wrapped for the day and the crew were on their way to town, Chance was drenched to the skin and shivering. It was still pouring rain. A definite chill had descended in the mountain air.

"I'm going to go up and get a shower," Chance told

Madison. He peeled off his slicker, hat and muddy boots on the porch.

"I'll make you some coffee," Madison said, kissing his cheek.

As it turned out, she did better than that. No sooner had Chance emerged from the shower and toweled off some fifteen minutes later than she was upstairs with dryer-warmed clothes and a cup of coffee laced liberally with bourbon. "Thought it might help warm you up a bit," she said, looking, acting and sounding like a wife.

Chance could only stare at her in wonderment. "Thanks." He was about to ask her to slip into the shower with him when she stepped out of reach.

"I'll be downstairs," she told him, her green eyes dancing with a mixture of mystery and anticipation. "Promise you won't keep me waiting?"

Wondering how he had ever managed without her, wondering how he ever would again, Chance nodded. "I promise."

CHANCE CAME DOWN to find Madison in the living room. She'd built a fire in the grate and set up a table for two in front of it. "Hungry?" she asked cheerfully.

Chance nodded, aware something smelled awfully good. "Want some help in there?" Feeling surprised and pleased at all the trouble she'd gone to, he nodded at the kitchen.

The model of efficiency, Madison shook her head. "Have a seat. I'll be right back." She returned with two steaming bowls of cream of potato soup, garnished with crispy bits of bacon and grated cheddar cheese, and two garden salads. Then went back and came in with two hamburgers broiled to perfection.

Was this what it would be like, Chance wondered, if Madison were his wife? There was no denying he could get used to this. He eyed her warily. "You don't have any more bad news for me, do you?"

Madison tensed and straightened. "No." She looked at him curiously as she set down their plates. "Why?"

Chance shrugged as he held her chair for her. He wondered what kind of honeymoon a woman like Madison would want. Something lively and exotic or quiet and private? Maybe a little bit of both? "I'm not used to being treated like royalty," he said.

Madison slipped into her seat. She sent him a sexy, beguiling smile that made him feel as if he wasn't moving too fast in hoping for a more traditional future.

"All I did was make you dinner," she protested.

Chance thought about how pretty she looked in a loose cotton shirt and jeans. "And put my clothes in the dryer to warm, and made me coffee with bourbon in it," he said, letting her know with a glance how much he appreciated it all. Madison was more suited to marriage than she knew. Maybe he was, too.

Madison lifted a brow as her bare feet came over to mingle with his. "No one's done these things for you before?"

No one had made him feel this cared for, this loved. He shook his head and took a spoonful of the hot, delicious soup. "I'm used to fending for myself."

Madison's lips took on a rueful curve as she crumbled saltine crackers in her soup. "Me, too."

Chance slathered mustard on his bun. "Speaking of fending for ourselves…"

"Hmm?"

Now was as good a time as any to start talking about the baby. And all the time between takes the last couple of weeks had given Chance plenty of opportunity to think about the things they had yet to discuss—things that shouldn't be put off indefinitely. "We haven't talked about how we're going to manage a baby," Chance said, and saw Madison tense slightly.

"I know they need clothes and diapers and a crib to sleep in," he continued. "But beyond that—"

"I'm sure there are lists in the baby departments of stores," Madison said. "But we've got plenty of time for that."

Did they? She was only going to be here a short while longer. Then, unless he could do something to get her to change her mind, or somehow include him in her life, he'd barely see her. The thought upset Chance more than he wanted to admit. He hadn't had enough time with Madison. Not nearly enough.

Madison added a triple layer of dill pickles to her burger. When the silence continued, she flashed him a curious look and cut straight to the chase. "What's on your mind, Chance?"

"I want to know if I should set up a nursery here."

Madison gave him a slow, measured look. "If you want me and the baby to visit—"

I want you to live here, Chance thought. But he knew it was too soon for him to say that.

Madison remained quiet, thinking, then sat back in her chair, looked him straight in the eye, and said, "Maybe we should actually get two sets of everything. One for my Dallas apartment and one for your ranch house here, since the baby will be in both places."

Disappointment knotted inside Chance. Maybe it was foolish of him, but he had hoped that Madison would have started to at least think about them living closer to each other. "That's practical," he agreed reluctantly. "And no doubt about it, I want our baby to have everything he or she needs."

"So do I," Madison agreed wholeheartedly. She sent Chance a level look. "That's only part of it, isn't it?"

Chance nodded. "I want our child to know he or she is loved by both of us. Not just be told it," he said quietly, "but to feel it. In here." He laid his hand over his heart. The way he hadn't since his mother died.

A troubled light came into Madison's eyes. "You don't think I can do that alone?"

"I don't think either of us can," he said flatly. "Not as a single parent." There wouldn't be enough hours in the day.

Madison pushed away her dinner abruptly. She had a panicked expression on her face. "I thought we had an agreement, Chance."

"No, Madison." Chance held his ground under her accusing glance. "You had an agreement. I just didn't argue with you at the time." And now that he and Madison were together as a couple, it was time they started dealing with reality. Time he convinced her to take a job in Wyoming, instead of remaining in Dallas once her ad campaign wrapped up.

Madison began to tremble even as her expression grew more determined. "Look, Chance, I don't want any uncertainty or angst in our child's life, either," she said angrily. "No broken dreams or crushed hopes. No fighting or lovelessness or infidelity." She stood and began to pace like a professor in front of a class. "If that means not staying together long enough to see our passion fade," she threatened softly, perfectly willing to sacrifice herself and her happiness for their child, "then so be it."

On the surface her declaration sounded noble. Chance knew her well enough to realize it was driven by pain and fear. "And you think ending our love affair before the baby's birth will do that?" Chance asked sarcastically.

Madison shrugged. "Don't you?"

CHAPTER TEN

"No," Chance said abruptly, knowing this discussion was not going the way he'd hoped. Madison's thinking—her desire to be practical and logical and adult about all of this—was driven more by her fear of being vulnerable than by what was in her heart. "I don't," he finished heavily.

Madison refused to meet his eyes. She turned her gaze to the fire blazing in the grate and the rain pouring down outside the Double Diamond ranch house. Briefly, her lashes fluttered closed. She opened her eyes, drew a long, bolstering breath, then continued in a rush. "Look, Chance, I accept our love affair as inevitable, destined even. And I know we have to devise some sort of plan for bringing up our baby and still having our careers."

Chance was the first to agree they had to make a living. At least one of them had to work, just as one of them had to be available to care for the baby. And since his business was less stressful and more secure, and financially very lucrative, given his success, the choice to him was obvious. But to do it that way was chauvinistic and old-fashioned, at least in Madison's point of view. He didn't want to think he was either. Which meant coming up with something else that would leave them all happy and yet together most of the time, too. Not an easy task, given Madison's single-mindedness and devotion to her career.

"But I don't want to talk about all that now." Madison shook her head and sighed as she sat across from him once more. "I don't want to talk about it until after the ad campaign is wrapped and ready to go,'' she finished with soft determination.

Chance could see Madison did not want to give up her career to stay home and take care of a child. If he were in her position and had worked as long and hard as she had to achieve success, he supposed he wouldn't, either. Which left them with quite a dilemma. One he knew was going to take some time and effort to resolve. He took her hand and covered it with his. He didn't want to fight with her, but now that they'd opened the door, he couldn't just walk away. ''Do you think that's wise?'' he asked mildly.

Madison studied him. The way she was looking at him, he knew she felt he was being unreasonable. ''You don't want to go on, knowing there's this problem ahead of us, do you?'' Contempt colored her low tone.

''I'd prefer to solve it now, yes,'' Chance said calmly. Problems didn't get solved by themselves. They just got bigger and less manageable. Outside, the storm picked up. Torrents of rain poured from the heavens. The wind howled in the trees.

He pushed back his chair, intending to draw her into his arms, but she was rising, too, and backing away from him. Something close to anger flashed in her eyes. ''I could make an agreement to end the physical side of our relationship before the baby comes and stick to that agreement, if it was for the good of our child.'' Her shoulders stiff, Madison picked up her plate and bowl and carried them to the kitchen.

Chance followed suit. ''So could I. But that isn't what either of us wants,'' he said fiercely.

''You're right about that. It isn't.'' Madison set her dishes in the sink with a loud thunk. Chance thought—but couldn't be sure—he saw tears shimmering in her eyes, but they were swiftly blinked back. ''But to tell you the truth,'' Madison said, doing her best to look as cool and unruffled as she did in any business meeting, ''I don't want to try and predict how you and I are going to feel six months— or even a year—from now, either.'' She tilted her head to his and turned to face him, the vulnerability she'd been hiding returning full force. She searched his eyes for some consensus and said in a trembling undertone that let him know just how reluctant she was to let him go, ''I'd rather just play it by ear and do what seems appropriate at the time.''

''So would I,'' Chance murmured as she went easily into his arms. Maybe it was because of the way he was brought up, he thought, stroking her hair, but he'd never had a very good handle on his emotions. And as for love, the expression of it, the duration of it, he knew very little. He suspected Madison was in the same boat. Her father's adultery had not left her feeling very loved, or their family very whole, either.

The question then was simple, Chance decided, still holding her close. Was what he and Madison felt for each other love? And if so, was it the kind of love that would endure through the birth of their child and beyond, for the rest of their lives? Was it the kind of deep, abiding love that would sustain them in good times and bad? The kind of love that would eventually make even the idea of going their separate ways impossible? The kind of love that would not just demand—but inspire—sacrifices of the weightiest kinds on both their parts?

He didn't have answers for any of that now. Maybe because so much had happened, and was still happening, in so very little time. But he also knew, as he lifted her chin to his and they began to kiss, whatever happened, he wanted to see it through.

''YOU HAVE TO GO back to Dallas?'' Chance asked as Madison pulled out her suitcase the following Thursday evening.

''Just for the weekend,'' Madison confirmed. ''I've got

to meet with the AMV marketing and sales departments, plus have dinner with some of the Southwest's biggest pickup truck dealers and give them an advance peek at the campaign we're going to be running for the Ranchero. I'm sure everything will be fine in my absence. I'll be back in time for the last of the filming next week.''

"And after that?" Chance asked.

"Back to Dallas to start putting the Ranchero commercials together."

Chance looked at the neatly typed pages on her bed. "Is this your schedule?"

Madison nodded. "Kit sent it up in the mail pouch yesterday afternoon, and Shawna gave it to me this morning."

Chance flipped through it. They had her scheduled from seven every morning until midnight, Friday through Sunday. "Do you work this hard all the time?" he asked casually, unable to help but be concerned. Was it safe for a pregnant woman to be working this hard?

"It depends. Sometimes." Madison looked up. She frowned at what she saw in his eyes. "You don't approve." It was more a statement than a question.

Chance was no stranger to hard work. He had put in mighty long hours during the years he had been building his business, and there were times when he still did. But that was then. This was now. And now he had as much part-time help as he needed.

"Just say what you're thinking," Madison told him tersely, tucking her hair behind her ear.

"Okay." Chance watched her transfer a stack of lingerie from her bureau to her suitcase. "I think your hours are incompatible with bringing up a baby."

She looked at him calmly. "Haven't you heard?" she returned lightly. "It's the quality of time you spend with a child, not the quantity."

"It's a lot of things," Chance said quietly, knowing even if she'd braced herself for this discussion with him, she hadn't braced herself for the reality of having a child. If she had, she would already be admitting it wasn't nearly that simple. Nor would it ever be. "Kids need more than a sense of obligation in their lives, Madison. They need love and tenderness and genuine care and affection from both their parents. They need time for stories, play times, picnics and heart-to-heart talks. Time for just hanging out and being with their mom and dad."

Madison went into the bathroom. "I'm prepared to let you participate in whatever activities interest you, Chance."

"It's a little more complicated than that, Madison," Chance snapped.

"Oh, really, and what makes you the expert?" she challenged as she bent over the tub to collect her shampoo and conditioner.

"My childhood." Chance watched as she made sure the bottles were capped tightly before sliding them into a plastic-lined toiletries bag. "My mom died when I was four. My dad never really got over it. And from that point on, he buried himself in his work. He met all my basic needs, but he never really had any time for me and he never expressed any love for me." It had been a miserable existence. Chance didn't want to see the same thing happen between Madison and their baby.

"I'm sorry." Madison paused to give him a brief, compassionate hug before moving past him. "But as I've told you before, our child will know he or she is loved."

"How—if you're not there to give that love?" Chance asked simply, wondering if she were really that naive, or just choosing to be for the sake of their argument. "This isn't some kind of part-time job you have, Madison. It's very demanding. And when you get this promotion you're up for—"

"It will be easier," Madison interrupted, going to the closet.

Like hell it would! "How do you figure that?" Hanging on to his temper by a thread, Chance watched her pull one of her smart linen pantsuits off a hanger.

Madison smiled as she folded the garments and slipped them into her suitcase. "Because once I am a vice president of Connelly and Associates, I'll have more control over my hours. I'll set my schedule instead of someone doing it for me. And I'll be able to have more personal staff. Instead of an intern helping me out, I'll have a permanent executive assistant, plus a secretary all my own."

Chance sighed. "You'll also have more responsibility."

Madison's lips tightened.

"As a VP, you'll be expected to bring in new accounts. Those potential clients will need wooing. Wining and dining."

Madison straightened slowly, the color draining from her face. He assumed she hadn't thought about this. She had. The knowledge hit him like a sucker punch to the gut. "And your point is?" she asked icily, resenting the blazes out of him for bringing this up.

Chance knew she didn't want to hear it, but it had to be said. "The job you have now and a baby are not compatible, Madison. And I think you should take a cold hard look at that fact before you accept a vice presidency."

Hurt flashed across her face. It was swiftly replaced by her trademark stubbornness. "I've worked long and hard for this."

"I know that," Chance said gently, his exasperation growing. "But you have to be realistic. And think about how much you'll have left over emotionally at the end of the day to give a child."

TRAFFIC WAS STOPPED in both directions as far as Madison could see on the Central Expressway in Dallas. She glanced at her watch. It was just her luck she'd get caught in a massive traffic jam en route to the restaurant where she was

supposed to meet the AMV dealers. She also had heartburn
and was so tired from the travel and the amount of work
she'd been doing lately that she ached.

This kind of stress could not be good for the baby, she
thought as her snazzy red sports car inched along behind
the minivan in front of her. Which reminded her. She
rubbed her hand across her tummy and the warm cozy
womb in which her baby slept. She was going to have to
turn this car in before the baby was born and get something
more suitable. Something safe. And practical. And big
enough to carry all the gear that babies seemed to require
these days. Stroller, car seat, diaper bag, playpen or port-
a-crib, plus assorted toys, maybe even a tricycle to ride in
the park.

To the right of Madison was a young mother in a small
sedan. She had an empty car seat in the back and looked
even more stressed out and impatient than Madison felt.
She kept glancing at her watch, too.

That could be me in a few months, Madison thought,
trying to get to the day-care center or baby-sitter to pick
up my child. Was that the kind of life she wanted for herself
and her baby? She frowned as the reporter in the traffic
helicopter above told the radio station listeners that traffic
was going to be backed up for the next three miles, due to
construction. Or did she want a life that included plenty of
time to read stories and go to the park and bake cookies
and bandage hurt knees?

Madison sighed and ran a hand through her hair. Her
baby—at first just a notion—was suddenly becoming very
real to her. It was too soon for her to feel movement in the
womb, but she had a mental image of her baby's tiny little
body, curled up snugly inside her, growing and changing
day by day. This baby was a part of her and a part of
Chance. Their baby was the miracle that had brought her
and Chance together and would continue to bind them for
all time. As she thought about it, she knew she didn't want

to miss a minute of this baby's childhood. She wanted to be there to see their baby's first steps, and hear his first words. To cuddle their baby in her arms and watch Chance do the same.

But how she could do that if she were on the road, filming commercials, or stuck in high-powered meetings, or flying off to meet with a client?

Madison sighed. Much as she hated to admit it, she knew Chance was right. It was time to start making some hard decisions about her life. She wanted to find a way to have it all, a romantic life and a satisfying career and maybe— one day in the very distant future—even a long-term relationship, one that might someday lead to an even more permanent arrangement with Chance, like marriage.

But first she was going to be awarded her vice presidency, she thought determinedly, because darn it all, she had earned it.

"I'M SO GLAD you're back!" Shawna whispered to Madison when she arrived at the ranch early Monday afternoon.

"Why?" Madison asked the young intern as she got out of the rental car she had driven from the airport. "What's going on?"

Shawna put her clipboard in front of her face. "Because Chance has been about as warm and cuddly as a big old grizzly bear, that's what!"

Her heartbeat picking up, Madison scanned the pasture where they were filming for any sign of Chance. She finally located him, deep in some sort of discussion with Vince, Ed and several crew members. To her dismay, none of the men looked happy. "He's refusing to cooperate again?" Madison guessed on a sigh.

Shawna handed Madison a list of phone messages. "He's cooperating. He's also in what seems like a permanent bad mood. And I think it's just 'cause you haven't been around to sort of soothe the savage beast in him."

Madison scanned the list of messages quickly, seeing if there were any that had to be returned immediately. "Surely you exaggerate."

Shawna gave Madison a look. "I may still be in college, but there are some things I know about, Madison. And lovesick guys happens to be one of them. If you ask me, Chance has been missing you desperately."

Just like I've been missing him, Madison thought, pleased to find she wasn't alone in that.

"And he's been taking it out on everyone around him," Shawna continued as Madison began walking toward the men.

"Well, we're almost done." Madison flipped her sunglasses over her eyes. "That ought to cheer him up."

Shawna gave Madison a skeptical look as she struggled to keep up. "Not if it means you're leaving and going back to Dallas permanently at the end of the week. He doesn't seem to be looking forward to that at all."

Madison looked up and saw them bringing in the snow machine. Thus far, they had filmed Chance driving the Ranchero on all sorts of terrain, in all sorts of weather. Except snow. Snow was on the schedule for this morning. Madison wished her schedule had allowed her and Chance a moment alone before they jumped headlong into the business part of their relationship. Alas, that wasn't to be. The group discussion had already broken up. Vince was stepping behind the camera, and Chance was leading a horse to the pasture, where several of his top horses were already making tracks through the half foot of snow the crew had laid down earlier.

As Madison neared Chance, she saw Ursula Rodriguez look at Vince. "What about the black stallion? I thought I made it clear, AMV wants Shiloh in this snow shot."

"Shiloh's not well-trained enough to be part of the commercial," Chance said as he slipped out of the pasture and closed the gate behind him.

Vince and Ursula exchanged looks. "I don't know what the problem is," Vince said furiously. "I saw you riding Shiloh this morning."

"And the sun rose in the east," Chance drawled sarcastically, his back still to Madison. Chance stared at Vince and braced his hands loosely on his waist. "What's your point?"

The air between the men was so fraught with tension it fairly crackled. "The point is, I think Shiloh would make an excellent addition to this frame," Vince said.

Chance shook his head curtly. "How many times and ways do I have to tell you people? I don't mix Shiloh in with the other horses."

"Just for a few minutes," Ursula pleaded.

"No," Chance said firmly.

Able to see a battle brewing, Madison lengthened her steps and joined them. "Chance is right. Shiloh is off-limits," she told the group. Ed and Ursula looked greatly displeased. Vince stared at Madison in frustration.

Chance turned to Madison, his expression gentle and welcoming. "When did you get back?" he asked quietly.

Aware others were watching them closely, Madison ignored the yearning of her heart—which told her to throw herself into his arms and kiss him warmly—and gave Chance a look of brisk efficiency. "Just now," she said matter-of-factly.

If Chance was upset by her cool greeting, he did not show it. He glanced at the pasture. "Mind if I speak to you privately for a few minutes?" he said. "I've got some legal stuff we need to go over. It's in the ranch house."

Madison looked at Vince. "Five minutes and no more," Vince snapped. He glared at Chance. "We'll send someone to get you as soon as the shot is set up."

Chance nodded. With snow on the ground and the temperature already inching up to seventy degrees, they'd need to move swiftly.

He wheeled around and headed for the ranch house in the distance. Madison fell in step beside him. "You know it's taking every ounce of self-control I have not to haul you into my arms and kiss you soundly, don't you?" Chance said, giving her a brief sidelong glance.

Madison swallowed and flashed Chance another quick, efficient smile. "I know," she said softly.

Chance took the steps leading to the house two at a time. He charged ahead to hold the door for her. Her heart pounding, Madison walked ever so casually into the ranch house. The second they had crossed the threshold and were out of view, Chance grabbed her wrist and tugged her into the kitchen, out of view of the windows. The next thing she knew, his arms were around her, and he was kissing her like there was no tomorrow.

"Damn, but I missed you," he whispered.

"And I missed you," Madison whispered. So much. She trembled with the joy she felt at holding him again, even as she knew their time was limited. "You said something about legal matters."

"I was going to ask you...." Chance stopped and grinned. "But now doesn't really seem the time." He bent his head and kissed her again. Even more thoroughly.

Dimly, Madison heard what sounded like pounding. Then Shawna Somersby's youthful voice. "Madison? Chance? Are you guys in there?"

Madison flattened her hands across Chance's chest and pushed away from him. Even as she rued the end of their private time, she struggled to pull herself together. Quickly, he scanned her face. "Better do something about your lipstick," he whispered.

Madison swore and blotted the moisture on her lips with her fingertips. "I don't have any here. It's in the car."

Chance smoothed her hair into place with his hand. "Maybe no one will notice."

Like hell they won't, Madison thought.

"I'll distract everyone. You get your purse."

"Thanks."

"Chance?" Shawna continued her pounding. "They're ready to start the filming now."

Chance strode out of the pantry and the kitchen, his boots moving commandingly across the wood floor. He opened the front door. "Sorry, Shawna. I didn't hear you."

"Where's Madison?" Shawna prodded curiously.

"Right behind you," Madison said cheerfully, hoping like heck that Shawna didn't notice she had gone into the house with her lipstick perfectly applied, only to come out with none on at all.

Unfortunately, she knew from the look Shawna gave her that she had noticed. Damn. She could only hope for the sake of her business reputation that Shawna wouldn't say anything to anyone.

Working to distract the young intern's attention, Chance took her elbow and propelled her down the steps. "Now, where am I supposed to be again?" he asked.

Shawna pointed. "Over there. Where the Ranchero is. Same old drill. When they yell action, you get in and drive to where the horses are. Once you get a little closer, they're going to start the snow machines up so it'll look like you're driving through a blizzard."

"Got it." While Chance headed for the truck, Madison hurried toward her rental car and the purse on the front seat.

Chance jumped in the pickup. The snow machines started up. And that was when they all heard it. The startled whinny. And saw the magnificent horse rear up in a flash of satiny black against the onslaught of snow. Madison and everyone else knew what had happened.

"How did Shiloh get in there?" Madison shouted. But even as she said it, she knew. Vince and Ursula had not taken no for an answer.

MADISON DIDN'T STOP to think. She ran in the direction of the pickup, the snow machine and the rearing, spinning stallion.

Chance had stopped the truck and leaped out. He was running through the snow spitting out of the thunderous machine toward the beautiful stallion. "Shut it off!" he yelled. But it was too late. Shiloh, spooked beyond reason, had created a stampede among the horses in the pasture. Clearly threatened and not about to run from a fight, he was suddenly headed straight for the snow machine and the entire crew.

Marshaling powerful muscles, Shiloh soared over the pasture fence, clearing it in a single bound. Too late, Madison realized Shiloh was coming straight at her. She would not have time to get out of the way.

Chance knew it, too.

In a split second, he changed directions, lunged away from Shiloh and straight for Madison. Swearing all the while, he grabbed her around the waist, simultaneously pushing her forward and spinning them around so their bodies slammed to the ground. Barely missing Shiloh's thundering hooves, she landed on top of him.

Shiloh shot past the cameras and headed for the distant mountains. Once he had cleared the area, the horses in the pasture settled down immediately. Among the crew, however, bedlam erupted.

"Are you all right?" Chance demanded.

Madison felt stunned. And numb. She swallowed hard. "I think so." At least nothing felt broken.

Gently, Chance slipped from beneath her. "Call a doctor!" he shouted. "Get one out here now!"

Ursula Rodriguez strode forward. "Aren't you overreacting a bit? She seems okay. You both do." Beside her, Ed Connelly nodded agreement, while in the distance Vince was yelling at everyone in shouting distance.

Chance's patience was exhausted. "You idiots! She's pregnant!" he fumed. "Get a doctor out here! Now!"

A HUSHED SILENCE fell over the group gathered around Madison and Chance.

"Pregnant!" Shawna echoed softly in shock. And Madison knew, as she struggled to sit up, that she had just failed as a role model for the young intern.

"Yes, pregnant," Chance snapped as everyone continued to blink in shock. "With my baby!" Giving her no chance to walk on her own, Chance swept Madison up in his arms and carried her to the house. He laid her gently on the sofa.

Seconds later, Shawna came dashing in, cell phone in hand. "They've got a doctor from the hospital emergency room on the way. He's bringing an ambulance, too, just in case it's needed."

"You feeling okay?" Chance grabbed an afghan off the back of the sofa and tucked it around Madison. "You want anything? A glass of water or a cup of tea?"

How about a new reputation? Or a way to turn back the clock and erase the one terrible mistake after another that she had made? Madison shook her head as tears continued to stream down her face. "No," she whispered hoarsely, shutting her eyes against Shawna's curious glance. "Nothing. Thanks."

"Are you in pain?" Chance whispered.

Madison shook her head again. "Just shaken up."

And scared that she might lose their baby.

CHANCE STAYED with Madison until the doctor arrived. To their mutual relief, he pronounced both Madison and the baby fine despite the tumble she had taken.

"I'm sorry about Shiloh getting mixed in with the other horses," Madison said to Chance as soon as the doctor had left.

"You have nothing to be sorry about," Chance said with gruff gentleness as he brought her a glass of milk and knelt before her. He kissed the back of her hand. "I'll go out and let everyone know you're okay."

"What about Shiloh?"

Chance tensed. "He'll be okay until I find him."

Madison drank some more milk then swung her knees off the sofa and put her feet flat on the floor. She shoved her hands through her hair. Although she was still shaky, she also knew they had a job to do. "That snow out there is probably melting like crazy. We better try and finish—"

Chance cut her off with a sharp look. "You stay here and finish your milk," he said heavily. "I'll take care of that."

While Madison sipped her milk, the sounds of activity outside picked up. Thinking the commercial filming was going to resume, she relaxed against the sofa. As soon as she finished her milk, she decided, she would go out to watch. Before she could do that, Ed came rushing in. To her dismay, he looked even more distressed than he had when Shiloh had jumped the pasture fence and thundered through the crew.

"How's the filming going?" Madison asked, putting her empty glass on the coffee table in front of her.

"It's not," Ed told her tersely, his face red. Her normally cool-as-a-cucumber boss looked like he wanted to punch something. "You don't know, do you?" he demanded furiously. Striding closer, he filled her in. "Chance Cartwright just invoked the property-damage clause in the contract. He's refusing to let us film anything else."

Considering what had happened to Shiloh, Madison could hardly blame him. Still, she knew what it had cost to operate the snow-making machine in the dead of summer. She put up a hand, sure she could work this out given a few minutes to talk to everyone. "He's upset by what happened, Ed."

"But everything's fine. You're fine. Your baby is fine," Ed protested.

"I know," Madison said, happy and relieved about that.

Madison knew from the look on Ed's face that they were going to have to talk about her unscripted love affair with Chance. Soon. On that topic, she had a heck of a lot of explaining to do. Right now, all Ed cared about was saving the account. The ethics of the situation would come in later.

"So get him un-upset," Ed ordered tersely.

Madison frowned. Although Chance was doing his best to keep his feelings in check around her, she knew how upset he was. "Realistically, I don't think that's going to happen today." *Maybe tomorrow, or the next.*

"Madison, this is a multimillion-dollar account and a major automobile manufacturer."

Madison had only to look in Ed's eyes to know that if she couldn't manage a save, all hopes of her being awarded the vice presidency were down the drain. The thought she might lose everything she'd worked for in the last ten years because she'd been more concerned with her love affair with Chance than the job she was supposed to be doing cut her to the quick. She knew the accident was as much her fault as anyone's, if not more. If she had been paying attention to what was going on instead of trying to steal a moment alone with Chance, Shiloh never would have gotten mixed up with the other horses. Madison would have seen to it.

"So you do whatever you have to do to save this account," Ed continued furiously, oblivious to the depth of Madison's guilt. "Use your sexual relationship, use the baby, use whatever it takes! But I want him calmed down and back filming those snow scenes for us ASAP!"

The front door opened and slammed behind them.

Chance stood there, looking from Madison to her boss and back again.

"Obviously, I didn't mean that the way it sounded," Ed

said quickly, his face turning even redder as he shot a look at Chance.

"Obviously, you did," Chance countered, colder than the snow outside. He regarded Madison and her boss with contempt, obviously recalling how Madison had bowed to Ed's wishes many times before. And why not? Madison thought angrily, resenting the fact Chance was forcing her to defend herself and her actions to him once again. "Making nice" with a client was all part of her job. Doing whatever it took to land or keep an account was the way she'd gotten involved with Chance in the first place! If it hadn't been for his determined resistance and her equally determined pursuit of him via the flirtatious letters, gifts and phone calls, if she hadn't bought him at the bachelor weekend and gotten passionately involved with him, none of this would have happened!

It was her passion for Chance that was the real culprit, Madison thought, guilt and remorse flooding her anew. If she had been doing her job the way she was supposed to, *none of this would have happened.* Shiloh wouldn't have been mixed in with the other horses, the filming wouldn't have been disrupted and people nearly hurt. Chance wouldn't have been angry. He wouldn't have tried to execute the quit clause he'd had written in his contract. The fact that this whole ad campaign was suddenly falling apart was her fault.

She'd made a big mistake.

Fortunately, for all their sakes, it wasn't too late to rectify that mistake.

Madison stood on legs that still felt a little like jelly and crossed to his side. "Chance, I know you're unhappy about what happened with Shiloh," she told him in the same gentle tone he had used on her many times when she'd been angry and uncertain. She looked deep into his eyes. "I am, too. But Ed's right—the snow is expensive and it's melting as we speak."

She took a deep breath and called on all her courage as she saw the anger in his eyes grow with every soothing word she spoke. Determinedly, she pushed on. "They can wrap this up quickly, without any harm to anyone. I know they can." She would talk to Ursula and Vince herself, make them see they'd have to do this in one or two takes at the very most if they wanted to salvage the ad campaign they'd been slaving over for weeks.

Chance turned on Madison. A muscle working convulsively in his jaw, he said, "I would think after what just happened that you of all people would want this bunch out of here now."

Madison swallowed. Chance was right. Had she lost the baby because of their foolhardiness, she would never have wanted to set eyes on any of them again. But she hadn't. And life went on. Just as before. Now she had to undo the damage her lack of attention had caused—she had to make things right for everyone.

Her heart pounding, she shot Chance a beseeching look. "There are months of work involved here. And not just mine," she told him calmly, forcing herself to meet her business obligations. "I've got a responsibility to the client and the company I work for—"

"What about your responsibility to me, Madison?" Chance interrupted.

"—to see this through to the end." Ignoring the scathing contempt in his eyes, she continued as if he hadn't spoken. "I don't want to do a job that is less than my best. And without those final scenes," she warned, practically begging Chance to see this her way and do what she asked of him one last time, "the commercial is not going to be our best."

CHAPTER ELEVEN

"I'D LIKE to speak to Madison alone," Chance said grimly, astounded she could think he would be able to forget what had just happened. Hadn't their time together taught her anything? The number-one lesson being that people and relationships were more important than any business deal.

Ed shot one last imploring look at Madison. "We'll be waiting for you," he said meaningfully, then slipped out the door.

Chance turned to Madison. To his surprise, she looked upset with him for demanding a moment alone with her.

Madison tilted her chin at Chance defiantly, hurt and confusion glimmering in her pretty green eyes. "I don't know what you thought you were trying to accomplish just now," she told him icily, looking more furious and disappointed in him than he had ever seen her, "but if you were trying to undermine my position at the agency and ruin my career by informing everyone publicly yet again that you and I have been sleeping together, then you've just done one heck of a job."

Chance grimaced. "I don't mind admitting I'm tired of hiding the fact you're my woman." That, he wanted to shout to the world. "But when it comes to ruining your career—" He stared at the fury in her eyes, then demanded tersely, "Why in blue blazes would I want to do that?"

"I don't know." Madison flung her arms up in a gesture of complete exasperation. "Maybe so you could have me and the baby all to yourself. And for the record—" Madison stomped closer, her temper growing hotter with every second that passed "—if that was your agenda, I think you may have just succeeded." She planted her hands on her slender hips and glared up at him. It seemed to be taking every ounce of self-control she had for her not to just haul off and slug him.

Chance knew the feeling. He'd like to shake some sense into her head, too.

"I don't deny I'd like to keep you both from harm," he retorted. The Ranchero commercial wasn't the real issue, and Madison knew it. The issue was them. She was looking for an excuse—any excuse—to cut and run, and in their current argument, she'd found it.

"Is that what you think you were doing just now by ordering my boss out of here? Keeping me and the baby from harm?" Her eyes locked on his in anger.

"As a matter of fact, yes, that's exactly what I was doing," Chance snapped, irritated she could be so quick to pretend their relationship was just an unimportant event in their lives and go back to doing business as usual for Connelly and Associates. No career, no matter how high-powered it was, was going to keep her warm at night or hold her when she needed to be held, love her when she needed to be loved. He'd hoped he had shown her that, but apparently not.

She uttered a weary laugh. "Pulling the plug on the ads serves your needs, Chance, not mine, and not the baby's." Madison arched a disapproving brow in his direction. "Not," she continued with no small trace of irony, "that I should be surprised about that, either. All you ever really cared about was the baby, anyway."

"I love you," Chance said gruffly, wishing he knew a way to get through to her, to make her see that loving each other was worth the risk.

She shook her head and laughed bitterly. "Yeah, you love me, all right, you just don't trust me enough to finish the filming without further calamity.'' Hurt shimmered in her eyes.

Chance stared at her. ''If that's the way you really see me—if it all comes down to business for you in the end—then I really have failed,'' he said bitterly. That meant he was just as inept and clueless at expressing love as his father had been. It meant he could no more forge a loving relationship with Madison than he'd been able to forge one with his father. And heaven knew he didn't need to repeat the misery of loving someone and knowing they loved him, deep down, but never being able to really connect....

''I know you care about me in your own way. Just as I care about you,'' Madison said carefully.

Chance heard the reservation in her low voice and reeled with the hurt of it. He had just told her he loved her for the very first time. He'd said the words out loud, and she had answered him as if she was negotiating her way through a business contract, as if she couldn't care less, as if his feelings didn't matter at all in the larger scheme of things, any more than their passion or their baby did. Their love for each other was never the bottom line in anything, nor—according to Madison—would it ever be.

''But what?'' he prodded, wondering what was coming next. The verbal equivalent of a Dear John letter? Would she tell him she had never and could never love him in return and suggest they should be friends?

Madison swallowed hard and shot him a frightened look. Color swept her cheeks. ''We have to be reasonable here,'' she said in a low, panicked voice. ''Since I met you, my whole life has been turned upside down. And so has yours!''

As much as Chance was loath to admit it, Madison knew it was true.

Because of Chance, she thought, her job no longer meant anything near what it had to her. All she really cared about was Chance and the baby. And yet, as the exec in charge of the Ranchero account, she had a responsibility to see things through. As mother to an unborn child, she had a tremendous responsibility to do whatever was necessary to hang on to her job, because now was no time for her to be out of work! Nor did she want to put her and her baby's fate in the hands of a man who might or might not choose to stay the course with her. Nine months was a long time, the eighteen or so years after that even longer. Thus far they'd known each other less than three months, and during half that time they'd been completely out of touch. Might still be if it weren't for the baby binding them.

With effort, Madison pulled herself together. Like it or not, she had to go back to the formula that had made her life work before. She faced Chance. "It's time I got this life of mine back on track." Time she provided some real security for herself and their baby. "I'm going to finish up here today, with or without your cooperation, and head on back to Dallas with the rest of the crew to see how much of my career I can actually salvage."

"And then what?" Chance snapped, assuming a militant stance and folding his arms.

Madison drew a stabilizing breath. "If and when I'm able to salvage what's left of my career, I'll be in touch and we'll see what we can work out regarding the baby."

"So in other words," Chance said grimly, "you're telling me to get lost."

"That's not how I'd put it," Madison said carefully.

"But it's the truth, isn't it?" Chance said. For him, her actions were a bitter replay of his past. She was doing exactly what his dad had done to him. Thwarting his attempts to be close to her. Pushing him away with both hands. Resisting intimacy on every level. He needed her to be here, physically and emotionally, to work this out. To put the three of them above business, above everything. He needed her to make the love in their life her first and most important priority—even if she was hurting, as both he and his father had been hurting after Chance's mother's death.

"Like it or not, I have to make a living, Chance," Madison said wearily. She moved to the window and stared at the crew standing idle, the snow melting on the ground, all of them waiting to see if she could pull a rabbit out of a hat and come up with some miracle fix.

But Chance knew none of that was important. The only thing that really mattered right now was what was going on in this room. "I could easily support us all, Madison," he told her wearily. There didn't need to be any cold, lonely nights in his family. It didn't have to be the way it had when he was growing up, with his father constantly using work as an excuse to keep his distance.

"But that's not what I want," Madison responded emotionally. She splayed both her hands against her chest. "Don't you understand? I have a career in Dallas. A home there. A life that makes sense to me."

"And this doesn't?" That took him by surprise. For him, their love, the passion between them, the baby they were expecting—they were the only things that made sense!

But not, he realized sadly, to Madison.

For the next minute, as an uncomfortable silence strung out between them, Madison lowered her lashes and looked anywhere but at him. "From the moment I met you at the auction," she murmured at last in a soft voice laced with regret, "I haven't been myself."

Nor had he. He'd been around long enough to know better than to put himself in a situation where his heart might get broken. But with Madison, all reason had gone out the window, replaced by gut-level feelings he'd been in no way prepared to handle.

Unfortunately, they couldn't undo what had already been done. He refused to pretend they could. "If you leave the ranch now, under these circumstances," he warned direly, "I can't see it as anything other than walking out on me."

He couldn't love someone again and not feel loved in re-turned. It was too painful. Worse, Chance had gotten through to Madison for a time, had established some real closeness and intimacy between them. He'd proved Madison was capable of loving him. She just chose not to do so. She was choosing to put her business career ahead of everything and everyone else.

"And I can't see your demand I stay as anything but an arbitrary command, one I can't possibly meet." She spread her hands wide, then let them drop ever so slowly to her sides. "So where does that leave us?" she asked sadly.

With his thumbs under her jaw, he tilted her head. "You tell me."

Silence fell between them. As he looked into her eyes, he saw the mounting sadness and knew it was over as well as she did. They just couldn't bring themselves to say the words out loud.

"WELL, I SOLD IT." Ursula sailed into Madison's office in a cloud of Shalimar perfume and dropped into a chair in front of her desk. "Reluctantly, I might add, but I sold it."

Madison smiled her gratitude at the thin, statuesque AMV exec. "Thanks."

Ursula patted her chignon with the flat of her hand, making sure every glossy black strand was in place. She shook her head at Madison. "Revising the Ranchero ad campaign this way is not going to help your career."

Madison sighed. "I know."

"Fortunately, the scenery is so beautiful there—the ad campaign so well done—it doesn't seem to hurt the Ranchero. Our market research shows that once people see the commercials they are still going to want the truck."

Thank goodness for focus groups, Madison thought. "I'm glad."

Ursula studied Madison. "What does Chance Cartwright think about what you did for him?"

Madison shifted uncomfortably in her chair. She plucked at the fabric of her loose-fitting linen shift. "He doesn't know yet."

Ursula flipped through her Filofax. Finding the date she wanted, she made a small notation next to it. "When are you going to tell him?"

Madison shrugged. The answer to that wasn't simple. "The next time I talk to him, I suppose."

"Which will be—"

"I'm not sure."

Ursula's gaze turned sympathetic. "I was engaged once a long time ago," she said softly.

"What happened?"

Ursula closed her Filofax with a decisive snap. "I kept putting my career first—to the point my relationship almost ceased to exist. Needless to say—" she lifted her shoulders in a small, elegant shrug "—my fiancé saw the light, gave me an ultimatum, which I politely but firmly refused to accept, and ended our engagement."

Madison studied the older woman. "What are you trying to tell me?"

"That men like Chance Cartwright don't come along very often in any woman's life," Ursula replied softly. "I didn't have a child to consider. You do."

Mustering every bit of composure she had, Madison pretended her heart was still intact. "It's better this way," she said, not sure who she was trying to convince, Ursula or herself.

"The two of you not in contact?" Ursula's expression became skeptical. "I don't see how."

Madison's hand went to her stomach, resting there protectively. She tried not to think about how much she already missed Chance, and it had only been a few days. "We'd just end up hurting each other."

Her expression said Ursula was not as sure about that. "You still have a baby—"

"We'll do right by him or her," Madison assured her blithely. "You'll see. We just need some time to get to the point where it isn't quite so awkward to talk to each other." *Where it doesn't hurt quite so much.*

Ursula was silent.

Shawna Somersby came in with papers for Madison to go over and the phone on Madison's desk began to blink, signaling she had two calls waiting.

Ursula rose gracefully. "You're at a crucial point in your life, Madison." She paused, her glance kind but direct. "Just make sure whatever decision you make is one you're going to be able to live with the rest of your life."

"SO THE FEE STRUCTURE is not going to change," Chance surmised after Ed Connelly finished going over the numbers with him.

"Right." Ed sipped the coffee Chance had made for them. "You'll still be able to give the Lost Springs Ranch for Boys the same amount of money. The only difference is you won't be asked to participate in any of the trade shows or any publicity for the Ranchero. You'll be pictured in the ads—along with the truck—and that's it. Any trade show appearances will be made by Rona Fitzgerald, and she'll be doing the voice-overs for the TV and radio ads, too. We're still in negotiations, but it looks like Rona is going to feature the new truck in an episode of her TV show. Her character will get a new Ranchero as part of the story line. In return, the AMV Corporation will supply them with Ranchero trucks to use on the set, and one for Rona's personal use, too."

"That'll make Rona happy. She really liked the Ranchero AMV gave me."

"That's what Madison said." Ed took one of the store-bought cookies Chance offered. "That's where she got the idea to approach Rona about being the pitch person for the new truck."

Chance knew how much Rona enjoyed doing commercials and being the center of attention—both on and off the set of her TV show. She was already planning to buy another horse or two from him with her earnings. "Seems like it's worked out for everyone, then," Chance said. He stared out at his ranch. The end of summer was a beautiful time of year in Wyoming, but this year he could hardly enjoy the temperate sunny days and crisp cool nights. Pushing his loneliness aside, he turned to Ed and gave him a rueful grin. "You don't know how happy it makes me to be able to remain relatively anonymous, after all's said and done, and not be turned into some instant celebrity."

"I have an inkling." Ed sat back in his chair and ran a hand over his balding head. "Although I'm not sure I'd feel the same way in your shoes. You had the opportunity to be the next Diet Cola man."

Chance recalled those commercials. The previously unknown male model had played a construction worker who stripped off his shirt every day at a certain time to drink a diet cola, while a group of female office workers ogled him from above. Instant fame, money and celebrity had followed. The guy had become a huge sex symbol almost overnight. "That's not how or why I want my fifteen minutes in the spotlight," Chance said dryly. He'd rather be known as a loving husband and father.

Ed helped himself to another cookie. "That's what Madison indicated when she helped convince Ursula—who helped convince the Ranchero people—that the truck should be the real star of the commercial, not the cowboy driving it around his ranch or the TV star pitching it."

Chance plucked a chocolate chip cookie from the cellophane package. "You don't agree?"

Ed shook his head. "I saw the commercial the way it was originally put together—before Rona was on board to introduce the truck and do the voice-overs. If Madison had kept the campaign the way it was, with the emphasis equally on you and the Ranchero, she would have been as famous as you would've been. Instead, she changed it to protect you and then insisted she could no longer work with you personally. Knowing that doing so—blatantly putting her personal feelings above the needs of the client—would cost her the vice presidency of Connelly and Associates.''

This was news. "Why would she do that?" Chance asked, not sure how he felt about it or what it really meant.

Ed shrugged. "I've been asking myself the very same question. For as long as I've known her, Madison has been after just this sort of recognition. And now that she finally had it within her grasp—'' Ed shook his head, looking completely baffled ''—she just walked away.''

"I CAN'T BELIEVE you're leaving before I am," Shawna said as Madison set the cardboard box on her desk and began emptying her middle desk drawer.

"Cheer up." Madison smiled at the intern. "The summer's almost over. You'll be headed back to college before you know it."

"I'd feel a lot better about it if you weren't quitting because of all the stuff that went wrong on the Ranchero account." Shawna's eyes filled with regret. "I mean—I know I made some mistakes, too, when I was helping you on that. Like giving Chance Cartwright that trade show schedule when he wasn't supposed to have it yet. I know that's one of the things he got so mad about, even before he threw everyone off his ranch."

Madison stopped Shawna's apology with a gentle look. "Your mistakes—and let's be honest, Shawna, there was really only one of any consequence—have nothing to do with my resigning."

Shawna blinked in confusion. "Then what does?" she persisted.

"I'd like the answer to that myself," a familiar voice said.

Madison turned to see Chance framed in the doorway to her office. He was dressed in a white cotton shirt, jeans, tweed sport coat, boots and Stetson. He looked more ruggedly handsome than ever, and at the sight of him so near, her breath caught in her chest. "Chance."

Chance looked at Shawna. He lifted his brow. "Maybe you'd like to give us some time alone?"

Shawna beamed. "Absolutely!"

Apparently unable to help herself, she leaned over and murmured in Madison's ear just loud enough for her to hear, "You go, girl!"

Madison's cheeks filled with warmth as Shawna dashed out of the office, stopping only long enough to shut the door quietly behind her.

Chance and Madison squared off. "So why are you quitting?" he asked with a studied casualness that sent her heart slamming against her ribs.

Deciding it was cowardly to continue hiding behind her desk, Madison stood and circled it to face him. She lifted her chin and, clinging to what little was left of her pride, confided matter-of-factly, "I decided you were right—this job and our baby aren't compatible. The hours are too long and there is definitely too much stress and pressure, too many decisions out of my control." She paused to wet her lips, not sure what he'd think of her plan, only knowing she still cared deeply about his opinion despite everything that had happened between them. Taking a deep breath, she plunged on. "I've decided to become a consultant and work out of my home."

Chance's lips curved in approval. "Sounds perfect for you," he said huskily, although he gave her the impression he wouldn't have cared what she had decided, one way or another.

Madison gulped. "I think it will be."

Chance took her hand between his own and squeezed it warmly. "Congratulations."

"Thanks." Knowing if they stood like that even one second longer she'd burst into tears, Madison swiftly withdrew her hand from his and went back to boxing up her things. "What are you doing here?" she asked over her shoulder.

Chance circled to stand in front of her, one shoulder braced against the wall. "Ed told me what you'd done in terms of retooling the Ranchero ads to keep me out of the spotlight while at the same time insuring that I would be able to earn some money from them to donate to the Lost Springs Ranch for Boys. I wanted to thank you."

"You're welcome." Madison continued filling the boxes with the awards she had taken down from the walls.

Chance pitched in to help. "So how you've been?" he asked quietly, with the considerateness of an old friend.

Sad. Lonely. Missing you more than I ever could have imagined possible. "Okay." Madison swallowed around the increasing knot of emotion in her throat. "How've you been?"

Chance shrugged aimlessly. "Okay. Busy."

Silence fell between them. Chance edged closer. "How's the baby?"

Madison straightened and smiled. "Growing like a weed, according to my obstetrician."

Chance's eyes sparkled with happiness, and his glance fell to her expanding belly. "Good."

Madison blushed. There was so much she wanted to say. So much she was afraid to say. But she knew she had to start somewhere or spend an entire lifetime regretting it. "Chance—"

He put a finger against her lips. An arm about her waist. The next thing she knew she was in his arms. And he was tilting her face to his. "I'm sorry," he whispered.

Madison's heart took a trembling leap as the love she felt for him—would always feel—bubbled up inside her. "For what?"

"For giving you ultimatums." Chance ran his hands warmly up and down her back. Soothing. Seducing. "For demanding everything ASAP. For being a jerk," he murmured hoarsely. "And not understanding how much your career meant to you."

Tears stung her eyes. "I'm sorry, too," Madison whispered thickly, as the tears streamed down her face. "For running out on you when I did."

Chance held her all the tighter. "Is that what you were doing?" he murmured, studying her upturned face. "Running?"

Madison nodded, knowing she needed to tell him this. She slipped her hands beneath his sport coat and splayed her fingertips across the hardness of his chest. "I felt so much for you, so fast, it scared me." She shook her head. "I didn't want to put everything I had, heart and soul, into making us a couple and the three of us a family. I—I wanted everything to stay the same in my life and yours so that if things didn't work out we could easily just slip back into our old lives, almost as if none of it had ever happened." She paused to take a breath, and at the same time searched his eyes. "Am I making sense?"

Chance inhaled deeply. He let his breath out slowly. "More than you know."

"But then I realized that couldn't happen," she said softly, feeling for the first time in a long time that things were going to be all right. "I realized that if we were going to be together, I had to make some choices. And some changes. I realized I had to stop holding part of myself back and start taking risks—the kind that would put my heart on the line."

Chance stroked a hand through her hair. "And that's why you quit your job here," he guessed tenderly.

Madison nodded. "Because I wanted to be with you. And if that wasn't possible, at least make it so you could be with our baby as much as you wanted. That's why I'm moving to Wyoming and opening my consulting business there.''

The pure joy she had expected to see on his face never came. Instead, his expression went from joyous to wary. ''Madison, you don't have to do all this,'' he said seriously. ''I could just as easily sell my ranch and move my horse training business down here.''

Madison paused, stunned. She knew how much the ranch meant to him—it was everything. ''You'd do that for me?'' she demanded hoarsely.

Chance nodded. ''I'd do anything to make you happy,'' he vowed seriously. He touched his index finger to her lips. ''There's only one condition.''

Madison tensed, hoping like heck these were terms she could meet, because she didn't want to lose him again, not ever. ''And that is?'' she asked tremulously.

''Marry me, Madison,'' Chance said, lifting her lips to his. ''Not because of the baby.'' He paused to give her a long, sexy kiss. ''Although that's a darn good reason in and of itself. But because—'' he paused to kiss her again ''—we belong together. Today, tomorrow and for all time.''

CHANCE SPREAD the blueprints across the kitchen table. ''So what do you think?'' he asked Madison after she'd had time to study the proposed addition to his house.

''I think it's perfect.'' She laced her arms around his neck and gave him a heartfelt hug. ''When it's finished we'll have two extra rooms upstairs. One for the baby—''

''And one for the baby's brother or sister,'' Chance cut in with a sly wink.

Madison grinned as she looked at the matching wedding rings they both wore. The thought that they might someday have two children—one planned, one not—delighted her, too.

''And downstairs I'll have my office as well as a playroom and nursery right next door," she continued enthusiastically as Chance sat in a chair and tugged her onto his lap.

"You don't mind working out of the ranch house?" Chance said.

Madison shook her head as she settled her weight comfortably across his thighs. "Not at all," she said, snuggling closer to his tall, strong frame. "In fact, it's a relief not to have to get dressed up in high heels and business clothes each day," she confessed with a sigh. Lovingly, she ran a hand across his chest. "Yet I still have all the creative work to keep me going on a professional level." And that was important, she thought. She wanted to keep working, just not in the same high-pressured way.

Chance grinned, all the love he felt for her reflected in her eyes. "You're really excited about taking on those local clients, aren't you?"

Madison nodded. In a way, it was like starting her professional life all over again. Yet she had so much more experience and knowledge, gleaned from her years of working within the business, to guide her this time. "To date, I've worked largely with major corporations, brand names. It will be a real challenge to help small businessmen and women come up with a catchy identity and promote their businesses within the local market."

"It sure hasn't taken you long to get started," Chance said.

No sooner had the two of them returned from their honeymoon than potential clients, having learned of her plans to start her own consulting firm in Wyoming, had started calling, asking Madison to design an ad campaign for them, something that would really put them on the map.

"Three clients so far," Madison recited happily as she linked fingers with him. A car wash, a bakery and a hardware store. "And three more thinking about signing up with me."

"Just don't work too hard," Chance said, pausing to kiss her tenderly. His hand smoothed over the slope of her gently rounded tummy.

"I won't."

Chance grinned. "Good. 'Cause—" he kissed his way up her neck, over to her ear, then lingered around her mouth, planting tiny kisses here and there that left her wanting more, much more "—I want you to have plenty of time for me."

Joy floated through Madison in boundless waves. "I'll always have time for you," she promised softly. And to prove it to him, she kissed him passionately.

Chance returned the affection languorously as he tunneled his hands through her hair and tilted her face to his. "Just as I'll always have time for you."

Madison sighed and cuddled against him. "We really do have it all, don't we?" she murmured, content.

Chance nodded and kissed her again, even more passionately, before promising softly, "That we do."

continues with

THE PERFECT SOLUTION

by

Day Leclaire

Flynn Morgan's weakness is a damsel in distress, and
Jane Dearly is that. Not only does she need his security
services, she needs a man to drag her away from her
laboratory now and then. Her guardians decide he'll make
the perfect birthday gift, but Jane is more interested in
Flynn as a subject for her latest experiments—
with love potions.

Available in April

Here's a preview!

"Jane Dearly? I'm Flynn Morgan. Your uncles sent me. I'm supposed to make an appointment with you to install a security system in your lab, but I heard it's your birthday today, so..." He whipped out the box of chocolates and bouquet of roses he held behind his back. When she failed to smile, he prompted, "These are for you. Happy birthday."

"I'm not interested in a security system."

"Your uncles are. That's why I'm here."

Her frown deepened. Definitely bad news. "Let me get this straight. My uncles hired you?"

"Right."

"For security?"

"You can't be too careful these days," he said.

Somehow the situation had taken a nosedive, though he couldn't figure out what he'd done wrong. Most women on the receiving end of chocolate and flowers not only smiled, they tumbled into his arms and thanked him with a full-blown kiss. The sort of full-blown kiss he'd like to experience with Jane. The sort he doubted he'd receive from her any time in the near future. The sort he *shouldn't* receive from a client unless he wanted to become reacquainted with Paulie's fist.

"That's why you were being so friendly? Because my uncles hired you?" She took a step closer, fanning her hands back and forth as though suffering from a hot flash. "No other reason?"

"It's your birthday, right?"

"So?"

"So…" He gave the box and flowers a little shake. Rose petals rained downward, settling at his feet. "So, I thought I'd bring you these."

"Why?"

He fought to enunciate through gritted teeth. "For. A. Birthday. Present. Are you familiar with that custom?"

"Yes." She eyed the flowers and grimaced. "For hot-house roses, these sure have a strong odor. Here. Let me get these out of the way." She grabbed the bouquet and held the flowers behind the door. "Now stand there and take a deep breath."

"Right." Flynn made a hasty reassessment of the situation. Tightly-wound scientist, gut-wrenching smile, gorgeous eyes—most of the time—and nutty as a sack of almonds. Damn.

"Are you breathing?"

"It's sort of automatic with me." She planted her hands on her hips and he released a sigh. She reminded him of the nun he'd suffered as a young schoolboy right before his days at Lost Springs Ranch—a tough old teacher who'd done her best to reform him with the painful end of a ruler. "Yes, I'm breathing."

"And?"

It took him sixty full seconds to realize that the truth might actually work to his advantage. "And I like your smile."

Unfortunately, the truth didn't work. Pink flared into her cheeks. At a guess, it wasn't because she had a tendency to blush. She confirmed it the instant she opened her mouth—the same mouth he'd have loved to explore in intimate detail. "You can't fool me. You're just saying that because you're hoping to sell your security equipment to my uncles."

"Not really," he said with absolute honesty.

"Tell my uncles I'm not interested in fooling with a security system right now. It's inconvenient. If they really want to help, they can get me a man. A *real* man."

With that she whipped around him and into her house, slamming the door behind her.

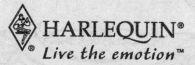

Harlequin Historicals®
Historical Romantic Adventure!

From rugged lawmen and valiant knights to defiant heiresses and spirited frontierswomen, Harlequin Historicals will capture your imagination with their dramatic scope, passion and adventure.

*Harlequin Historicals...
they're too good to miss!*

HHDIR104

e♦HARLEQUIN.com

The Ultimate Destination for Women's Fiction

Visit eHarlequin.com's Bookstore today for today's most popular books at great prices.

- An extensive selection of romance books by top authors!

- Choose our convenient "bill me" option. No credit card required.

- New releases, Themed Collections and hard-to-find backlist.

- A sneak peek at upcoming books.

- Check out book excerpts, book summaries and Reader Recommendations from other members and post your own too.

- Find out what everybody's reading in Bestsellers.

- Save BIG with everyday discounts and exclusive online offers!

- Our Category Legend will help you select reading that's exactly right for you!

- Visit our Bargain Outlet often for huge savings and special offers!

- Sweepstakes offers. Enter for your chance to win special prizes, autographed books and more.

Your purchases are 100% guaranteed—so shop online at www.eHarlequin.com today!